"Well, Mister Parker," she said quietly...

"It took an awful lot to get you to say my Christian name, didn't it? Seraph Raber and his five guns, the state of Texas, Wyoming, Montana, the Sioux nation... I guess I needed a little bit of help."

She reached up and touched his face with one black-gloved hand. "It was wrong of me to mention the gun you never wear. The truth is, I'm proud of you for that. Forgive me. I will take you up on your proposition, and if you give me one hour, the children and I will be packed and ready for the Union Pacific Railroad. But, Z, there is just one small thing you'll have to agree to."

Zeph's head was spinning from the play-out of his anger, from her quiet words and from her gloved hand pressing against his cheek. "What's that?" he managed to get out.

"You have to come with me to Pennsylvania. And you have to come as my husband."

Born and raised in Canada, **Murray Pura** has lived in the USA, the UK and the Middle East. With over two dozen works of fiction and nonfiction to his credit, he has published with HarperCollins, HarperOne, Baker, Barbour, Zondervan and several other publishing houses. He works in many genres, including historical fiction, classic or literary fiction, romance, and Amish fiction. Currently, Pura lives and writes at his home by the Canadian Rockies.

A BRIDE'S FLIGHT

Murray Pura

Recycling programs
for this product may
not exist in your area.

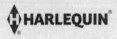

ISBN-13: 978-1-335-60511-5

A Bride's Flight

First published as A Bride's Flight from Virginia City, Montana in 2012
by Barbour Publishing.

This edition published in 2021.

Copyright © 2012 by Murray Pura

This edition published by arrangement with Harlequin Books S.A.

For questions and comments about the quality of this book,
please contact us at CustomerService@Harlequin.com.

Harlequin Enterprises ULC
22 Adelaide St. West, 40th Floor
Toronto, Ontario M5H 4E3, Canada
www.Harlequin.com

Printed in U.S.A.

A BRIDE'S FLIGHT

For Lyyndae
My wife & my friend & the first reader
of all my stories

Chapter One

Charlotte Spence lay in her comfortable down bed with the big goose-feather pillows a few minutes longer and listened to the grandfather clock downstairs strike the hour—one, two, three, four, five. Not for the first time, she wondered how she was able to sleep through those loud gongs in the dead of night. She closed her eyes again and whispered a quick prayer.

Lord, it's Your day. Give me the strength and wisdom I need. Open the gates You want opened, close the ones You don't. In Christ's name. Amen.

She stepped out of bed in her blue flannel nightgown and went to the washstand. Lighting an oil lamp and setting it on a nearby table, she washed her face and hands then crossed over to the dresser where she sat down and began to brush out her long blond hair while she read from the Bible. She was working her way through Psalm 119.

My soul is continually in my hand:
Yet I do not forget thy law.
The wicked have laid a snare for me:

Yet I erred not from thy precepts.
Thy testimonies I have taken as an heritage for
ever: For they are the rejoicing of my heart.
I have inclined mine heart to perform thy statutes
always: Even unto the end.

"There's a thought, Lord," she said out loud. "Your words and promises as my heritage—not beef cattle and acres of land and abundant water. Those are wonderful. But to think of You as my heritage! That's something that goes beyond horses and ranching and wide open spaces." She suddenly recalled a verse she'd read the morning before: "I have seen an end of all perfection: but thy commandment is exceeding broad."

Going to the closet, she glanced at the calendar on the wall with its engraving of a cowboy on a wildly bucking horse. It was Tuesday, February 2, 1875. She would be riding, not going to church, so she looked to her thick woolen riding skirts with leggings and her heavy jackets and sweaters. Above zero or not, she picked out warm gear and her blue woolen coat. After she had finished dressing, she crossed to the window and glanced out. It was still dark and would be for several more hours, but she could see by the stars it promised to be a clear morning. A thermometer was fastened to the outside of the window frame, and she squinted at it—ten above. An unexpected warm spell in the dead of winter. *The west wind brought the mild weather,* she thought to herself as she went back to the dresser and mirror to pin up her hair. *It shook the house all night.*

She left her room and went down the stairs, holding the lamp in her hand. The rich smell of fresh coffee brought her into the kitchen. It was empty at this hour, but by six o'clock all her hands would be trooping through the back door and sitting down at the large table for breakfast. Most of them had already been on the range for an hour or more. She poured herself a cup of coffee from a big pot on the woodstove. As she drank it, standing close to the stove's heat, she caught the scent of eggs and bacon and beans from the warming oven.

Pete always made good, strong coffee, but his meals were even better. And his biscuits were legendary. Turning this over in her mind, she opened the small door of the warming oven and plucked two buttermilk biscuits from a plate heaped high, dropping them into a pocket. *Filching,* her mother would say. She smiled and put the coffee cup in the sink. On the way out of the kitchen, she took a red apple from a basket. Then paused and went back to the warming oven to filch two more biscuits. "It will be a long morning's ride," she said to the empty kitchen.

She brought a Winchester 1873 carbine down from a gun rack in the hall and checked to make sure it was loaded, then opened a drawer under the rack and put a box of 44-40 cartridges in her jacket pocket. A light-brown Stetson was hanging from a peg by the front door, and she placed it on her head. Two high leather boots were standing on the floor beneath the hat. She sat in a chair and tugged them on. Then she took a black scarf and wound it about her neck. It might be ten above, but a stiff breeze could still cut like a bowie knife. She stepped onto the porch, pulling on a pair of leather gloves, and two of her men swept off their hats as they stood talking with the cook.

"Miss Spence," the three men said at the same time.

"Mr. Laycock. Mr. Martin. Pete. Are you about ready to ring that piece of scrap iron for breakfast?"

"We are," grinned Pete. "I hope you grabbed a bite before the boys ride in. They won't leave a crumb."

"I don't need anything, Pete, thanks," she said, the biscuits still warm in her skirt pocket.

"Save you a plate for when you get back in?"

"That's kind of you. Yes, please." She turned to Laycock and Martin. "May I?"

"Why, sure." Laycock handed her the striker. "I hardly ever get to do it anymore."

The iron she was going to hit was the rim off a wheel from one of the first wagons her brother Ricky had used on the Spence ranch. It was still sturdy as a rock. She bent her arm and banged the iron bar against it. The rim rang clear and sharp through the star-nicked air. The shock went right up her arm to her shoulder, but she knew one blow wasn't enough. She swung the striker back and forth inside the wheel rim as fast as she could so that the ringing was loud and unmistakable no matter where her hands might be. Then she handed the striker back to Layton.

"That's certainly enough to raise the dead," she said with a laugh.

"The boys will come pelting in from all four corners," agreed Laycock.

"So how are things?" she asked the men. "Anything I should know about?"

"We're getting some early calves," replied Laycock. "This mild spell sure helps us out on that score."

"I'll keep an eye out for the young ones then. I'm

going to do my monthly ride over the ranch this morning."

"Yes, ma'am, you look like you're loaded for bear."

"Anything else?" she asked.

"There's been predators," Martin spoke up. "We haven't found anything that's been killed yet, but the tracks are plentiful. Fox. Coyote. Maybe a cat. Can't tell for sure; the tracks were messed up."

"By what?"

"Horse hooves."

"Whose horse hooves?"

Laycock and Martin glanced at each other.

"We don't rightly know, Miss Spence," Martin finally responded. "But we do know one thing. It's none of our boys."

"How many riders?"

"Half a dozen. Maybe a few more. Traveling fast. Headin' north. The tracks are a couple of days old."

Charlotte stared at him. "Are any cattle missing?"

"Boys are doing a head count. So far, so good. But we ain't got to every part of the herd."

"Where are these tracks?"

"Couple miles west. By Lookoff."

"The marshal hasn't sent us word about rustlers in the vicinity, has he?"

"No, ma'am."

"Let the men get a hot meal in their stomachs before they do any more of that counting. The sun will be up soon, and that will make their job a lot easier." She smiled brightly. "Well, perhaps my ride won't be uneventful."

Laycock and Martin glanced at each other a second time.

This time Laycock spoke up, Stetson still in his hands.

"Miss Spence, perhaps it'd be best if one of the boys was to ride with you. Gallagher, say, or Scotty."

"Ride with me?" Charlotte looked at him in surprise, her eyes opening wide. "Whatever for?"

"Well, there could be the panther; that's reason enough. But a group of riders belting out across our land headed for who knows where? Sounds like outlaws."

Charlotte made a face. "You don't really think so."

"Me and Martin and the rest of the hands think it's a pretty safe bet. There's been talk."

"What kind of talk?"

"About marauders in the neighborhood. About squatters being burned out down on the flats."

Charlotte's eyebrows came together sharply. "Were people killed?"

"Some say no. Others say it was bad."

"But the marshal hasn't said anything about it?"

"It's just rumors, ma'am. I expect we'll hear something, one way or the other, when Marshal Parker gets to the bottom of it."

"'The west wind carries blue skies and blue skies carry lies,'" Charlotte recited. "My mother again. It seems I'm always quoting her."

Martin smiled. "Wish we'd had a chance to meet her."

"So do I, Mr. Martin." She tugged on the brim of her Stetson. "I'd better be on my way. If things are as bad as you say, the men will never let me out of sight of the ranch house."

"You should reconsider," urged Laycock.

"I am twenty-five years old. I've been riding this land since I was a teenage girl. Even Jesse James and his barbarians couldn't keep me off God's good gift to the Spence family and its hands. I'll be back by noon." She glanced at the cook. "I hope the food will be hot, Pete."

"Hot, thick, and three plates full," he responded.

Charlotte was striding across the yard to the stables. "Three plates? Are you trying to fatten me up for the kill?"

Her saddle was hanging clean and dry from a brass hook on the wall. She lit an oil lamp by the door and carried it close to where Daybreak stood in her stall, watching her mistress with large dark eyes. Charlotte brought out the apple.

"Here's a treat, girl. Let's have a good ride together, all right?"

The palomino mare chewed and slobbered over the red apple before taking it into her mouth and working over what was left of it. Charlotte came into the stall and put a saddle blanket and saddle on its back, tightening the cinch under the horse's stomach. Then she slid the carbine into a scabbard. Leading Daybreak out of her stall, she spoke to the other horses that stood watching everything carefully and nickering their comments. At the door to the stable, Charlotte paused and looked out.

Men were riding up to the ranch house, hitching their horses to the rail, then walking around to the back where they'd head in, wash their hands, and sit at the kitchen table for the morning meal. Even those who'd been too far off to hear her striking the wheel rim knew to be at the table by six. The ranch house shone like a star, with oil lamps burning in all its ground-floor windows, drawing the cowboys in from miles around. She smiled as she listened to their banter.

"What you been doing all morning, Scotty? Grabbing some more shut-eye in the hills back yonder?"

"Billy, I could be asleep in the saddle and still work more cattle, and work 'em better, than you sitting wide-awake and ramrod stiff on that itsy-bitsy pony of yours."

"Pony? You say Bill's got a pony? Here all along I could have sworn it was a mule."

"Oh, he's got both. Rides the pony on Tuesdays and Thursdays and the mule the rest of the time."

"Glad you cleared that up, Scotty. I thought Billy Gallagher was two different men on two different nags and drawing two different paychecks from the Spence outfit."

"So I am, you worn-out old cowpokes. Why, Charlotte Spence has made Billy number one foreman and Billy number two head wrangler—I aim to retire a rich man in a few more months."

"You fellahs can stand here and spin your yarns right through breakfast if that's what pleases you. But me, I'll take bacon and beans over a cowboy's dreams. *Adiós.*"

Charlotte waited a bit longer, until she was sure all the men had ridden in and were seated at the table. Then she led Daybreak from the stable and swung up into the saddle. Urging the mare into a trot, she went across the yard and headed for the eastern end of the ranch. She was pretty sure Laycock and Martin would tell the hands she was headed west to Lookoff and send a few of them out that way to keep an eye on her. Charlotte had every intention of having a look at the panther tracks herself, as well as the trail of the riders her foremen thought might be outlaws, but not until she was sure she could be up there on her own. Her ranch hands were all good men, but she had to make sure they understood she could handle things without their help. Otherwise, how could she command their obedience and respect? Picking up the fence line, she followed it north under the winter stars. Yes, it was mild out for early February, but she still felt a sting on her cheeks.

For two hours she crossed streams that were running or partly frozen in the dark, found healthy calves with their mothers, and spotted knots and clusters of her herd happy to find good grass where the snow had melted back. Eventually she made her way up a ridge where there was a tall pinnacle of rock she called the Sentinel. She hardly ever mentioned the place to others, even though it was one of her favorite spots on the ranch, simply because she wanted to have it to herself. Her foreman wouldn't think to send Scotty or Gallagher here.

She sat back in her saddle and brought two buttermilk biscuits from her pocket. Cold as ice, they still tasted pretty good. As she chewed and swallowed, the sun rose like a great yellow and orange ball over the valley and hurled bright light at the Rocky Mountains to the west. The sight made her stop eating and hold in her breath. The white snow on the peaks burned like a world on fire. Was there any part of America more overflowing with grandeur, more rugged, and more beautiful than the Montana Territory?

"And God said, 'Let there be light and plenty of it!'" she called, her words echoing back twice over. "And so there was light! Light that had no end! Light that could not be stopped!" She laughed in sheer delight and went back to her biscuits while she looked over the land that was spread out beneath her. Sweet Blue Meadows. Two Back Valley. The Shining Mountains. What a location her brother Ricky had found to build the Spence ranch. What a gift. It was impossible to get tired of gazing out over heartland that was God's land, land He had shared with the creatures made in His image, the human race. All kinds of people loved Montana—Indian, white, black, Chinese, Spanish. Sometimes they fought, sometimes they lived in peace. But they held in common their respect and passion for the rocks, grass, earth, and boundless sky.

Then, as the sun fully emerged, bringing the blue sky with it and making everything gleam, a feeling of deep sadness rushed through Charlotte. The sensation was so strong it made her wince. Her father and mother were dead. All her brothers and sisters were dead. No one sat on his horse beside her, loving God and God's land as she did, loving her, gazing at her with a fascination that told her he cared more for her beauty than that of the great mountains themselves. The big ranch house was empty except when her hired hands rode in for their three squares a day—no children slid down its banisters or chased each other through its halls or hollered through its windows and doorways. For a few minutes she let tears streak over her face. So much to enjoy and no man, no family, to enjoy it with. For a few moments she let the faces of various men drift through her thoughts. Many of them had been handsome but were not men of faith. Others followed God but did not know their way around a lasso or branding iron or beef cattle. Still others seemed to love the idea of being connected to Charlotte Spence and the Spence ranch but did not know how to love her.

She leaned into the saddle horn with her gloved hands. No, nothing had worked out. Well, she'd had her cry. She flicked the mare's reins. There was no use in carrying on like this. She was a woman alone and had to get used to it.

To make her way to Lookoff she had to come down from the Sentinel and the ridge, so she coaxed Daybreak along a trail that led to the valley bottom. Then she walked the palomino through thickets and scattered boulders. There was still snow on the highlands, so she didn't think all the tracks would have disappeared with the thaw. Her brother had taught her how to read signs, and she was curious to see what she would come up with when she examined the pugmarks—mountain lion, panther, something that wasn't even remotely like a cat?

The crying of a calf jolted her out of her thoughts. She put her horse into a trot and saw the calf standing by a large rock, its young eyes wide in terror, bawling for help. Without even thinking about it, Charlotte slid the Winchester from its scabbard and walked the horse closer. Now she saw the body of a cow just beyond where the calf was tottering on its thin legs. Instinctively she knew it was the calf's mother. Then a head lifted from the far side of the carcass. A mountain lion.

Charlotte barely had time to take it all in before the big cat growled deep in its chest and sprang, bounding over the dead body and making for the horse. Daybreak reared just as Charlotte fired, and the shot went wild. The mare kicked out at the lion with her front hooves. The cat darted around to the horse's back, and Daybreak whirled and struck with her hind legs, missing the mountain lion but throwing Charlotte to the ground. Just missing a pile of rocks, she rolled and took dirt and grass into her mouth. The palomino ran off, squealing loudly, and the lion turned to Charlotte, its eyes spitting fury. She had trouble bringing the Winchester to bear, the barrel sticking into the soft soil. The cat was going to pounce.

Jesus, help me. Help me.

The lion was on top of her, roaring and trying to bite through her neck and head. She yanked the barrel clear and shoved it into the cat's snarling mouth. Her finger was outside the trigger guard, and she wasn't able to fire. The cat thrust claws at her face, and Charlotte twisted her head and shoulders. This movement jerked her finger onto the trigger. She squeezed.

The blast made her ears sting. She was able to work the lever and fire again. Then the weight and hot breath of the lion were on her face, and she almost passed out.

The lion was not biting or moving. Charlotte tried to push herself out from underneath, but it took some time. Finally, she was free and sat back, trying to get a lungful of air and staring at the animal, her carbine still in her hands. As frightened as she was, she could not help but marvel at the mountain lion's strong body and long tail, at its wild and powerful beauty. She bent her head and leaned it against the warm Winchester barrel.

I wish it had never hunted my cattle. I wish it had never strayed onto our range. But thank You, God, that I'm alive. Thank You.

Finally, she climbed to her feet and glanced around for Daybreak. The mare was about a hundred feet away, her head turned toward her mistress and the cat. Charlotte slowly walked to her, speaking softly.

"It's all right, girl. The lion won't bother you anymore. Don't run. You're safe. Yes, it's me."

The mare didn't move, but rubbed its nose on Charlotte's arm and snuffled against the sleeve of her thick winter jacket. Charlotte put her head against the mare's and closed her eyes. "We're both alive. We made it. Rest easy, girl. Thank God, we're both okay."

The crying of the calf made her look up.

"That's enough excitement for today," she said to Daybreak. "Let's get the calf back to the ranch and get it some milk. Keep it alive. It's all about life, girl, all about keeping things alive."

Not wanting to take the mare close to the cat's body, she tied the horse's reins to a nearby aspen and then walked over to get the calf. It was happy to be picked up and comforted, burying its little head in Charlotte's chest. Then she came back to Daybreak, took the reins in her hand while holding the calf tightly with the other, and after a couple of tries, got up into the saddle. The calf cried out at this but once the horse started moving, the rocking motion seemed to comfort it. Charlotte kept to the valley floor and moved the palomino along at a slow trot. It would take a couple of hours to reach the main ranch.

"You hold on, young one," Charlotte whispered to the calf. "I intend to take good care of a little orphan like you."

The calf was asleep but alive when Charlotte walked Daybreak into the yard in front of the house. It was about ten o'clock, she reckoned. She never used a watch while out on horseback but preferred to estimate time by the position of the sun. Billy Gallagher was sitting on his horse and gulping down a mug full of coffee Pete had just handed up to him when they both saw her. Billy was off his horse and at her side in an instant.

"What happened to you?" he asked, reaching up for the calf.

Charlotte placed it in his arms. "I guess I ran into that mountain lion of yours."

"Where?"

"Just below the Sentinel. It killed the calf's mother."

"What happened to the cat?"

"It's dead."

"Are you cut? Are you bleeding anywhere?"

"I don't know."

"You look like you took a tumble down a mountain slope."

Pete helped her down from the mare. "Better let me look you over. Come inside."

She looked at Billy. "The calf needs warm milk."

"Did it have a few days to feed off its mother?"

"I think so. She's pretty sturdy."

Billy nodded. "I'll take care of it." He headed toward the barn.

"What about Daybreak?" called Charlotte.

"I'll take care of her, too. Don't fret. Let Pete clean you up." It didn't take long for word to get around the ranch that the Spence outfit's ramrod had tangled with a mountain lion, and the mountain lion had come up short. Not only that, but Charlotte Spence hardly had a nick on her despite firing off two rounds with the lion pretty much sitting on her head. Charlotte lay down for an hour in her room but heard the ruckus when the hands came in for lunch. Scotty had brought in the cat, and most of the men would have seen it when they rode up. She could tell that the talk around the table was louder than usual and pushed herself off the bed.

I had plans to do chores in town this afternoon. A brush with a mountain lion shouldn't change that. And the boys will want to see me.

She put on a blue dress with lace at the collar, pinned up her hair, and headed down the staircase. The men all stood up when she entered the kitchen, dropping their forks and knives and asking after her health. She smiled. They treated her like one of their sisters.

"Boys, I'm fine. It was a good bit of excitement, I can tell you that, but I'm none the worse for wear. Pete has given me a clean bill of health, haven't you, Pete?"

Pete was wearing a large apron and placing another pot of coffee on the table. "A few thumps and bumps, but she's sturdy as an oak."

"There you are. So thank you all for your concern, but please, sit down and finish your meals. How is the calf, Mr. Gallagher?"

"Top notch, Miss Spence. Drank her fill and more. She'll be all right."

"That's good news. And Daybreak?"

"Not a scratch on her, Miss Spence. I rubbed her down and gave her some oats, and she's resting in her stall."

"Thank you very much. You're a good man." She looked around the table. "You're all good men. I'm blessed to have such a solid outfit to keep the Spence ranch up and running."

"Our pleasure, ma'am," said Laycock.

"And now, if you don't mind, I'll need the black hitched up to my Philadelphia buggy, Mr. Martin, for I have some matters in town to attend to."

"Miss Spence," Martin protested, "are you sure you're fit for that?"

"I certainly am. After all, the excitement only lasted a minute or two. I'm rested up. Pete stood over me and forced me to eat hot buttermilk biscuits with gravy to restore my strength, and now I need to get into Iron Springs before this lovely February day is gone forever. I assure you, gentlemen, that considering the morning I had, an afternoon in town is going to prove most uneventful."

She was on her way in ten minutes, the black stepping smartly along the road into Iron Springs, the dark buggy rolling smoothly through the puddles and mud behind it. Charlotte was wearing a bonnet and leaning back, comfortably holding the traces in her hands. She thought about her work at the library, some sewing items and fabric she meant to purchase at the general store, and whether today was a good time to discuss some issues with her attorney, Mr. King.

A bird burst across her path and startled her. For some reason, a face popped into her head immediately afterwards. A man she had been interested in once. Zephaniah Parker. A kind man. A strong man. A young man about her age, who had his own small ranch and ran it well. A man who honored God. She bit her lower lip and thought about him for a few minutes. Then she shook her head in annoyance and flicked the reins. She had hardly seen him more than once or twice over the past year, and for all she knew, he didn't even live in the region anymore. She might never see him again and that was that.

"God's will be done," she murmured to herself and turned her mind back to the sorts of fabrics she needed to pick out at the store and which sorts of buttons would go best with what colors.

Chapter Two

Zeph eased his horse over the ridge and down the slope.

Cricket was making a lot of noise and grumbling into her bit. She didn't like the slush, and she liked the ice even less.

"I know it," Zeph said to her as she blew loudly through her nostrils. "But I'm keeping us off the trail because it's even worse. We'll be into some open grass in a bit."

The sky was so blue and so bright it hurt Zeph's eyes. It was February and ought to have been colder, but a thaw had come in with the west wind and melted all the snow back. Zeph liked the break from below zero, and so did his cattle, but when it cooled off at night you wound up with too many patches of ice—bad for horses, bad for the cows.

Cricket snapped her head back.

"Whoa!" called Zeph. "What was that for? You got grass under your hooves now."

She reared. Zeph stared all around, trying to find out what was spooking her. All he saw was a thin line of smoke off to the left, coming from behind a clump of gray cottonwoods with their bare branches all tangled. That's where some of the new homesteaders from out east had settled in back before Christmas. That wouldn't be it. He looked down—there weren't any snakes out in February, even during a thaw. What was going on with his mare?

She balked, didn't want to go any farther. Zeph swung down and held her reins while he inspected the ground in front of them. Just dead winter grasses, brown as dust. Wet some from snowmelt, but that was about it. He got down on one knee—and saw the bloody footprint.

Not large. No boot. High arch. The wound seemed to be in the back by the heel. He squinted ahead. There were more of them, crossing over the grass and soft snow. Cricket protested, but he tugged her forward as he followed the prints.

"Two of 'em," he said out loud.

The two sets of tracks were obvious in the snow. The blood was pretty fresh. He kept walking, pulling Cricket along. The prints went into a gully. Cricket snorted. She had seen the two heads first.

"Hello!" Zeph called. "You all right?"

The heads ducked out of sight.

Zeph tilted his brown Stetson back and scratched at his head.

"One of you looks to have a cut. I have some bandage in my saddlebag. Good clean cloth."

Still no answer. He rubbed his jaw and thought for a moment.

"I'm Zephaniah Parker. I own the Bar Zee, just a few miles west of here in the Two Back Valley. I'm out looking for strays. Been living by the mountains for five or six years. My brother's the preacher at the church in town. And my other brother's the federal marshal. You can come out. I'm not gonna hurt you."

After a moment a boy stood up, tall and skinny, about twelve, Zeph figured. He seemed to totter on one leg. He didn't say anything. Then a girl stood up and clutched the boy's hand. She was half a foot shorter, straw-blond hair, maybe ten or eleven. Neither of them smiled.

"Can I come closer?" asked Zeph. "Take a look at that foot?"

The boy nodded. "All right."

Cricket had calmed down, and Zeph brought her over to the gully and wrapped her reins around some thick scrub. He smiled at the girl and boy. Up close now, he could see their faces were scratched, their cheeks hollow; they looked tired and gaunt. He rummaged around in one of his saddlebags while Cricket munched grass. He finally held up some strips of white cotton cloth.

"Told you I had some." He knelt by the boy.

"You wanna show me your sore foot?"

The boy lifted his left foot, and Zeph saw the cut on the heel. It was pretty clean from all the melted snow, but he wiped some mud and grass away before he started wrapping.

"Neither of you have shoes?"

"No," said the boy.

"What happened to 'em?"

"I don't know."

Zeph shrugged, finished the wrapping, and stood up. "The next thing is to get you home. Where are your parents? They'll likely be worried about you, won't they?"

The two kids stared right through Zeph. He'd seen that look before on ten- or twelve-year-olds, but that was back during the war and coming through a town that had been fought over by both sides. He glanced at the pencil line of gray smoke.

"That your place over there? Your mom and dad with the new settlers?"

Still neither of them spoke. Zeph looked more closely at the girl. Her eyes were bluer than the sky. But the skin around them was swollen and red. She'd been crying, a lot.

"You don't need to be scared," he said to her gently. "I'll get you back to your folks just as soon as you tell me where they are."

"We hain't got folks," she said. "We hain't got a home."

Zeph smiled as warmly as he could. "Now, what do you mean by that? Everybody's got folks and a home."

"We hain't."

Her voice had a trace of an accent. From another country. One part of Zeph's mind worked on that while another part tried to figure out what to do next.

"Well, look, I tell you what, let's go to that farm over there behind the cottonwoods, and maybe they can help us out. Do you know them?"

The girl began to cry. She buried her head in the boy's arm.

Now what did I say? Zeph asked himself.

"Mister Parker," said the boy, "we can't go there."

"Why not?"

"We can't."

Zeph looked up at the sun. It was about three o'clock. "The sun'll be down in a few hours. We've got to get to someplace. Now Cricket here'll take you both easy. How about we go into town and get you some food and a safe place to stay, and then we'll figure out the rest of it?"

"Don't leave us!" the girl suddenly blurted, tears running muddy down her cheeks.

Zeph shook his head. "I won't leave you. I'll stick right with you. Now let's get you up on Cricket and into town. You hungry?"

"Yah, sir," she answered.

"What would you like to eat?"

"Potatoes and meat."

"I guess it'll be easy enough to rustle up some of that. You got a name, young lady?"

She didn't answer. He held out his hand to help her onto Cricket, and she slowly stepped forward and took it. He hoisted her into the saddle. She was as light as a snowflake.

"No name?" he asked again.

But she just sat on the horse and clung to its mane.

The boy came up and put one hand on the pommel. "I can get up myself, Mister Parker."

"Help yourself."

The boy winced when his left foot touched the stirrup, but he swung his leg over Cricket as if he'd been born to the saddle. *He has that accent, too,* thought Zeph. *What is it?*

Zeph started leading Cricket cross-country and to their right.

"You like horses, boy?"

"Yes."

"Have any of your own at your place?"

The boy didn't answer.

Zeph walked for a while in silence. The sun dipped lower. "We're not far from the town," he told them. "We cut across the fields like this, and we'll be there in another hour. You seen it yet? Not a bad little place. Iron Springs. For the iron ore the miners been pulling out of the earth. Used to be a lot of gold here in the '60s. I think we're making more money now off the iron and the beef. You'll catch sight of it in a little while."

"Thank you, Mister Parker."

"You're welcome, son. How about you? Your folks drop you into this world without a name, too?"

But the boy didn't say anything. Zeph looked at his dark hair and green eyes a moment and then glanced ahead.

"Well, I got to call you something. How about I give you each a nickname? So I don't have to say, 'hey, boy' or 'hey, girl' the whole time?"

They didn't respond.

"I come from out of Wyoming. They've got some nice towns there. I grew up just north of what's now Cheyenne, the Magic City of the Plains. If you don't mind, young lady, I'll call you Cheyenne Wyoming. That'll be your name just for this trip. Is that all right with you?"

She stared straight ahead.

Zeph nodded. "Glad you like it. Now, son, do you want a town name, too?"

"It doesn't matter."

That accent again. Zeph had his head down while they plowed through a snowdrift.

"There's a man I greatly admire that I met in Wyoming a few years ago. Cody was his name. He rode for the Pony Express when he was hardly older than you. Then he was a scout. They gave him the Medal of Honor for the work he did. How about we hang his name on you until we reach town?"

"All right."

"Well, there we have it then. Cody Wyoming and Cheyenne Wyoming. Brother and sister. I guess I should have asked—you are brother and sister, aren't you?"

But no one spoke. And Zeph did not open his mouth again until the three of them spotted the riders coming at them over the snow and the dead grass. There looked to be six or seven men, and they were riding hard. Zeph was sure he recognized the lead horse.

Cricket reared. Zeph glanced behind him. Both the kids had jumped off the horse and were running away as fast as they could.

Chapter Three

"Hey! Wait! What are you doing?" Zeph shouted.

But they didn't stop. Zeph dropped Cricket's reins and lit out after them. The boy was already staggering because of his wounded foot, yet he showed no signs of stopping. The girl was racing ahead of him, blond hair flying.

Zeph got to the boy first, because he had collapsed in the snow, blood all over his foot.

"What are you running for?"

"They'll kill us!"

"Who's gonna kill you?"

"Those riders killed our families, and they're going to kill us, too! They said they would!"

"No one's gonna kill anybody, boy. Those are men from town, and the lead rider is my own brother, the federal marshal. They won't hurt you. Now stay put before that foot of yours falls off."

Zeph went after the girl as the riders bore down on them. He caught her and wrapped his arms around her as she kicked and screamed.

"Nay! Nay! Nay!" She shrieked and sobbed.

"Settle down!" snapped Zeph, struggling to hold on to her. "Nobody's gonna hurt you. Those are men from town. It's the marshal and a bunch of others, all good men who have kids of their own."

"They'll shoot us!"

"No, they won't!"

She broke free and ran a few yards before Zeph grabbed her around the waist again and picked her up off the ground, legs and arms swinging. The riders reined up right in front of them. "Looks like you got a handful there, Z," said his brother the marshal.

"You could say that."

"What's going on?"

"Matt, I don't know what's going on. I found these kids over by the new homesteads a couple of hours ago, and nothing's made sense since."

"The new homesteads?"

"Yeah. Down in the flats by the river."

"Young lady," said Matt kindly, "I am the federal marshal, and I am here to help you. All of us are. We rode out to give you as much help as we can. That's why I'm here talking to you right now."

She had stopped squirming and was looking up at him through the blond hair that had fallen down over her face. The marshal took off his hat.

"I am Matthew Parker, but you can call me Matt. The man that's got ahold of you is my younger brother, Zephaniah T. Parker. Now this here"—the marshal swept his hat back toward the men sitting on their horses behind him—"this here with the long black coat is another one of my brothers, Jude, and he is the preacher in town, and these other three are all brothers, too. We got a special on brothers today. This is William King, and Samuel and Wyatt."

The man with the thick black beard smiled with a big row of white teeth and lifted his black Stetson. "Billy King," he said, "barrister and solicitor and attorney-at-law for the Montana Territory. I have long sticks of peppermint candy in my coat pocket. Would you like one? Or are you too old for that sort of stuff? I usually keep 'em for myself; it's my belief they make me smarter, but sometimes I share if I run into someone special."

He swung down off his large black horse and stood by the little girl. He took a long red and white stick of candy from inside his sheepskin jacket and offered it to her in his gloved hand. Zeph had set her down. Slowly she reached out and took the candy.

"Thank you, sir," she said.

"You're very welcome, young lady. Would you like to walk with me and give one to your brother?"

She nodded, and they headed back across the snow to where two other men were off their horses and looking at the boy's foot. The marshal watched them for a moment then tilted his Stetson back and scratched at his head and sandy-blond hair.

"We got news by telegraph that some marauders were in our neck of the woods. Then Abe Whittaker came in and told us he'd heard shooting down in the flats the day before yesterday. So I got some of the boys together, and we were heading out there to take a look. You see anything?"

Zeph shook his head. "Just these two kids."

Matt glanced over at them. "They say much?"

"They don't say anything at all, not where they live or who their folks are, nothin'."

Matt rubbed his jaw. "See any smoke?"

"No. Well, a bit from a chimney, I guess; that's all."

"Abe figured the homesteaders were burned out."

"Did he see that?"

Matt shrugged. "You know Abe. He tells you what he wants when he wants. I don't know what else he knows. But he's got that dugout by the river, so he must've seen something." He pulled his hat down again. "Now, look, we got to get out there before it's dark. We brought along three extra horses, so why don't you take the gray here and put the kids on it? Then you can get back on Cricket and all ride into Iron Springs and get warmed up."

"That's where I was heading, Matt."

"Well, now you can do it faster."

"Why'd you need all those extra horses anyway?"

"Why do you think? The telegram said it was Seraph Raber's crew."

"Raber. The Angel of Death. They sure?"

"Whoever they are, they've left a trail of dead bodies between here and Dakota. Looks like Raber's work. No one likes killing as much as him." Matt glanced down at Zeph's waist. "No gun, I see."

"No need, brother."

"Suppose Raber jumped you while you were taking care of the kids? How would you have saved them then? The war's been over a long time, Z."

"Not long enough."

"Just get 'em into town."

Matt pulled away with the others. Only Jude held back. "You all right?" asked Jude.

"My boots are wet, and my feet are cold and sore. Getting back on my horse will make a world of a difference."

"You given any thought about where you'll put the kids up?"

"Some."

Jude suddenly smiled. The silver conchas on his black Stetson winked in the falling sun. "What about a good church woman like Charlotte Spence?"

Zeph reddened. "Charlotte. I guess she'd do. The kids had better mind their p's and q's."

"Are you telling me she never crossed your mind?"

"Not much has been crossing my mind lately. The ranch is a lot of work."

Jude turned his horse to join the others. "She's out and around. Saw her on Main Street before we left. I guess you know what she looks like. Take the kids to Miss Charlotte Spence, brother."

Ten minutes later they walked the two horses into Iron Springs, the boy and the girl on the gray mare, Zeph back on Cricket. There was maybe an hour of sunlight left, Zeph figured. The town was hopping— wagons, men on horseback, people heading back and forth across Main Street from one shop to another.

"I guess the good weather's brought everybody out of hibernation," Zeph said.

The boy and girl rode silently on their horse, but at least, Zeph thought, they didn't act as scared as they'd been. He saw them taking in all the activity and doubted they'd even been in the town before. If they were with the new homesteaders they may not have had the chance yet.

"Pferdewagen!" shouted the girl, pointing.

"What?" Zeph looked at her and then looked where she was pointing. There was a cluster of wagons. He didn't see anything unusual. But the boy was excited, too.

"*Pferdewagen*, yah," he said, rising up in the stirrups, even with his sore foot.

"What are you two talking about?" demanded Zeph.

They both pointed—and smiled for the first time. Emerging from the knot of wagons came a shiny black horse stepping smartly and pulling a black buggy. Zeph knew the horse and buggy well.

"Charlotte Spence," he said under his breath.

And then it hit him. The accent under some of the kids' words was the same accent Charlotte had under some of her words. It was a little like the Germans he'd heard speaking English in Wyoming. And this "Pferde" whatever they were squawking about, that sure sounded like the real thing, the way cattleman Wolfgang Mueller used to talk when he was with his buddies from overseas.

"Zephaniah Truett Parker, what on earth are you doing sitting in the middle of the street with those two children?"

Charlotte Spence, in a blue dress with lace at the collar and a matching lace-trimmed blue bonnet, pulled her buggy up in front of them, smiling. She leaned out from under the roof of the carriage. The sun struck her golden eyebrows and sky-blue eyes. Zeph looked down at the ground.

"Well? Isn't anyone going to speak to me?"

Zeph sat up and lifted his hat off his head and gave her a crooked smile. "Miss Spence."

"Who are the children, Zephaniah? Aren't you going to introduce me?"

"This is Miss Charlotte Spence. She has a spread outside of town. She is also Iron Springs's librarian. You can say hello."

The girl poked her head out from behind the boy's shoulders.

"Pferdewagen," she said and nodded. *"Vorsintflutlich."*

The woman's eyes widened. "What did you say?" But the girl ducked behind the boy's back again. "What did she say, Zephaniah?"

"I don't know, Miss Spence—"

"Oh, stop that. My name is Charlotte."

"It seems to me she's talking like a cattleman I knew in Wyoming, a gentleman from Germany by the name of Mueller."

"Who are these children? Where are they from?"

"It's hard to say, Miss Spence. I found them wandering in the scrub not far from the river and the new homesteads."

"Well, where are their parents?"

"I don't know. They won't tell me."

Charlotte Spence placed one high, black, tightly laced boot into a puddle of mud and melted snow and then the other. She came up to the children on their horse and stood stroking the gray's neck. Part of her face was in shadow and part in the light. Zeph tried to keep himself from looking at the small freckles sprinkled across her nose and just under her eyes.

"I am Miss Spence, and you may call me Miss Charlotte," she said to the boy and girl, with her brightest smile. "I know the words you are using very well. Would you like to have a ride in the horse and buggy?"

The boy shrugged, but the girl smiled and nodded.

"Well, then, you must tell me your names and where you are from. That's only polite."

Neither of the children spoke for a moment. Then the boy said, "I am Cody Wyoming. And this is Cheyenne, my sister."

Miss Spence blinked. "Pardon me?"

"We are Cody and Cheyenne Wyoming."

Miss Spence looked up at Zeph and he looked away. A smile curled her lips once again.

"Very well, Cody and Cheyenne, it's a pleasure to meet you. And where did you say you were from?"

The boy and girl said nothing.

"Where did you learn those words you just used?" Silence.

"Well, let me tell you a secret. I learned those words from my grandmother. Did you learn them from your grandmother?"

"I learned them from my aunt Rosa," the boy said.

"And where is your aunt Rosa?"

"Pennsylvania."

Miss Spence nodded. "I know the words because I am from Pennsylvania, too. I grew up there. And I rode in the horse and buggies like you did all the time."

She looked at Zeph. "Until you find their parents, these children are staying with me."

Chapter Four

The sun was just coming up, the weather was still mild, and Zeph let Cricket plod slowly through the mud and puddles back to town. His ranch was only about two miles out. It used to be five miles, but things had started changing again in the last three years, especially with talk of the Union Pacific putting a branch line through. That hadn't happened yet, but the town was prospering just the same.

He'd left Byrd and Holly, his ranch hands, to take care of the day's chores. He needed to see his brother Matt and find out what was going on with the homesteaders and what they'd found out. Were the kids' parents alive? Were any of the homesteaders alive? Then he'd need to swing by Sweet Blue Meadows and the Spence ranch to see how Charlotte was making out. It was the polite thing to do.

So she'd been born and raised in Pennsylvania. He'd always thought her family had hailed from Texas. Did that mean her father and brothers had been Pennsylvanians, too? They'd fought on the side of the Union. All of them killed except the one brother who made his way to the Montana Territory and started the Spence ranching operation—and finally died of his wounds and left it all to Charlotte. Who now ran the whole thing with a ten-man crew as if she were the legendary brother himself. Ricky Spence, who could handle Indians and outlaws and hard men with one hand, and cows and bulls and beef shipments with the other.

He'd met Ricky twice. Once at a meeting to press the Union Pacific into building the connection to Iron Springs they'd always said they would, the other time when they were both part of a posse hunting down a gang that had robbed a gold shipment out of Virginia City, just south of them. Ricky coughed up a lot of blood on that ride. Zeph had made sure he got back to the Spence homestead all right. That was four years ago. Ricky never left the house again.

Zeph remembered how Charlotte stood with the lamp while he walked with Ricky up the steps to the porch. Blood was running down the front of Ricky's jacket. Zeph got him in the door, but no farther. Charlotte blocked his path.

"I'll take it from here, Mister Parker." Her voice had been like iron. But as he turned to go back down the steps she grasped his arm. Her eyes were a soft blue and gold, the lamp just inches from her face. In almost a whisper she said, "Thank you, Z."

Only his brothers called him Z. And she'd never called him that again. He shrugged. It had been the kind of sweet moment that got a man's hopes up. But after Ricky's death, she was a stranger. He saw her at the library, where he only went to take out books he thought might impress her, and at meetings of the Stock Growers Association, but he was Mister Parker or Zephaniah Truett Parker from then on, and they hardly said more than two words to each other.

Until yesterday. That was the most time they'd spent with one another in years. He guessed he could thank the kids for that. She loved kids. People in town wondered why she hadn't applied for the position of schoolteacher. But she loved horses and cattle and her homestead, too. She could only do so much and do it well. She knew where to draw the line.

Cricket had stopped in front of the marshal's office. Matt's horse Union was already there.

"How'd you know I wanted to go here?" asked Zeph. Cricket let him wind her reins around the hitching post, and then she nuzzled the roan gelding. Zeph stretched and walked in the door. He hoped Matt had a fresh pot of coffee.

He did, but it was almost empty. Zeph squeezed one small cup out of it. Better than nothing. Matt looked like he'd barely slept.

"How's Sally?" asked Zeph.

"Worried."

"About what?"

"Me setting up a posse to go after Raber."

"Is that what you're doing?"

"Not much choice." Matt leaned back in the chair behind his desk and looked at the ceiling. "Three families were in there, Z. Billy King did all the deeds, all legit. From Pennsylvania. They got this far without a scratch. And then Raber comes through. Killed everyone—women, men, children. Lots of hooves cutting up the mud and snow. Five or six riders. The kids said they were in the thick brush. They saw the outlaws, but the outlaws never spotted them. And that's about all they said."

"So they saw most of the killings?"

"I believe they did." Matt sat up. "I've sent out telegrams trying to locate next of kin. I expect we'll hear back later today or tomorrow. King had their names: Kauffman, Troyer, Miller. Bird in Hand. Lancaster County. Funny handle for a town. Heard of it?"

Zeph shook his head. "Did he have the kids' names?"

"No, none of that. Just the adults'." Matt got to his feet. "Trail'll be cold. I could use a decent tracker."

"I'm in—you know that."

Matt nodded. "We've got to bury them first. Jude'll do a service this afternoon. In the town cemetery. Least we can do. We'll head out at first light tomorrow. Pack for a couple of weeks. If they've left the Montana Territory, we can leave it up to someone else. I telegraphed the federal marshal who's at Lewiston in the Idaho Territory."

"Who's gonna watch the town?"

"Leaving my deputy here. You know, Luke, the new man." Zeph put down his cup.

"Want me to brew another pot?" asked Matt.

"No, I'm heading up to Spence's."

"Yeah. I should head up there myself and look in on them. Doc Brainerd's been in to see the kids."

"When was that?"

"Last night."

"What'd he tell you?"

"They're doing fine, considering what they went through. Charlotte Spence couldn't be happier, Doc says. Treating them like her own."

The ranch was three miles north. Two of the hired men, Laycock and Martin, met them at the main house.

"Was it Raber?" asked Laycock.

"Yeah," said Matt. "You know his trademark. No one left alive."

"How'd these kids get out then?"

"The gang never saw them. They were hiding in the bushes. You think they'd talk about what they saw?"

"I don't think Miss Spence will let you ask them," said Martin. "She wants to get their minds off all that."

"Fair enough. But no one's ever seen Seraph Raber's face. He could've stayed at the Ten Gallon Hat last night, and nobody would've been the wiser. Would be something if the kids could tell us what he looks like."

"Matt," said Laycock, "Miss Spence was wondering if Raber knows those two kids are alive."

"Who knows?"

"Because if he did, he might come back for them." Matt looked hard at Laycock.

"Especially if he thinks the kids saw his face," Laycock finished.

Matt nodded. "Yeah. She's right. He could. You got your boys ready for that?"

"Ever since she brought 'em home."

"Sometimes I think she should be marshal."

The men smiled. Matt and Zeph headed up the steps and knocked on the door.

Charlotte had been watching Zephaniah and Matt ride in from a window. She was glad to see both of them but, she admitted to herself, if Matt had come alone, it wouldn't have been good enough. Pausing to check her hair in the hall mirror, she answered the door in her yellow cotton skirt and white blouse. Her hair was pulled back and she wore silver earrings. She gave them a smile.

"Marshal. Zephaniah Parker. Please come in."

They took off their hats and stepped into the hall then paused a moment to glance around at the large front room with its massive fireplace and rugs. She knew Zeph hadn't been inside for a long time and watched him marvel at the high ceilings and oak walls and floors, the chandeliers, the couches, and the huge buffalo head over the mantel.

"It's beautiful, Miss Spence," he said to her.

Zephaniah Parker and his polite manners that went far and beyond the call of duty!

"Matt," she teased, "can I get you to arrest him if he calls me Miss Spence once more?"

"I'll ask Judge Skinner. There could be something on the books."

"I'm Charlotte, Zephaniah Parker. Especially to you."

As she turned her back to lead the way into another room, she saw Matt raise his eyebrows at his brother, and Zeph shrug. Well, Zeph, she thought, it's still the season to keep you guessing, because I'm not sure of how I feel about you myself. The children were sitting and eating a breakfast the cook, Pete Sampson, had served up: ham, eggs, bacon, toast, big jars of jam, a pitcher of milk. They both smiled at Zeph. She could see right away that he approved of the transformation she'd wrought in them—they'd both had baths, their hair was clean and combed, and the girl had blue ribbons in hers and was wearing a blue dress. Looking at the boy in the shirt and denim pants she'd purchased in town, she realized there was quite a change from the bedraggled young man Zeph had brought into Iron Springs the day before.

"Marshal," she said with a playful curtsy, "may I introduce to you Cody and Cheyenne Wyoming?"

Matt inclined his head. "We've met. First time I've heard their names though."

"Oh, their names are a surprise to everyone," she said, "but they insist on using them." She glanced at Zeph. "You both know Pete? Would you men like some of his excellent food or magnificent coffee?"

"That's kind of you, Charlotte," said Matt, "but I'd appreciate a word with you alone, if I may. Perhaps Z could spend some time with Cody and Cheyenne while we talk?"

"Fine with me," said Zeph, pulling a chair up to the table. "Take all the time you want. Fill me up a plate, Pete. I'm starved. You starved, Cody?"

"I was once." The boy smiled. "But not anymore."

"How about you, Cheyenne?"

"The men keep us safe here, Mister Parker, don't they?"

Zeph looked at her and nodded. "You bet. Miss Spence hires only the bravest and the best."

Pete leaned over Zeph's shoulder with a plate heaped with pancakes and sausages. "How's that, Zeph?"

"Why, thank you, Pete, that'll do for a start. Any maple syrup around here, Cody?"

Charlotte led the marshal into the parlor with its antelope heads on the walls and dark-brown sofa and chairs and piano. She closed the door firmly and then leaned her back against it.

"What do you have to tell me, Marshal?"

"The kids were part of a group of families that came here from Pennsylvania, town named Bird in Hand. Their folks were all killed."

"Indians?"

"White men, Charlotte. The Raber Gang."

She felt ice in her chest when he used the name. "The Angel of Death."

"Yes, ma'am. I'm getting a posse together, and we'll be going after them at first light. Zeph will be my tracker."

"Is he any good at that?"

She saw Matt's eyes narrow. "Yes, he is, Charlotte. Any better, and I'd swear he's got Sioux or Apache in his veins."

"Why aren't you going after them today?"

"We'll do the funeral for the families this afternoon. Set everything else to rights before we head out. Could be gone for weeks."

"I see. Anything else?"

"Well, we're trying to get ahold of the children's kin, so we've sent out a telegram. The families were the Millers, Troyers, and Kaufmanns."

Charlotte passed a hand over her face. But she forced herself to speak up. "I hope you are successful, Marshal."

"Are you feeling all right, Charlotte?"

She lifted her head. "I'm perfectly fine, Matt. Is there anything else?"

"I was wondering if you would be attending the funeral with the children—"

She shook her head. "No, Matt, they've been through so much already. Next week will be soon enough for them to pay their respects."

"I understand. There is also the possibility of the Raber Gang coming for the children. We don't know if the kids saw any of their faces. It might be best if we moved them into Iron Springs for the time being, so we can offer them better protection."

Charlotte stopped leaning against the door and stood straight. She felt a strange knot of anger in her stomach, what friends and family called "Charlotte getting her Spence up."

"We can take care of them perfectly fine here. There's no need to disturb them further by running them into town. They're just getting settled in."

"Yes, ma'am. I don't suppose you'd let me have a chance to ask them what they saw and if they can identify any of the outlaws?"

The anger was in Charlotte's head now. "Certainly not, Matt. You should know me better than to ask. The children need to recover from their ordeal, not keep being reminded of it. You do your job and find the killers and leave those children alone."

"Yes, Miss Spence."

Charlotte led the way back to the kitchen. Her face was set like stone. Matt stood awkwardly behind her, his face looking like a hat someone had crumpled in their hands.

"Best we be moving on, Z," Matt said.

"All right," responded Zeph, getting to his feet. "I'll be back, you two, so make sure you have plenty of adventures to tell me about next time I come around."

"We will!" said Cheyenne.

Charlotte walked the men to the door.

"Thank you for coming, gentlemen. Zephaniah, I hope

you will make your way here again tomorrow. I think it's important for the children's recovery to see you."

"It will be my pleasure—"

"Charlotte," she said.

"Miss Spence."

She smiled sadly and shook her head. "You're incorrigible."

"Will we see you this afternoon?" asked Zeph.

"No, your brother and I have discussed that. I think it's best the children stay here and keep putting all that behind them. A day will come when they can say a proper good-bye to their parents and relatives. But not today. Thank you again."

She shut the door firmly. Zeph could hear it being locked and then double-locked from inside.

"Well?" he asked his brother as they walked their horses back into town.

"That woman," answered Matt, "isn't afraid of anything, and she's sure not afraid of Seraphim Raber. She wouldn't budge from that house if a whole army was coming after her."

"That doesn't surprise me. Pete Sampson told me she shot and killed a mountain lion yesterday."

"What?"

"Yes, sir. Right after her horse had thrown her."

Matt whistled. "I guess that about says it all when it comes to Miss Charlotte Spence."

Zeph squinted ahead. "There's someone riding this way, Matt. They're in a lot of hurry."

Matt stared. "It's my deputy."

They spurred their horses forward. When the three reined up in the middle of the road, Zeph could see the young deputy's face was gray and tight.

"What is it, Luke?" demanded Matt.

"I've got bad news and worse news. Which do you want?"

"Dish it all out."

"We got three telegrams since you went to Spence's. Heard back from the law in Lancaster County. Those three families were excommunicated or something, kicked out of their church, but the relatives told the sheriff they'd take the kids back."

"Not so bad. What else?"

"Raber hit settlements near Copper Creek, three days' ride north. Burned two out, took some cattle, killed seven settlers. And Marshal Baker and his deputy, Ned Green."

Zeph glanced quickly at his brother. Matt had counted both those men as two of his closest friends. Ned had stood as best man when he married Sally. Matt clenched his teeth, and Zeph saw his knuckles whiten on his reins.

"Go on," Matt whispered.

"Witnesses said Raber had five riders with him. And tracks have them headed back this way."

Matt nodded. Zeph could see his mind was working fast. "You said there were three telegrams."

"Billy King and me didn't believe the third was genuine, so we cabled back to the station at Copper Creek. They said it was the real article. Some of Raber's men had put guns to their heads."

"All right. What'd it say?"

"Short and sweet. 'Give us the two kids, or we kill the woman and anybody else we can get our hands on in Iron Springs.'"

Chapter Five

The sun was slanting through the Colorado blue spruce that lined one side of the cemetery. As Jude spoke, Zeph looked over the crowd. He figured there were about a hundred and fifty people or more. Carriages were lined up on the road. He could remember a time when Charlotte Spence was the only one with a carriage. Not any more. He guessed Iron Springs was getting sophisticated. Not so bad a thing, maybe. What were they at now, five hundred, six hundred? In the '60s, when he'd first come out, there'd been two thousand, on account of the gold strikes in the region. Lots of tents and lean-tos. Now there was less gold and more iron, and people had gone north to Helena. Virginia City had lost a lot of people, too. The difference was, Iron Springs wasn't all built on gold, so folks were trickling back in. He knew for a fact that Matt was still getting run off his feet and had requested the town increase his budget to allow him to hire more deputies like he'd had during the gold rush. His brother had kind of hinted Zeph should be one of them this time around. But Zeph was happy with the Bar Zee for now and hoped Matt wouldn't ask, at least not right away.

Matt had deputized about a dozen citizens because of the danger from Seraphim Raber, and the town council had agreed to pay them a dollar a day if they supplied their own firearms and ammunition. Zeph saw them standing at various places at the edge of the crowd: three-piece black suits and derbies, every one of them, with shiny new badges on their lapels. They all had Winchesters, too, most of them brand-new 1873s, some with the octagonal barrel; but others had carbines with the 20-inch round barrel that had just come out the year before. There were a couple of 1866 Yellow Boys, too, with their distinctive brassy looking gun-metal frames.

"Hey," he whispered to Matt, as they stood together with their Stetsons in their hands, "I thought they were supposed to supply their own firearms?"

Matt kept staring at Jude. "I had a couple of crates in the cellar."

"What about the duds?"

"Nobody said I couldn't give 'em uniforms. The tailor donated the suits. Had spares."

"In all the right sizes? Are you playing politics with this Raber thing?"

"Just want the citizens of Iron Springs to see how good it looks and feels to have their own police force."

"Anything in it for the tailor?"

"Shhh. Your brother's praying."

Zeph dropped his head and prayed, too. It was the way they'd been raised in Wyoming—not to believe in God and church and prayer for show, like some people, but to mean it and to live it.

"Lord, we believe these people would have made good neighbors," Jude prayed, "and good citizens. We believe their children would have made good playmates for our children. Now let their bodies rest under these beautiful blue mountains that You made for our joy, and may their souls rest with You in heaven until the day comes when You wed body and soul once again in a new earth and a new heaven. And Lord, deliver us from the evil that harmed them. We ask this in the name of Jesus our Savior, amen."

"Amen" rumbled through the large mass of people as if distant thunder had pealed through the hills. Eleven pine cones sat ready next to mounds of earth. Zeph had helped dig two of the graves and then raced back to the Bar Zee for a change of clothes. The earth had softened up, so the work hadn't been too hard.

Matt slapped him in the stomach with his hat. "You're looking like a deputy today yourself, except for the Stetson."

"Black suit's all I got."

"Where you headed now? Your ranch?"

"Not mine. Guess I'll pay Miss Spence an extra visit today and explain about those telegrams."

"No need to go there. She's here. She watched the whole thing from Lincoln Creek Ridge."

Zeph glanced up at the grassy hill that overlooked the cemetery and the town, high and sharp and away to the east. Matt's eagle eye hadn't missed a thing. Charlotte was up there, so were the horse and buggy, so were the kids; but so were two deputies, one on horseback, another in back of a clump of bushes.

"She changed her mind," said Zeph in genuine surprise.

Matt smiled. "Free country."

Zeph walked past the usual cluster that gathered around a popular minister and shook Jude's hand— "Thank you, brother"—then made his way through the tangle of townspeople and carriages to Cricket, hitched back and away, behind a tall blue spruce. He swung into the saddle and walked her up the bridle path to the top of the ridge, passing the two deputies who were making their way down, both mounted now. He reined in by the buggy.

Charlotte and Cheyenne were in black dresses with black bonnets and no lace. Cody was in a black suit that looked like it had come from the scissors of the same tailor who made the outfits for the deputies, except he wore a black Stetson with a simple silver band. Where did she come up with all these clothes? Zeph removed his hat.

"Miss Spence."

She inclined her head. "Mister Parker."

"Cody. Cheyenne. I am sorry for today. God bless you."

"They are alive in heaven," said Cheyenne, looking up at him.

Zeph nodded. "I believe that."

Charlotte put her arms around Cody and Cheyenne. "We decided to come, but to have our own private ceremony up here."

"A good plan."

"We listened to your brother's words. He has always been a fine preacher."

"Yes, he has."

She studied Zeph's face. He noticed that her eyes looked violet.

"Do you have something to tell me?" she asked.

"I do."

"Well, climb down and we can step over there. You children don't mind if Mister Parker and I have a short chat, do you?"

"No, ma'am," said Cody.

"Miss Charlotte," she corrected. "Miss Charlotte, ma'am."

She waited for Zeph by a large boulder with a bronze plate embedded in it which he'd never bothered to read. The sun poured down over her and caught a wisp of blond hair that had escaped the edge of her bonnet, igniting it like a match. The mountains were blue and white behind her, a perfect backdrop, he thought, for her granite strength and her striking blue eyes. She smiled as he approached, squaring his hat on his head.

"What do you think of the view?"

"It's beautiful up here," he said, but he did not take his eyes off her.

She shook her head. "I meant the mountains."

"I've seen the mountains."

She averted her face quickly and began to walk. "I used to come up here with Ricky. We both liked it so much, especially at sunset when the snow turns so many bright colors: pink, scarlet, gold, green. He'd say, 'Char, you have to bring your beau up here some day,' and I'd tell him, 'Ricky, you have to bring your bride.' But he never had that chance."

"Well, Miss Spence, I'm sure you will have yours."

"Miss Spence. I suppose it's too much to ask that up here on Lincoln Creek Ridge you might use my Christian name?"

"Matt asked me to talk to you."

"Matt? You mean you can't decide to talk to me on your own?"

Zeph caught the edge in her voice. "I didn't mean it that way. I would have come out to the ranch to see you and the kids tomorrow like you wanted."

"Like I wanted? Do you want it?"

Zeph swallowed. *Okay,* he thought, *here goes.*

"Any excuse to get out to the Spence Ranch and see you is a good excuse, Miss Spence."

She lifted her head. Then her voice and the stiffness in her body gentled. "Thank you, Z."

The blood started roaring in his head, but he knew he had to stay calm and not blurt something foolish. If anything was to come of Miss Charlotte Spence and Mister Zephaniah T. Parker, there was still a long way to go. And there were other matters that had to be attended to right now.

"Miss Spence, three telegrams came in this morning. One of them was from Lancaster County. The sheriff there told us the three families were part of a church in that county, at a place called Bird in Hand, but that they'd been asked to leave the church—excommunicated, I guess, was the high-grade Wells Fargo word he used."

Her face and eyes darkened again. "Yes. I know the word. And they weren't asked. They were ordered." There was that sharp steel in her voice again.

"They did say they'd take the children back," he added.

"Did they? Did it ever occur to them the children might not want to go back to such people? That they might find more love and a better life out here?"

"There was another telegram, too. It was from Seraph Raber—"

"I'm not afraid of Seraphim Raber!"

"He said he wanted us to turn over the two kids, or he'd kill you—"

"I am not afraid of Seraphim Raber!"

Zeph thought she was going to start shouting and pummeling him with her fists. "And that he'd kill as many citizens of Iron Springs as he could."

She was silent. They stopped walking.

"We figure he has about five in his gang, Miss Spence, six counting himself. If he comes against us, there'll be a lot of bloodshed, his and ours. He telegraphed from Copper Creek. It'll take them three days to get back here. Four or five if the weather turns nasty."

Her voice was cold, and her blue eyes like new ice. "What are you suggesting I do with the children, Mister Parker?"

"We can get you safe to the railhead in Ogden, Utah, in less than three days. Why don't you take the children east to their kin and stay with them for a spell?"

"He thinks the children have seen his face?"

"I'll bet he doesn't know for sure. But he's never left anyone alive, ever. He doesn't want them drawing a picture and having it plastered all over the West."

"What's to stop them from drawing a picture in Pennsylvania? What's to stop him from following those children all the way to Lancaster County with a gun in his pocket?"

"I don't believe he'll take it that far."

"You don't believe he will? Do you know him well

enough to say that with a certainty? Do you know what's in a man's heart?"

"I don't, Miss Spence, but it's a chance we have to take."

"A chance you have to take? Or a chance the children and I will have to take? I notice you don't even wear a gun!"

The blood was roaring in his head again, but it was different this time. Zeph clenched and unclenched his fingers. *Lord, help me,* he prayed. He knew he shouldn't say anything. He knew he should bite his tongue and swallow his anger. But she'd pushed him too far.

"Miss Spence," he said, struggling to keep his voice down, mindful that the children were only a little ways behind them, "if it came down to fighting for a woman like you, I'd take on the state of Texas and all of Wyoming and Montana Territory and the entire Lakota nation, if I had to, and not think twice. The only way Seraphim Raber would get to you is through my dead body. The trouble is, I can't protect you and Cody and Cheyenne and five hundred people from Raber's gunmen and neither can Matt, no matter how many men he deputizes. If you're here three days from now, they'll burn your ranch and shoot up the town, kill decent folk and settlers and little old grandmothers and all your hired men, whatever it takes to get to the kids and make sure they don't make a sketch of Raber's face. Now you may not like it, but we're gonna save lives by putting you on the Union Pacific to Pennsylvania, and you're gonna stay out east until we telegraph you that it's safe. And you know that it won't ever be safe for you or the kids until Raber's locked up or hung, and that's what I'm gonna work on next. But first, I'm putting you on that eastbound train if I have to tie you to my saddle like a sack of white flour. Do you hear me, Charlotte?"

Zeph blew out his breath, and his eyes and hands were twitching. *You fool,* his head was raving, *you crazy fool, you've done it now. You've lost Miss Charlotte Spence for sure, and there's nothing you're ever going to be able to say or do that'll win her back.*

Charlotte's eyes were fixed on him. Zeph couldn't tell what color they were—in fact, he couldn't see any color.

"Well, Mister Parker," she said quietly, "it took an awful lot to get you to say my Christian name, didn't it? Seraph Raber and his five guns, the state of Texas, Wyoming, Montana, the Sioux nation… I guess I needed a little bit of help."

She reached up and touched his face with one black-gloved hand. "It was wrong of me to mention the gun you never wear. The truth is, I'm proud of you for that. Forgive me. I will take you up on your proposition, and if you give me one hour, the children and I will be packed and ready for the Union Pacific Railroad. But, Z, there is just one small thing you'll have to agree to."

Zeph's head was spinning from the play-out of his anger, from her quiet words, and from her gloved hand pressing against his cheek. "What's that?" he managed to get out.

"You have to come with me to Pennsylvania. And you have to come as my husband."

Chapter Six

Charlotte laughed as she looked at his face. "Z, I don't think your body knows whether to leap for joy or run and hide. Oh, forgive me, I have a mischievous streak I haven't been able to do much with since my brother died, but I just had to put it out that way to see how you'd feel about getting hitched. It's all right, Z, I didn't mean we had to get married for real. I just meant it's going to have to look that way to others, and Cheyenne and Cody are going to have to act like they're our children. Isn't that the safest way to get to Pennsylvania?"

She could see that a lot of things were going through Zeph's head, and she let him take a moment to let them settle down. She knew she'd shown a side of herself he'd never seen before and that he wasn't sure how to deal with it. Finally, he spoke up.

"A family of four wouldn't get any second looks, you're right about that."

"Is that a yes?"

"A yes to what?"

"A yes to my proposal."

Zeph took a good look at her face instead of looking down or away or over her shoulder. She made up her mind to hold his gaze. It felt different and it felt strange, but she found she also liked the sensation it gave her. She watched him muster up the words to respond to her.

"It's a yes to your plan as far as it goes."

"And do you have a plan that takes it further?"

"I got a plan that takes us to Ogden, Utah, and tickets on the transcontinental railroad."

"What do you propose?"

"The stage doesn't come into Iron Springs until noon tomorrow, and it's a milk run. Goes north for two or three more hours to Picture Butte and Nine Forks. It doesn't turn around till it's had a supper stop at Purple Springs. It's too slow. Now if we can get into Virginia City at six tomorrow morning, there's an express taking gold out. It won't stop except to change horses and drivers until it reaches Ogden. It'll have extra guards, and all of them armed to the teeth. I say we make sure we're on it."

"The four of us are going to ride down to Virginia City tonight?"

"No, there'll be six or seven of us. Matt won't let us head south on our own. Ninety minutes we'll be there, and we'll make ourselves comfortable. Once we're on the stage, the deputies will head back here."

Charlotte looked at the sun on the mountain peaks. "How long to Ogden?"

"It's an express. We go all day and night. A couple of days. We should be on the train before Raber reaches Iron Springs. By that time his people will know we're gone."

"What people?"

"Raber's got to have some friends in Iron Springs. How else would he know those two kids are alive and staying with a woman?"

Charlotte frowned and crossed her arms over her chest to rub her shoulders. "That God's earth should have such kind of people." She looked at Zeph. "Are we going to make it, Z?"

She saw him swallow hard. "You can depend on it, Charlotte."

She gave a little smile and glanced down to the cemetery. "The graves are filled in. I told the children I would take them down there once everyone had left." She turned to Cody and Cheyenne, who were standing about fifty feet behind her and Zeph and just waiting. "We can head down now. Please get in the buggy."

Zeph rode alongside as they wound down to the town and pulled up by the cemetery's black iron gates. Charlotte brought a bag with her as they climbed out. Zeph walked with them.

The wooden marker for each of the graves was the same: KAUFFMAN, TROYER, MILLER, FEBRUARY 1875, WITH JESUS.

On two of them were the additional words: A CHILD. Zeph removed his hat.

Charlotte took Cheyenne and Cody to each grave, where they placed a hand-sewn cross made out of quilt material they had stiffened with wood. When the children were bent down by one marker and planting a cross in the earth, Charlotte stood by Zeph and whispered, "They could not tell one person from another?"

"There was no one that could identify the bodies. Who knew them? And some had no faces."

Charlotte bit her lip. "That there should be such people who would do that to others."

A loud rumble made them glance toward Main Street. Freight wagons carrying iron ore thundered past on their way to the railroad spur at Vermillion. Zeph and Charlotte looked at one another. Zeph shook his head.

"The train can only handle ore and cattle. There's no room for people."

"I know," she said.

"And it's slow. Very slow."

"I know."

The children had taken a cross to one of the child markers. "I don't know when's a good time to ask this," said Zeph.

"Ask what?"

"Do you think—is Cody—is Cheyenne—did they see the men's faces? Could they—would they—try to draw any of them for Matt?"

She stared up at him. "Oh, Zephaniah, you know they're not up to that. It's enough to say a quiet goodbye without upsetting them about making drawings of those horrible beasts."

"I know, Charlotte. I hate to ask. But those men will be riding in here in a few days, and they could walk their horses bold as brass down Main Street, and nobody would know a thing. They could place men with rifles in doorways and rooftops and back alleys, and not a person would look twice until the shooting started. I know the kids have been through something no boy or girl should have to see. I don't want them to keep reliving it. But I don't want more good people to die on account of Seraphim Raber, either."

Charlotte looked at the children coming back toward them and blew out her breath. "I will talk to them about it when we're alone at the ranch. I haven't asked them if the men were masked. It's not something I wish to bring up. But you're right. Others deserve a chance to live."

The children's eyes were wet. Charlotte put her arms around their thin shoulders. "You have been very kind to them all. They look down and see that. The crosses are as beautiful as flowers. Wouldn't you agree, Mister Parker?"

"They are handsome. I don't know too many resting places that have such special colors by them."

"Thank you, Mister Parker. Would you children like a prayer to be said?"

"Yah, please," said Cheyenne softly. Cody hesitated and then nodded.

"Mister Parker, would you?" asked Charlotte.

He bowed his head. The others bowed their heads with him. "Lord, thank You for Cody and Cheyenne. Thank You that they were spared. Thank You that their family and friends are at peace and with You. Thank You for the beauty of this resting place. Thank You that tomorrow's sun will come up for Cheyenne and Cody and their good friend, Miss Spence. The Lord is our Shepherd. Amen."

As they climbed into the buggy, Charlotte said, "I will need time to speak with the children about all the plans, time to pack some food and clothing."

Zeph nodded. "We'll come by at eight tonight. Pack some winter clothes. I'm sure this warm spell won't last forever."

"No, it certainly won't. Well, I'll look for you in a

few hours then. Make sure you book us some seats on the stage."

"That's done."

"Pardon me?"

"I said, that's done."

Charlotte had the reins in her hand and was about to move into the roadway. She felt a mixture of surprise, delight, and anger flow over her features. "How did you manage that?"

"Matt set it up, Charlotte, not me, so don't get excited—"

"I am not getting excited."

"He had it so two deputies would be going with you all the way to Pennsylvania—there was never any talk of me."

"So he purchased five tickets?"

"The town did, yes."

Charlotte thought for a moment. "You think you can take the place of two men?" The corners of her mouth moved upward ever so slightly.

"Dunning and Doede are all right."

She laughed. "Strange sounding name—Dough Dee."

"Strange name, good man. But I guess I can do the work of ten of him when it comes to Charlotte Spence and her brood." Charlotte called out to her horse and pulled into the street.

"We'll take you up on that, Mister Parker."

He watched them roll between wagons and men on horseback and disappear around a bend of stone buildings and tall roofs. Then he walked Cricket over to Matt's and tied her next to Union. He stood a moment, looking at the pieces of rock that made up Matt's office and jail—it had been one of seven banks in Iron Springs during the gold rush of the '60s and was built like a fort—then he opened the door.

Matt was standing by his rack of rifles and levering each one to make sure they were loaded and the action was smooth. Two deputies sat drinking coffee in their black suits and derby hats.

"Zeph," they both said at once.

"Mister Dunning. Mister Doede."

Matt glanced over at him. "Well?"

"She's never even talked with them about what happened. Doesn't know if the gang wore masks or if the kids could tell who the leader was. Hard stuff to bring up, Matt."

"I know it."

"She said she'd try and go over it with them tonight before we showed up. Maybe there'll be drawings, maybe not."

Matt nodded. "So how does she feel about going to Ogden?"

"She's okay with it. I told her eight o'clock. Who's coming?"

Matt inclined his head. "My two men here, of course, Dunning and Doede. Jude. Billy King."

Zeph coughed. "There's been something of a change in plans, Matt."

"What change?"

"She wants me to go with her to Pennsylvania. Wants us to act like we're a family of four. She thought that would be better."

Matt looked at him. "She did, did she? And what do you think?"

"I think she's hit on a good idea."

"Is that right? Tell me, Z, did you put up much of an argument?"

Zeph shrugged and looked at a new wanted poster on the wall behind the desk. From the corner of his eye, he saw Dunning and Doede exchange glances and sip their coffee. For the first time he noticed how huge their handlebar moustaches were. "Sorry to disappoint you two gents," he said.

They both smiled at the same time and raised their cups. "She is a handsome woman," said Dunning, "and I had a hankering to see Pittsburgh."

"On the other hand," said Doede, "we didn't want to miss the show here, either."

"No, we didn't."

"Good luck, Zeph," they both said at the same time.

"Thank you, boys."

Matt had his hands on his hips. "So it's all settled. Charlotte Spence travels a few thousand miles with my kid brother—"

"Jude's younger."

"—and a gang of cutthroats hunting them down, and this kid brother is going to protect them without the benefit of a badge, a pistol, or even a slingshot."

Dunning and Doede laughed.

Zeph glared. "I'll make out all right."

"Will you?"

"I came through the war without a scratch, didn't I?"

Matt was thinking. "I can't go with you. And I guess I got to thank you for freeing me up two more guns"— he nodded toward the two deputies—"but there is a thing or two I can do."

He opened a drawer in his desk and pulled out a badge. "Oh, no—" Zeph started to protest.

"Oh, yes," said Matt, pinning the badge to Zeph's black suit. "You either go as the law, or you don't go at all. I mean it."

"All right," Zeph grunted.

Matt picked up a black book off his desk. "Put your hand on this Bible and swear to uphold the laws of Iron Springs and the Montana Territory."

Zeph placed his right hand on the leather Bible. "I swear."

"And the laws of the United States and every federal jurisdiction."

"I swear."

"So help you God."

"What, am I on trial or something?"

"So help you God."

"So help me God."

Dunning and Doede raised their coffee cups in salute.

Matt opened another drawer with a key. He pulled out a holster with a six-gun.

"No!" Zeph almost shouted and backed toward the door.

Matt ignored him. "You don't have to wear it. You can leave it in your luggage until you need it; I don't care. Heck, maybe you'll never need it. It'd be nice to live in your kind of world, where there's never a villain and no one ever gets hurt or killed."

"I'm not taking it, Matt."

"You will. You're a peace officer now. It's the law." He thrust it at Zeph. "Take it. Maybe you didn't notice. It's Dad's. The 1858 Remington he always swore by.

You don't think he'd want you to have it if he knew the sort of journey you're setting out on tonight?"

Zeph took the gun from Matt's hands and looked at it—the long dark octagonal barrel, eight inches, some engraving on the frame and cylinder, the grips white elk horn. It was Remington's New Army, and it had been converted from a pistol that fired lead balls, like a Civil War musket, to one that fired six .44 caliber cartridges. He caught a whiff of burnt powder and new leather and his dad's rich pipe tobacco, and saw him smiling at the dinner table and teasing Mom about something with the Remington in its holster hanging off the back of his chair. "I remember. He used to plink tin cans when he wanted to relax."

"Yeah." Matt smiled. "You shove it in your bedroll and I'll relax, too."

Zeph held on to the gun and holster. "I'll keep it because it's Dad's. But I ain't going to use it. Not ever."

"Tell me your stories when you're back in Iron Springs safe and sound." Matt snatched a piece of telegram paper off his desk. "I forgot. We heard back from Fort Abraham Lincoln."

"They're too far."

"I know they're too far. But Custer's keen. If Raber sets foot in Dakota again, they'll send a platoon of troopers to run him down. A personal guarantee."

Zeph shrugged. "He'll cut straight down to Utah and the railroad once he knows the kids aren't in Iron Springs."

"Or try to head you off through Wyoming." Matt pulled another scrap of telegram paper from his shirt pocket. "We heard back from Fort Laramie. They keep on eye on the railway anyhow. Said they'll be ready to respond if they hear from us. They're harboring a grudge against Raber. Appears he shot down two of their troopers last fall."

"Good to know the bluecoats'll be out and around. Thank you, brother."

"I guess you'd better have a talk with Byrd and Holly about the Bar Zee. No telling when you'll be back from Pennsylvania. See you at Spence's at eight?"

"Yeah. I'll be there. Gentlemen." Dunning and Doede both raised a hand.

When Zeph had Cricket a mile out of town and headed for Two Back Valley, he reined up, twisted his body around, and dug into the saddlebag on his left. He came up with his dad's pistol and holster. Pulling the gun, he flipped open the cylinder gate and pushed against the ejector rod under the barrel. One, two, three, four, five rounds. That was all his dad loaded into the Remington. The hammer was always on an empty chamber, so he didn't shoot his foot off when he tugged the gun free. He stuck the Remington back in its holster and shoved both into the saddlebag as deep as they would go. Then he cinched the bag down tight.

He kept riding toward the Bar Zee. Behind him the bullets were scattered in a circle and sinking into the mud and snowmelt and hoofprints. The sun was going down red. He'd see Charlotte Spence in two or three hours and then spend maybe three or four months with her if he was lucky. Or blessed. *Now that would be a mighty nice way to spend the winter and spring, if it's okay with You, Lord.* Zeph began to whistle as Cricket jogged toward the mountains.

Chapter Seven

Charlotte pulled aside one of the drapes at her third-floor bedroom window and looked down into the yard at the front of her house. Several men were riding up. Laycock held a lantern toward their faces. His other hand held a shotgun. She wasn't alarmed. She had spotted Zeph right away.

He was taller than Matt, but Jude had a few inches on him. His teeth were whiter and straighter than either of his brothers and his shoulders broader. His hair was a nicer shade of brown. She made a face. His shoulders and teeth and height weren't the important things. She liked his spirit. All the brothers had nice smiles and easy voices and pleasant personalities, but Zeph was something special.

She'd known it from the time he'd helped her brother Ricky on that posse. No, she'd known it before that. And when Cody and Cheyenne told her how he'd rescued them, how gentle he'd been, how he'd named them, it only confirmed what she already believed—that Zeph was strong, gentle, and caring, a true man. She had thanked God in her prayers that evening that he was the one accompanying her to Lancaster County and not a pair of strangers with badges and guns.

Years ago she had hoped to spend more time with him. But Ricky's long illness and death had made that impossible. So had all the years since then she'd spent running the ranch from dawn to dusk. There had been no opportunity for long evening rides and talks; she could only dream about such things.

Until now. Circumstances had combined to bring Zeph and her together in such a way they would have plenty of time not only to talk, but to see what the other person was like under all sorts of conditions and in all kinds of moods. Now she would truly get to know him and find out if he was the man she thought he was. What Raber had done to Cody and Cheyenne's family was unspeakable. But the good that God was starting to bring out of it was a gift.

Still, there was the promise she had made, a promise she could not break. There was a war going on inside her, and it had been going on for years. She had always liked Zephaniah. One moment she desperately wanted something to happen between them. The next she knew they could never be a couple, ever. It was why she had always kept Zephaniah at arm's length. She had to. A promise had been made at her brother's deathbed. Yet she still wanted to be close to Zephaniah. She shook her head. There was no easy way to solve her dilemma. She fixed a bonnet on her head, her long blond hair already pinned up. The luggage was by the front door with Martin who, to all appearances, was guarding it with an old buffalo gun his grandfather had owned. She carried a lamp into Cheyenne's room. The girl was sitting on her bed in a charcoal dress and bonnet

like Charlotte's, no ribbons. Together they knocked on
Cody's door. He opened it, dressed in the same clothes
he had worn to the funeral that afternoon, but the hat
on his head was not a Stetson; it was flat-crowned and
broad-brimmed, not nearly as interesting to look at.
Charlotte nodded and smiled even though Cody was
pouting about the hat. *I don't want people to find you
or your clothing interesting,* she thought. *I don't want
any of them to notice you at all.*

"Miss Spence?" Martin called up the staircase.

"We're coming!"

"They're here."

The three of them descended the staircase. Marshal
Parker stood just inside the open door, hat in his hands.

"How are you, Charlotte?"

"Perfectly fine, Marshal."

"We have the girl riding with you. We can fit a side
saddle if—"

"Not at all. I'm dressed for riding under my skirts.
Perhaps I'll be mistaken for a man by anyone who's
out looking for us."

"Maybe. The bonnet will be a giveaway though,
even in the dark."

"Then I'll take mine off. And Cheyenne's."

"That's fine. We also have a couple of packhorses
to carry your luggage."

"Thank you, Matt. There is a good amount of it.
But I *am* thinking of three or four months. My, it's
getting chilly."

"There's a cold front moving in from the northeast.
I brought some sheep-fleece jackets along. It might
make the ride more comfortable for the three of you."

She laughed. "And I'll look even more like a man." Matt smiled. "It'll help."

They came down the front steps. Zeph had the jackets ready for her and the children. He helped Cheyenne with hers and then held Charlotte's open. She liked his touch as he tugged the sleeves over her arms. Cody had already pulled his on over his suit.

"Cody," said Zeph, "Cheyenne, you know Mister King, and these two deputies are Mister Dunning and Mister Doede. They'll be riding with us tonight."

The deputies raised their derby hats.

"You two have handsome mustaches," said Charlotte.

"Thank you, ma'am," they responded, one after the other.

"And this is Pastor Jude," continued Zeph. "He's also riding with us to Virginia City. You remember him?"

"He prayed for everyone," said Cheyenne.

"That's right. Cody, this is your horse over here, Raincloud. Think you can handle him?"

In the lantern light all of them could see Cody's pleasure at being given the tall dapple gray. "Yes, sir."

"Charlotte, this is your buckskin. What do you think, Cheyenne? Isn't she a beauty?"

Cheyenne nodded and smiled. "Yah, sir."

"Her name's Marigold." He helped Cheyenne into the saddle. "There you go, m'lady."

Charlotte put her left boot into the stirrup. "Will you ride beside us, Mister Parker? Or should I say Deputy Marshal Parker?" She had caught sight of the badge.

"Matt's idea," he muttered, "and only temporary." Charlotte looked down from Marigold at Laycock and

Martin. "Tell the men I appreciate all they are doing for the Spence Ranch. But I do not wish that to include getting themselves shot. If Raber's men show up, I don't want any of you to stand in the way. Let Raber do what he wants, so long as no one is hurt."

They touched the brims of their hats.

"Yes, ma'am," said Laycock. "We'll look forward to the day you return."

"As will I."

She walked Marigold over to Matt. "Marshal, I have spoken with the children. They are looking forward to seeing their aunt Rosa again, so this long trip is something they are glad to take. As for drawing likenesses of the men, well, that is not something they feel they are able to do right now. But they understand how it might help you, and they are going to try and remember what some of them looked like and put charcoal to paper. When that happens, and I believe it will, I shall have the sketches sent to you by the fastest means at my disposal."

Matt nodded.

As Charlotte turned her horse toward the road, she said in a quiet voice, "None of the men were masked, Matt, and neither was the leader that they called Angel."

As she headed out with the others, Charlotte wondered if her ranch hands would listen to what she had told Martin and Laycock. Somehow she doubted it. She prayed they would make it through the next few days without a scratch. Then she wondered if that was too much to ask of God under the circumstances, given the kind of men who worked for her—loyal to a fault, hardworking, proud and brave—and the kind of men they would be facing—vicious, treacherous, and bloodthirsty. She shook her head and wished, not for the first time, that God would scour evil from the earth the way she scoured grime from her pots and pans. Then a place like Sweet Blue Meadows, already a jewel, would be a paradise without end.

But that's heaven, Charlotte, she said to herself, *and you're not in heaven yet.*

A mile from her ranch, they veered west toward the Rockies and a stretch of forest, taking a little-used track left over from the gold rush days. This route would bypass the town and any of its citizens who might be up and watching the main roads. *Who would be watching for us?* she wondered again. *Who would help a man like Seraph Raber harm two innocent children?*

She felt someone's eyes on her. It was not an unpleasant sensation, as sometimes it could be, so she let the feeling linger a moment before she turned her head. She hoped it would be Zephaniah Parker, and she was rewarded with his concerned face and smile.

"Are you worried about me, Mister Parker?" she asked. "No more than usual, considering what we're going through right now," Zeph answered, "but you did seem awfully far away."

"Did I? Perhaps I'm missing Sweet Blue already and wishing we were to Pennsylvania and back again. Do you recall the day you first came to this place?"

They spoke softly in the dark, and their horses trotted quietly through the rocks and pines alongside the others.

She saw Zeph nod slightly. "It was '69. Thousands of people living up and down the valleys here then. Some had gone up to Helena when they had their strike in '64, but men were still pulling a decent amount of gold out of the hills in Iron Springs and Virginia City. Matt was already here. He had dreams of making it rich and buying a big spread in Texas. When Jude and I showed up, he was a deputy, and it's been the law for him ever since."

"What about you?"

"Jude was talking about being a circuit rider with the Methodist Church, and I guess I just wanted to make enough gold to get my own place in California. We hit pay dirt all right, not a lot, but Jude decided to start a church with his cut. He put that whole building up on his own, and I bought the land I turned into the Bar Zee. Funny, I never thought about California again, and he never thought about circuit riding. This place got a hold of all three of us and never let go. Maybe it's the water."

She was sure he was smiling in the dark; she could *feel* him smiling in the dark. "Your mother and father never wanted to join their sons?"

"Well, Mom passed away just after the war—at least she got to see us home to our little ranch safe and sound, and Dad, it seemed as if he never wanted to leave her side. So we'd visit him once a year, stage and train. We never could talk him into leaving Wyoming. Died in '73. I believe he would have loved all the mountains here and the valleys and the streams. He was always one for hunting and getting away from the crowds."

He glanced up at the stars, and she knew he was wondering how the view would have made his father feel.

"I guess I'm talking too much," he apologized.

"Not at all," she responded. "It makes the time pass. Please, go on."

"Well, Cheyenne was growing too cramped for Dad. They started her up in '67, just south of our place. He liked going into town at first, but he must've seen where it was heading, four thousand people in the first few months." *Now,* she thought, *he is shrugging his shoulders in that cute way he has.* "Couldn't get him out here, though. Matt got married in Cheyenne for Dad's sake, and Sally didn't mind. I would like for Dad to have seen the Bar Zee, and he would have been proud to watch Jude preach at his own pulpit in his own church. These things don't always work out, do they?"

"No," she said, and she thought of her father and brothers never coming home from the war, never stepping through the door again, only Ricky making it out with a bullet in his lung, a bullet that wouldn't let him alone until it had finished what it started.

"I hate war," she said suddenly and more loudly than she meant.

Zeph was silent for a bit, and then he said to her, "I'm sorry, Charlotte. I believe your family would have liked the Sweet Blue."

Charlotte wrestled with all kinds of memories and feelings that usually she would just hold inside. But this was the ride she'd wanted to take with Zeph for years, this was the time God had given her, and she felt she needed to make as much use of it as she could.

"You warm enough, Cheyenne?" she suddenly asked the girl snuggled up against her.

"Yah, Miss Charlotte."

"All this grown-up talk isn't boring you?"

"I don't listen to much of it."

Charlotte laughed. "The perfect audience, Z."

They rode for a while without talking. She glanced around her and finally found Cody riding with Billy King. King was leading one of the packhorses, and she spotted Jude leading the other. Then she returned to the thoughts she'd thrust away a few minutes before and decided it was time to offer them to Zephaniah Parker to see what he would make of them, and of her, once she'd finished.

"Do you know what Amish is?" she asked him.

"No, I don't," he answered.

"Mennonite?"

He seemed to hesitate. "A fellow in our platoon during the war said he had Mennonite roots. Said they didn't believe in wars and violence and that his family had been real disappointed in him for joining up."

She nodded. "It's like that. The Amish broke away from the Mennonites because they wanted to be even more strict. Jacob Amman felt people should be shunned if they broke the rules of the church. Ignored. Not spoken to. Cut off. Until they repented of what they'd done wrong, and then they could be brought back into fellowship again."

She looked over at him. He had brought Cricket in closer. She took a deep breath. "I'm Amish, Z, Amish born and raised. You said once I had a sweet accent. I grew up speaking Pennsylvania Dutch. English was my second language. We were part of an Amish community in Bird in Hand in Lancaster County, the same community Cody and Cheyenne are from. I had a happy childhood, Z. There is a great deal of gentleness and love among the Amish. But my father felt it was wrong for the South to force slavery on other people. So he joined the Union army to resist them. And my brothers did, too."

She rode in silence for several minutes. All of a sudden she felt a reluctance to continue talking about her family. It was more painful to bring it up than she'd thought it would be.

"I suppose I'm boring you," she said, with an irritability she didn't mean to direct at him.

"No, ma'am. Nothing that interests you could be boring to me."

"Is that right?" she snapped. *Calm down, Charlotte,* she told herself, *there's no need to get your Spence up.* "Please do not call me ma'am again."

He was quiet for a moment and then said, "I won't."

Still irritable, she decided to plunge on in defiance of her misgivings for starting the conversation at all.

"Perhaps it wasn't all about the South bullying people. My father did not feel there should be two countries. He was very much against that. But the church was against war and warned Father that if he left to fight he would be shunned, our whole family would be shunned. He was a proud man and was convinced that God had told him to take up arms against slavery. Told the elders he was done with being Amish and being part of the colony. Took steps to make sure his family would be taken care of if the elders really did turn the church against his family. Then he and my brothers went to Philadelphia to enlist."

Again she grew silent, struggling with her memories.

Zephaniah thought she was done. "Did the church turn its back on you?"

Charlotte flared. "I will tell this in my own way

and my own time. I am not a rush ahead, restless spirit like you."

"I'm sorry—"

"Just stop. Yes, the church turned its back on us. Satisfied? From that time on, my mother and I and my sister, Mary, were shunned by the other Amish. No one would even say hello to us. We still lived among them—Mother wouldn't leave the house Father had built—but there was no friendship, no sense of family or community or love. Mother might have taken us to Virginia if Virginia hadn't been one great battlefield during those years. She had family there. I saw a few acts of kindness from the Amish, usually from the family Father had asked to keep an eye on us. But even when my sister, Mary, grew ill and died, there was little support."

Charlotte had been telling her story without looking at Zeph. Now she stole a glance to see if he was even listening. His eyes were locked onto her. It was obvious he was taking in every word she spoke.

"I watched Mother wither. When we received the news that Father had been killed, and then the same terrible news about each of my brothers, it was just as if the Confederate army had plunged a bayonet into her own chest. She gave up and lay down, and would not rise. An Amish family took me in after her death. These were the people Father had asked to help us. I was thirteen, and I remember how very lonely I felt, and frightened, but they were kind to me and did not seem to care that my family was excommunicated." She was angry that she felt tears on her face. Crying was not a luxury she afforded herself. Looking up at the night sky, she swiped at her eyes with the palm of her hand. *Oh, you've come this far,* she said to herself impatiently, *you might as well be done with it.*

"We did not know Ricky had survived," she went on, "but he came one day to our door and took me in his arms and thanked the Amish family; then he said we were leaving Pennsylvania and going west and starting fresh. We came here in '66, and Ricky struck gold. He poured it all into me and the ranch at Sweet Blue. So, you see, I understand something of what the parents of these children have gone through, how awful the shunning must have been to make them pick up and leave the Amish community and travel here by wagon to start again. The only reason I am taking them to Lancaster County is because Seraph Raber will kill them if I don't.

"When this is over, I pray they will want to come back and live on the Sweet Blue. To tell you the truth, if it were just about me, I would prefer to stay here and face Raber and his savages than travel to Pennsylvania and face the people who destroyed my family. But there are others to think of. Cheyenne here, asleep against my chest. Cody. The women and men and children of Iron Springs. That's why I'm going to Ogden with you, Z, and for no other reason. I swore to God I'd never return to Lancaster County. Never."

I will not look him in the face, she said as she stared straight ahead at the winding gold rush trail, *I will not let him see my tears and my pain.* But she did turn to him in the hope that he could do something, anything, about the anguish she had locked in her heart for a lifetime and buried in beef cattle and stock prices and horses and fencing. His face was a pale blur, and she could not read his eyes through her tears.

Suddenly she hated herself for having told him, for letting him see her weakness. With a small cry that was a mix of anger and despair, she spurred her horse into a fast gallop into the night.

"I know that."

"I've prayed so many times for strength—"

"You have the strength of mountains."

Horses galloped around the bend toward them. Charlotte sat upright and kissed Cheyenne. Matt reined up in front of her.

"What's wrong?" he demanded, his pistol still in his hand. "You two gone loco? They'll hear you for miles!"

Zeph held up a hand to Matt's anger. "Easy, brother. Her horse got spooked. That's all. It was a mountain cat."

"I didn't hear any cat."

"It didn't make a sound. Went across the track right in front of her."

"I never saw a thing."

"It moved fast, and it was so low to the ground it looked like a snake."

Matt stared at him. Zeph glanced away and looked at Charlotte. He could see her eyes were swollen, but he could also see heart and strength pouring back into them. Matt holstered his gun and touched his hat brim.

"Sorry, Charlotte. I don't like running the pack-horses. And that whole episode made me near jump out of my skin."

"Me, too," she said.

There were a few chuckles. Zeph let out his breath softly. "No harm done," announced Matt. "We're miles past Iron Springs and in the middle of nowhere. In fact, that little run bought us some time. I reckon we'll be into Virginia City a lot sooner than we thought. That's what we call good news in the Montana Territory."

They counted heads and moved on, walking their horses. Zeph stayed close to Charlotte. She pulled away from the group, and he followed her. Cheyenne had her head on Charlotte's chest and was looking up at the stars glittering between the evergreen boughs.

"Thank you, Z," Charlotte said.

"No need to thank me for saying what was right."

"A mountain lion?"

He saw her small smile. "Well, there was something there."

She shook her head. A few pins came loose, and some of her hair tumbled and got wrapped up in moonlight. It took Zeph's breath away. She didn't notice. Cricket and Marigold plodded side by side. Zeph started to whistle quietly and looked up.

"I see those stars, too, Cheyenne."

"I'm looking for the Big Dipper."

"Hard to spot when so many branches get in the way. Hey, now, did you see that?"

"Yah, a shooting star."

"Make a wish on it, and everything'll turn out all right."

Charlotte glanced at him. "You believe that?"

Zeph shrugged. "A wish can be a prayer. Prayer moves mountain peaks, a preacher once told me."

She smiled and looked up, too. "I used to think summer in Pennsylvania was crowded with stars. The first night Ricky took me to Sweet Blue and said he'd bought it for me, there were so many stars it was like gold dust. I swear I could hardly see any dark patches in between. It made me dizzy. I laughed and spun and fell down in the grass and mountain flowers like a schoolgirl."

"I'd like to have seen that."

"It wasn't so long ago. I think I could do it again. In the right place."

The words "with the right man" weren't spoken, but they floated in the night air between them like snowflakes. They gazed at each other. Her eyes and face gleamed in the silver light that fell down through the crisscross pattern of branches and twigs.

"There she is," one of the men said.

Matt trotted ahead of them into Virginia City. They saw a lot of light and heard a lot of noise farther down the street, but where they came in was dark and silent. One lamp burned in one window. The sign on the building read: WELLS, FARGO & CO., OVERLAND MAIL EXPRESS. Next to it was SR BUFORD & Co. All their windows black and unlit.

Dunning and Doede swung down, Winchesters at the ready, and Dunning opened the Wells Fargo door. He leaned in and said a few words. A man with a smaller mustache than Dunning's came out. He was thin and dressed in a white shirt and gray flannel pants. He spotted Matt and reached up to shake his hand.

"Marshal. Welcome to the capital of the Montana Territory."

"Mister Wilson. These are my brothers, Jude and Zephaniah. And this is Miss Charlotte Spence and the two children, Cheyenne and Cody. Behind me is Mister William King. The men on the ground with you are two of my special deputies, Mister Doede and Mister Dunning."

"It's good to have you here safe and sound," said Wilson. "I'm the assistant to Mister H. B. Parsons, who is the Wells Fargo agent for Virginia City. Everything is ready to roll for six sharp, so I'll just show you to your beds, and you can get settled in for the night. I've got a room set up in back for Miss Spence and her wards and another for the men. Are you staying over, Marshal?"

"I'm afraid not. Neither is Mister King. But I believe Jude and my two deputies will be with you until the stage leaves in the morning."

"Capital. I only have two cots for the men, however."

Dunning and Doede shook their heads.

"We'll be up all night, Mister Wilson," said Dunning. "No rest for the wicked," grinned Doede.

"You do have the fixings for black coffee?" asked Dunning, looking a bit worried.

"All in there on the stove, Deputy."

"Coffee," said Doede with a smile, slinging his Winchester over his shoulder.

Matt looked at Zeph. "Need anything?"

"I'm all right."

"Charlotte?"

"I feel like I'm in good hands, thank you, Matt."

"Then we'll see you back in Iron Springs."

Matt wheeled his horse and headed back into the night, leading Cricket and Marigold. Billy King had the two packhorses that had been unloaded of their baggage. He raised his hat—"God bless you, folks, God bless you, Cody, Cheyenne. I pray time flows like a fast river for us all while we're apart"—and followed Matt north on the gold rush trail. Zeph walked into the station and helped everyone get settled in. It didn't take long. Dunning parked himself outside Charlotte and Cheyenne's door, tipped back in a broad oak chair

Zeph had found, Winchester in his lap, coffee mug in one fist. Doede sat in a rocker by the other door, sipping at his coffee and watching Jude put his feet up on the express agent's desk and place a nickel-plated six-gun on the large green blotter.

"Pistol-packin' preacher?" asked Doede, surprised.

Jude smiled, his hat with the silver conchas tilted forward over his eyes. "Only in the Montana Territory. And it's never loaded. Sometimes looks are enough."

Doede and Dunning glanced at each other and shrugged.

Zeph watched Wilson stoke the stove and put on a fresh pot of coffee. He wiped his hands on a cloth.

"Anything else I can do for you gentlemen?"

Jude said nothing. Dunning and Doede shook their heads. "I'm all right," said Zeph.

Wilson rapped lightly on Charlotte's door. "Miss Spence?"

"Yes?"

"Is there anything else I can do for you?"

"I'm quite comfortable, Mister Wilson, thank you."

"Good night, then."

Wilson turned to Zeph. "Is the boy comfortable?"

Zeph carefully opened the door and poked his head into Cody's room. "Half asleep already."

"Then I'll be locking all of you in the building for the night," said Wilson.

"Fine."

"There is one thing, Mister Parker."

"What's that?"

Wilson pulled a telegram out of his pants pocket. "This came addressed to you this evening."

The telegram was folded once. Zeph opened it.

PARKER
II KINGS 19:35
ANGEL

Zeph looked up. "Do you happen to have a Bible handy, Mister Wilson?"

Wilson nodded. "Of course. But I took the trouble to find the reference and write it out for you."

Zeph took the note Wilson handed to him. It was printed in clear dark letters.

And it came to pass that night, that the angel of the LORD went out, and smote in the camp of the Assyrians an hundred fourscore and five thousand: and when they arose early in the morning, behold, they were all dead corpses.

Zeph felt a crawling in his stomach. "When did this come in, Mister Wilson?"

"Two hours ago."

"From which telegraph station?"

"Mister Parker," Wilson said quietly, "it came from Iron Springs."

Chapter Nine

The man had taken a stained pillowcase and cut one hole for an eye and another for a mouth. He thrust the barrel of his pistol into Zeph's ribs and said, "It is the Lord's will you die and all those with you. You know that."

"I need to see your face to be sure it's you," Zeph answered calmly.

The man nodded. "All right. Then you will know for certain this is the work of the Lord."

He drew off his hood, and Zeph expected hair and teeth and bulging eyes. What he saw was a face as handsome as the dawn. The man smiled, "No, I'm not a monster, am I? Are you convinced now that your death is ordained by the hand of God?"

Zeph didn't know what to say, he was so surprised by the man's beauty. Then the gun barrel dug into his body once again, and the roar of a gun blast filled his head.

Zeph jerked upright as the stagecoach lurched and banged. Charlotte was asleep across from him in the dark, Cheyenne snuggled with her, thick quilts pulled up to their chins. Cody snored softly, with his head against Zeph's left shoulder. The guard on the other side of Cody caught Zeph's eye.

"A nasty bump, sir," he said in a low voice. "Lots of stones on the road between Virginia City and Eagle Rock. Hard to avoid them all when you're trying to make time."

Zeph grunted. He opened the wooden shutter over the stage window on his right. Trees and rocky slopes rushed past. Snow was swirling down in circles, white spots against the gray and the green.

"How far to Taylor's Crossing?"

"We're doing well, sir. Eagle Rock is only a few hours. Then a change of horses. New driver. They'll replace us as well."

Zeph closed the shutter to keep out the cold air. "Does the snow slow us down?" he asked.

"Not much. A bit. It's the ice that causes the wrecks."

Zeph slid farther down into the blue point blanket that covered him and Cody. The stage rattled and jolted through the Idaho Territory.

If it slows us down, it will slow them down, he thought. *And even if the stage is hauling us and our luggage and a gold shipment, the four horses can make better time than a crowd of riders.*

He did not believe the gang had already reached Iron Springs. Raber couldn't be in Copper Creek one day, hundreds of miles north, and Iron Springs the next. It was someone in Iron Springs, Raber's accomplice, sending a telegram on ahead and trying to unnerve him.

It couldn't be Dunning or Doede. Or Billy King. Or Matt or Jude.

As if it would be one of my brothers.

There was hardly any way to narrow it down. It could be virtually anybody. Raber was probably paying him in gold. Why else would someone take the risk of getting his neck stretched on the end of a rope? Who did he know that needed the money that badly?

But what if there was more than one person involved? What if there were two or three?

That was a game Zeph didn't want to play. Once he thought there might be more than one, any of the people he knew and trusted could be guilty. Then Dunning and Doede could be in on it. Or Billy King and his brothers, Sam and Wyatt. Or Martin and Laycock. Or Byrd and Holly. He could go crazy trying to figure it out, and he'd be suspicious of everyone that crossed his path.

He tried to sleep again, but the stage banged and thumped and shook, and sleep would not come.

He was tired enough. Once he'd read the Bible passage the night before, he'd known it would eat at him for hours, just as the person who sent the telegram intended it should. He'd tossed and turned all night and never found a comfortable position for his body. A part of his mind expected the splintering of wood and the crash of firearms as Raber's killers forced their way into the Wells Fargo office. Suppose Raber did have hired guns that he'd telegraphed in this neck of the woods? More than once, Zeph's thoughts had turned to his father's Remington New Army buried in his saddlebag. But he knew it was empty, and the threat of a gun would not stop Raber's madmen, it would just incite them to shoot.

Before dawn Wilson had woken them up, cooked a

breakfast of ham and eggs, and made sure their luggage was packed into the leather boot at the rear of the stage. The driver and three guards had been booked into one of the quieter hotels and shown up around five thirty. The driver had downed a cup of coffee with Dunning and Doede, and then they'd helped him hitch up the team of four chestnut horses. Tipping their derbies, the deputies had ridden off with two mugs of fresh coffee and Wilson's blessing.

Jude had pulled a small Bible out of one of the pockets in his long black coat and given it to Zeph. "One for the road, brother."

Zeph saw right away it was the one Jude had carried with him during the war, the Bible he'd seen Jude reading by the campfires at night. "I can't take this," he'd argued. "This is your talisman, your keepsake."

Jude had laughed. "God's my talisman, brother. This is just a book of paper and ink. It's the taking into yourself of what it talks about that's key. Open it now and then. I pray you'll find the words you need when the ride gets the roughest."

They'd shaken hands.

"I'll read it, brother," Zeph had said.

Now Zeph dug under the point blanket as he sat inside the stage and came up with his brother's war Bible. It was well-worn around the edges, and some of the binding was loose. It smelled of black powder and woodsmoke and gun grease. It naturally fell open to a number of different passages that Jude had obviously read several times over. He picked one. "Fret not thyself because of evildoers, neither be thou envious against the workers of iniquity. For they shall soon be cut down like the grass, and wither as the green herb."

"What are you reading, Z?"

Charlotte was smiling at him in the dimness, a crack of white light from the window shutter drawing a pale line down one side of her face.

"Nothing," he said.

"It's something. Isn't that the little Bible your brother gave you?"

He nodded.

"Read it to me."

He read her the first two verses from Psalm 37.

She stared at him. "Are you fretting because of evildoers?"

"No," he lied.

She looked skeptical, but chose to let it go. "Would you look up something for me?"

"Sure."

"Can you read Psalm 91 to me?"

It was marked with dark powder smudges that held forever Jude's fingerprints.

"'Thou shalt not be afraid for the terror by night; nor for the arrow that flieth by day,'" he read out loud, speaking in a soft voice that he hoped would not wake Cody or Cheyenne. "'Only with thine eyes shalt thou behold and see the reward of the wicked. Because thou hast made the Lord, which is my refuge, even the most High, thy habitation; There shall no evil befall thee, neither shall any plague come nigh thy dwelling. For he shall give his angels charge over thee, to keep thee in all thy ways.'"

"You see, Z," Charlotte spoke up, "there are the

good angels, too, and I believe they're stronger than the evil ones."

Zeph suddenly remembered his dream. "Do you think the people that do evil deeds actually start to look evil?"

Charlotte gazed at him a few moments before answering. "You mean do I think Seraphim Raber must be an ugly man because of all the wicked things he has done? Well, he might look like the handsomest man in the world if you saw him fishing off a bridge in his straw hat and brown boots with the sun setting just over his shoulder. But if you looked into his eyes and down into his heart, you would see nothing but filth and corruption. By their fruits you shall know them. The apples from his tree are covered with worms and wasps."

A sudden venom had come into Charlotte's voice. She turned her face away. "Still, even men like that, they say, we need to pray for. Resist their evil, but pray for their souls."

Before Zeph could think of a response, the driver bawled out, "Eagle Rock, formerly Taylor's Crossing," and the stage thundered over a wooden bridge.

While the team was being changed, Zeph and Charlotte and the children stepped out of the stage and stretched their legs. The sky was the color of lead, and a cool wind was blowing from the north, but no one was anxious to sit back down anytime soon and get jolted and tossed about for another twelve or fourteen hours. Yet the changeover of the horses and the men would be swift.

"Where's your badge, Mister Parker?" asked Cody.

"In my pocket for now."

"I thought it was great."

"Did you? Tell me, what do you think of the stage-coach ride so far?"

"It's like the Conestoga wagons we used to come here from Pennsylvania," the boy grumbled. "You feel like a sack of apples getting bounced up and down."

"Well, in the summer," Zeph responded, "there'd be heat and dust and mosquitoes and horseflies. This is probably a little bit better."

Cody was remembering, Zeph could see, the Conestogas rumbling through the heat and flies of the plains. Then the light went out of his eyes as his remembering took him too far.

"I'm sorry," Zeph said.

"I slept very well." Cheyenne suddenly spoke up. "I felt like I was being rocked in a cradle."

Zeph put one hand on her shoulder, smiling. "You would make a good advertisement for the company that builds the Concord coaches. 'Travel across the most rugged roads in America and sleep like a baby the whole way.'"

"I *was* sleeping the whole way, wasn't I?"

"You were."

Charlotte had been tugging at their luggage, which was stored in the boot at the back of the coach, grunting and complaining as she dug past item after item. Finally she found what she wanted and brought over a parcel wrapped in white paper and tied with twine. She put it into Zeph's hands.

"Here."

"What is it?"

"In another day or so we'll be in Utah and boarding the train for Chicago. We have to look like a family."

"We do look like a family."

"No, the children and I look like a family, because we are dressed the same and look very plain. You look like a cowboy—"

"I am a cowboy!"

"—and your scarf and boots and Levi Strauss waist overalls will have to be stored away until we return. Until then, we must look ordinary."

Zeph stared at the package as if it might jump up and bite him. "What's in it?"

"Go inside the Wells Fargo at once and find a room to change in. We will wait for you here."

Zeph returned in ten minutes, just as the guards were clambering up onto the coach and the driver was asking Charlotte to get the children inside. Gone was his brown Stetson. In its place was a flat, black, broad-brimmed hat, exactly like Cody's. A baggy jacket over a gray shirt and baggy pants and black shoes completed his outfit. He looked sadly at his cowboy boots and shirt and Levi Strauss pants.

"I've only had the pants for a year," he protested. "They're the new ones with the rivets, and I've broken them in. They fit like a glove."

"Well," said Charlotte, "the pants I made for you fit like a glove, too, just a very big glove."

Cody laughed. They so rarely heard him laugh that Zeph and Charlotte stopped talking to look at him and watch his green eyes flash.

"Where do you think she gets all these clothes?" Zeph asked him.

Cody was still smiling. "The Hunkpapa Sioux."

"I told you," Charlotte said, taking Zeph's cowboy clothing from him, "I made them for you."

"You sew?"

"And even bake. And break broncs. And sing in the church choir."

She walked back over to the coach boot and tucked Zeph's hat and clothing inside and refastened the leather cover and straps. It was beginning to snow again, and she opened the door to the stage with a flourish. "Let's carry on with the show."

They squeezed in next to a new guard, who had already made himself comfortable. He lifted his derby hat to Charlotte and Cheyenne. "Ladies, I am Slick, and I will keep you safe until we reach Ogden."

"Hello, Slick!" beamed Cheyenne.

"Hullo, my girl. How has your trip been so far?"

"It's been like traveling across America in a cradle."

Slick looked at her in astonishment. "Is that so? Well, I hope your presence will bring a little of that cradle into the coach for my poor bones. Not that I'm allowed to sleep. But a guard should always be relaxed right up until the very moment he's needed. He functions better that way."

The stage began to move, and the horses trotted more and more briskly and finally started to run. The five of them began to sway and bounce.

"You see, sir?" grinned Cheyenne.

"You're right, I feel like I am six weeks old once again."

"This is my brother, Cody. And my mother and father. We are the Wyomings."

My, my, thought Charlotte, *look who is bursting out of her shell.*

"The Wyomings? They name the territory after your family?"

"Maybe, sir."

"Well, I am Slick Doolan. That's my whole handle. Pleased to meet y'all."

He leaned over to shake Zeph's hand. Before Zeph could open his mouth to introduce himself, Charlotte reached between them, and took Slick's hand.

"Mister Doolan. My husband, Fremont, and I are very glad to have such a pleasant personality as yourself for our guard."

"Why, thank you…"

"Conner."

"Missus Conner. That's something different."

"My parents wanted a boy," she said with a playful pout. "When I came out they'd put so much work into planning for a little man they were reluctant to backtrack. So I got the name, a blue crib, and a blue set of pajamas."

"Well, you seem to have done all right by it all. If you don't mind my saying, Mister Wyoming."

"Fremont," Zeph grunted.

"Fremont, if you don't mind my saying, she is purtier than the blue Wyoming Rockies in the springtime. You're a lucky man."

"Oh, he knows it," said Charlotte, lightly slapping Zeph's hand.

"I do know it," said Zeph.

"And, young lady," said Slick to Cheyenne, "I guess you will grow up to be as beautiful as your mother."

"Thank you, sir."

Suddenly the stage lurched and swerved and came to a dead stop. Charlotte was pitched into Zeph and Cheyenne into Cody. Slick banged open his window shutter with his shotgun barrel and took a look. It was getting dark, and the snow was pouring down. He blew out his breath in a sudden burst.

"Well," he said slowly, "I guess we got trouble."

Chapter Ten

Zeph felt his whole body tense. "What kind of trouble?" Slick leaned back in his seat and closed the shutter.

"You can't see more than a foot in front of you. We're locked in a bad squall, and it could blow for hours. I been in 'em before on this stretch. Either we sit tight, or somebody gets out and walks the horses forward. If we were on a straight run through the plains, he'd keep 'em moving slow. But here we got to worry about drop-offs and cliffs. He wouldn't be able to spot them in time."

"Will we be all right if we just stay put?" asked Charlotte.

"Maybe. Blows too long and the temperature drops out of sight, different story." Slick didn't look too happy.

"So one of you can lead the team on foot?" asked Zeph. He doubted Raber was being held up by a snowstorm.

Slick groaned. "That's the problem. Tess and Marble hate me. Always try and take bites out of me. So that won't work. Bert and Stoner up top, well, they hate horses to begin with, and the horses know it. They get down there with 'em and the team'll either kick 'em both to death, or bolt, or both. Stan's great with horses, but he's the driver. We gotta have him on the reins." He closed his eyes. "Lord above, we are stuck and we're stuck bad."

"You ever walked out of one of these squalls?" Zeph's mind was racing, looking for a solution.

"Sure, sure. You get the right person walking ahead with the team. A lot of times these storms are, you know, locals, you're out of 'em in one or two miles. But you got to have the walker. Try and run the team without someone checking what's ahead, and you'll have a wreck. I picked up the pieces of one that went right over a riverbank and another that went into a rock wall when the team panicked. You got to take it slow and sure and steady."

"I'll do it," said Zeph. He pulled on his sheepskin coat and opened the coach door.

The snow and wind caught him full in the face and took his breath away. His broad-brimmed hat vanished. He hunched over and stumbled to the front of the coach and glanced up at the guard sitting next to the driver. He was wrapped in a blanket and looked like a snowdrift.

"I'm a rancher in the Montana Territory," he called up. "Got about a hundred horses. I'll be your walker."

The guard didn't even turn his head. But the driver leaned over. "Go easy. Take the harness of the lead horse on the right. Gelding named Marble. But you got to go easy. I'll work with you best I can. Name's Stan."

"Fremont."

Chapter Eight

"What's going on?" snapped Matt. His pistol was out of his holster in a flash.

But Zeph had dug in his heels and was pounding after the buckskin. He was worried about rocks, potholes, and low branches. Cricket's breath came in white spurts. Charlotte might have been upset, but she had not lost her head and panicked. He saw her bent over her horse's neck as if she were on a racetrack.

"Let's fly, Crick," he said into his horse's left ear. Cricket surged and was at Charlotte's side in moments. "Charlotte!" he called.

But she would not look up.

"Charlotte! Slow up before you and the girl take a tree limb in the head! Slow up! I admire you for the courage it took to tell me the things you did!"

He reached over and grabbed her reins and started hauling back on Cricket's. The buckskin fought the bit, but Cricket's weight began to throw her backward, and she slid to a stop, breath tumbling like pent-up steam from her nostrils. Cheyenne was crying. Charlotte held her. "It's been hard; it's been very hard, Z."

"You need something for your head, or you'll lose your ears. Here."

He took off his hat and threw it down. It was so heavy with snow the wind couldn't catch it.

Zeph planted it firmly on his head. "What about you?" he shouted.

"I got another under my feet."

It was completely dark now. The only brightness was the snow and the horses' breath. Zeph got up beside Marble, who stood rigid. He was talking softly the whole time he approached the horse from behind. He kept using the same subdued tone once he was beside Marble and didn't touch her.

After about five minutes the guard beside the driver began to get impatient, and Zeph heard him mutter, "Get him outta there, he don't know what he's doing."

Stan snapped, "Shut up, Stoner. This'll likely be the farmer that saves your dude hide from becoming winterkill."

Zeph waited until Marble was interested in what was in his jacket pocket. When the gelding began to nuzzle the pocket, Zeph pulled out an apple and let the horse take a big bite. When it had finished the apple off, there was another. Then Zeph began to walk forward. The horse moved with him and, after some reluctance, so did the whole team.

He did not do anything more than place his hand on Marble's shoulder. He could see that Stan held the reins loosely. Zeph put his head up to squint into the snow-blown night, then down to blink his eyes clear and look at the roadway. It was only a walking pace, but Marble took longer and longer strides, and Zeph had to work harder to keep up. After a few minutes he was warmer due to the extra exertion, so he didn't complain or urge the team to slow down. After about half an hour, he gave Marble another apple. Now he had a friend for life.

Zeph had taken gloves out of his coat pocket and pulled them onto his hands using his teeth. He wished he had a scarf to wrap over his face, but he found that Marble would let him lean his head gently against his neck. The warmth of the horse's flesh and breath did wonders to relieve the stabs and pinches of pain he felt on his nose and cheeks and forehead.

Think of hot things, he said to himself, *think of the Utah desert in summer or a dry August wind in Wyoming or the hot springs at Yellowstone melting back the snow and ice. Think of thick woolen blankets and heated bricks at the foot of your bed and patchwork quilts as heavy as iron ore. Warm spiced milk. Hot coffee. Apple pie and raisin pie just pulled out of the oven. A wood fire and venison roasting on it.*

Marble snorted and reared. Zeph's right foot went into nothing. He began to fall and grasped desperately at the horse's traces. Marble didn't fight his grip or panic, but pulled slowly, snorting the whole time, and dragged Zeph back over the edge. Zeph got to his feet, head spinning, and embraced the horse, who permitted it. He had a final apple and gave it to the large sorrel with a whispered, "Thank you."

They moved forward again, except that Zeph swung left to avoid the drop-off, and the team swung with him. Snow that had gone up his sleeves, down his neck, and into his loose pants chilled him until it melted and dried against his skin. Marble began to walk more briskly, and Zeph half-ran for ten minutes to get his blood pumping. His eyelashes started to collect ice, and he had to rub his gloved hands over them to keep his eyes from freezing shut. He touched a gloved hand to his mouth and came away with spots of blood—his lips were chapped and torn. *One foot in front of the other,* he said to himself. The wind shrieked and bit.

He stumbled. Hung on to Marble's traces. Felt an arm go through his. Caught a scent that made him think of oranges and cinnamon and chocolate.

"Fremont?" he asked through chapped lips. "Why that for my name?"

"Fremont's Peak," Charlotte answered.

They walked together and the team kept pace. "Conner?"

"Fort Conner."

"I know Fort Conner. Guess I should be happy you didn't take all your names from Yellowstone Park: Elephant Back, Fire Hole, Lower Geyser Basin."

"How about Stinking Fork?"

"If you knew Charlotte Spence's wicked sense of humor, you'd thank the Lord for small mercies."

He glanced over and saw her laugh to herself at that. The snow was already thick on her clothing.

"What's this about a hundred horses?" she teased.

"If I have a good spring there'll be eleven. I guess a hundred sounded better."

"Are there any apples left in my travel bag?"

"Not sure about that."

"I thought you were having trouble tying your shoes in the stage. I didn't know you were helping yourself to apples from my luggage."

"I *was* having trouble tying my shoes."

"Oh."

"I never wear shoes."

"One day I'd like to be married—"

"Amazing what a snowstorm and shoelaces will bring to mind."

"—and for my honeymoon, I want to spend a whole month, maybe a whole spring, summer, and fall, just riding and camping in Yellowstone. That would be the best wedding gift a husband could give me. Other than himself, that is."

Zeph blinked his eyes several times to clear the snow and get a look at her face as she said all this. Did she mean it? Or was she passing the time? And why was she telling him?

"Doesn't sound like a difficult honeymoon to make happen," he responded. "Be sure your wishes are clear to the gentleman who wins your hand."

"Oh, they will be. There is a problem, however."

"What's that?"

"I'm married to a man already."

"You are?" Zeph couldn't tell if she was still joking.

"I am. Fremont Wyoming. We have two children. And, do you know, I cannot recall a wedding ceremony or cradles or cribs, and I certainly cannot recall a honeymoon. I don't believe there ever was one."

"How did you let that slip past you?"

"I think the marriage just came upon me too fast. I was overwhelmed. A husband, a son, a daughter, it all happened at once. There never was time for a honeymoon."

"A woman like Conner Wyoming, I think she'd rectify that."

"Hold up!" called Stan from the driver's box. "We're clear!" Zeph and Charlotte stopped walking and so did the team. Stars were shining like lanterns. The moon was shaped like a silver cradle. The wind had dropped to a cool breeze. The road ahead was open and dry.

"Looks like we came down some," remarked Zeph.

Stan nodded. "A drop in elevation did the trick." He climbed down from the coach and shook Zeph's hand. "I'm obliged to you, young man. Missus."

Looking like walking, talking snowmen, Stoner and another man got off the coach and came over. "Thank you, mister," said Stoner.

"Name's Bert. You got a way with those beasts," said the second man, his beard glittering with icicles. "You ought to be head wrangler with some big outfit down in Pecos, Texas."

"I'd like that warmth right about now," Zeph replied.

Bert grinned through the ice. "So would I."

"You're quite the lady, missus," said Stoner. He took off his hat and whacked it against his leg. Snow flew in all directions.

Charlotte inclined her head. "Thank you."

"Both of you got a way about you," nodded Stan. "Nice to see a couple that got so much in common hitched and filling up the West with children."

"We have always thanked God for our marriage," said Charlotte.

"We got time for coffee?" called Slick as he opened the coach door for Cody and Cheyenne.

"Why, you got your fixin's?"

"I do."

Slick had a sack out of which he pulled wood, newspaper, matches, coffee, a coffeepot, brown sugar, and tin cups. "A habit I picked up during my gold rush days." He lit a fire at the side of the road, melted snow in the pot, boiled it, added the coffee grounds, let it steep, added sugar, and started pouring.

"The kids have some?" he asked Charlotte. "A little bit would do them no harm. And I have some cocoa to sprinkle into it, for Slick and those under twenty only." He winked, producing a can and a thick block wrapped in paper.

"What's in the paper, Slick?" asked Stoner.

"Only for those under twenty, ladies and gentlemen."

He opened the paper, broke off chunks of dark chocolate, and dropped them first into Cheyenne's cup and then Cody's. "Give it a minute to melt some," he told them.

Stan laughed and tilted back his hat. "Slick, I got to say, you are some ball of fire."

Bert snorted. "Missed your calling. Should've opened up a stage station. People'd take the trip through Apache country just to sit down to one of your hot drinks."

"When I retire from keeping you alive, Bert."

Zeph sipped at his cup. The heat was giving him new life. Charlotte still had her arm through his. A scarf was wound around her head, just leaving a space for her eyes, nose, and mouth. Snow was melting on the scarf and the loose strands of hair that had slipped out from under.

Moonlight and starlight always found her eyes. She was more beautiful than God's heaven and earth. Now how was he supposed to tell her something like that with all these men standing around and the horses snorting and blowing and stamping and steaming? He gazed at the mountains to the east.

"Were you going to say something?" she asked.

"The moon makes the mountains look like mother of pearl."

"Is that what it was?"

"And you," he said so the others could not hear. "The moon makes me see a beauty in you I've never seen anywhere else on earth."

Her lips parted, but she didn't answer him. Instead she looked away.

Stan glanced over and poured the dregs of his coffee on the ground. "Let's get on board, ladies and gents. Mister and Missus Wyoming have a train to catch in Utah."

Chapter Eleven

The locomotive stood hissing and trembling, like a blackened and smoking arrowhead quivering on a bowstring, ready to let fly at the snow-capped Rockies and the hundreds of miles of open plain that stretched east of them.

Zeph and Cody stood together and stared at it. *US GRANT* was painted in white italic script on the side of the locomotive's cab.

"Is that the president?" asked Cody.

"That's right," replied Zeph. "Though maybe this locomotive was commissioned while he was still commanding the Union army."

"That is simon-pure."

A man in striped overalls with a striped hat, clean white shirt, and bright-red scarf climbed down from the cab, pulled off one of his thick tan gloves, and put out a hand for Zeph to shake. He turned and shook Cody's hand, too, a big smile playing over his sun- and wind-burnt face.

"Bobby E. Clements," he said with a grin, "kind of like Bobby E. Lee, what folk in Carolina called me during the war, though now most call me by the name the railroad hung around my neck, Cannonball Clements."

"Fremont Wyoming. And my son, Cody."

"Proud to meet you. You two on board?"

"All the way to Omaha," said Zeph.

"I take her more than halfway to Cheyenne. Cody, I will cut her slick as river water through the valley, you'll have a fine ride."

"Will we see buffalo?" asked Cody.

"Buffalo? Well, who knows. Now and then we might see a small herd south of the tracks. I see any coming up, I'll blow the whistle four times, how's about that?"

Cody smiled. "Thank you, sir."

"I heard you talking while I was up in the cab. You bet, Mister Wyoming, the Union Pacific had this engine named for the president before he ever was a president. Might seem funny to have an old Rebel like me driving a locomotive named after a Yankee general, but I got no quarrels with Grant. He treated Lee fair at Appomattox. Treated us all fair, for that matter, back in '65."

Zeph thought he was going to say something else about how Grant had treated the South since '69 when he'd become president, but Cannonball squinted up at the sun and shook his head. "It ain't all what presidents do or don't do that makes the South what it is, or the whole country for that matter. We do plenty of harm on our own." He looked Zeph in the eye. "I don't think much of these armed gangs decidin' who gets to vote and who doesn't in Carolina. I won't go back unless my own people make it right. Maybe I'll never go back. I guess I'm three parts a westerner by now, anyhow."

He walked over and patted the side of the US Grant.

"She's a good one. Danforth Locomotive Works, four drivers five foot in diameter, twenty-four inch length of stroke. There's ones with more drivers, but Grant holds her own. She does well, very well."

"Cannonball!" called the fireman from the cab. He had his pocket watch open in his hand. "We're burnin' daylight."

"Easy, Dan," said Cannonball. "We'll make it up."

He shook hands with Cody and Zeph again. "You two enjoy the trip. Got sleepers?"

Zeph nodded.

"The rails'll rock you like babies. Good day, gentlemen."

Cannonball climbed back up into the cab. Zeph put his arm around Cody, and they started walking back to their car where Charlotte and Cheyenne were waiting. The air had frost in it, but the day was not uncomfortable.

"How long will it take for us to reach Omaha?" asked Cody.

"I'd say about three days."

"It took us a lot longer to come out by wagon from Pennsylvania."

"I guess it did. Train goes from California to New York in a week and a day."

Charlotte was at the window, smiling down. They could just make out her voice. "I thought we might have to haul everything out of the baggage car and wait for the next train east."

"We met the engineer!" said Cody excitedly. "A very nice man named Cannonball. He will blow the whistle four times when he sees buffalo!"

"Will he?" Charlotte laughed. "I hope he doesn't spot a herd at midnight."

Zeph and Cody swung up into the car and sat in their seats facing Charlotte and Cheyenne. The car was crowded with people heading east for Cheyenne, Omaha, Chicago, and New York. Charlotte handed them each an orange. Cody's eyes lit up.

"Something special," she said, offering the boy her black-handled John Petty and Sons pen-knife. "Real William Wolfskill oranges from Los Angeles, California."

Zeph glanced at the knife. "Where's that from?"

"It was Ricky's. He had it in the army."

"Sheffield, England?"

Charlotte looked over at him. "What a question. I never examined it with a magnifying glass. I just use it."

Zeph took out his own pocketknife, a J.M. Vance with a spear point and a small saw people called a cock spur. *V & Co* was stamped on the blade. He began to peel his orange. He noticed that Cody was more interested in the knives than he was in the oranges.

"Where did you find the fruit?" Zeph asked Charlotte.

She was helping Cheyenne use another knife that looked to be German made with mother of pearl handles. "There was a market downtown. I purchased more apples, too. In case we run into another blizzard."

Zeph grunted. "You think the locomotive will eat apples?"

"The engineer might."

Cody opened the knife Charlotte had given him and

started poking at the skin on his orange, but he kept glancing up at Zeph.

"What is it, boy?" Zeph finally asked, popping a few orange segments into his mouth.

"What do you use the saw for?"

"Every now and then it cuts something better than the straight edge of the big blade."

"Where did you get it from, Mister—"

"What's that, son?" Zeph interrupted.

"Pa, where did you buy it from?" Cody's face reddened.

"Well, I picked it up in Pennsylvania, Cody." Zeph winked to ease the boy's discomfort at calling him Pa for the first time. "Here. Made in Philadelphia. Why don't you try it on that William Wolfskill?" He folded in the blade and saw and handed the pocketknife to the boy.

Cody's discomfort vanished as he held Zeph's knife with the warm honey bone handles.

"Thank you… Pa."

"You're welcome, son."

Charlotte glanced up from Cheyenne's orange. "I didn't know you'd been to Pennsylvania."

Zeph finished eating his orange and looked out the window at Ogden. "I've been."

"You've never mentioned it. Here I thought we had a great surprise in store for you."

Zeph could see she was miffed. He stared out the window at two men hitching a horse to a small wagon. "Sorry."

"When was that?"

Zeph watched the men load what looked to be sacks of lettuce into the wagon. "The war."

She sat stock-still for a moment and took this bit of information in. Cheyenne slipped the knife from Charlotte's hands and cut away at the orange.

"Gettysburg," Charlotte finally said. "That's right."

Now it was her turn to look out the window at the men loading the wagon. "My father was killed at that battle."

Zeph didn't know what to say. "I didn't want to be there, Conner."

"Nor did he."

The edge was back in her voice. There was nothing he could do. It was over and done. Was she going to sit there and worry whether he was the man her father died beside? He thought it best to stand up.

"Wonder why we haven't started yet?" he said out loud.

A man in a white suit and gold paisley vest turned around and glanced up at him. "I just asked the conductor the same question. Apparently they're taking another stack of wood into the tender."

Zeph eased himself into the aisle. Charlotte reached out a hand.

"Where are you going?"

"The smoking car."

"But you don't smoke."

"Maybe Fremont Wyoming does."

She got up and slipped her arm through his. "I'll walk with you," she said.

"Are you sure you want to?"

"Perfectly sure. Cody, help your sister finish peeling her orange."

"All right... Ma."

They walked arm in arm down the aisle of the car.

There was scarcely room to do this, but Charlotte was determined. Zeph kept banging into seats and people's knees and elbows. The smoking car had about half a dozen men in it who all stood up as Charlotte swept through.

"Good afternoon, gentlemen," she said.

In another car they sat down briefly in a set of vacant seats. She took his hand and squeezed it. Her eyes were dark violet.

"I am sorry. You were not responsible for the war or my father's death. You caught me off guard, that's all. I didn't know about Gettysburg."

"I don't talk about it."

"Is that battle the reason you won't wear a gun?"

"One reason."

"But a big reason."

"Yes."

"I admire you all the more for it." Zeph looked down at the floor.

"Is there something else bothering you?" she asked.

Zeph lifted his eyes to hers. "When you and Cheyenne were having baths, Cody and I walked to the telegraph office."

Charlotte's gaze became more intense. "Was there something there?"

He nodded.

"Another Bible passage?"

"No. Nothing from Raber. This one was from Matt."

"What did he say?"

"The gang never came by Iron Springs. Matter of fact, they never came within a hundred miles of Iron Springs."

"Then where are they?"

"Nobody knows." He took her hands in his. "We have to stick together on this, Conner."

"I'm sorry. I didn't realize you had been in Pennsylvania during the war. I hate that conflict and everything about it. It was jarring to think about Gettysburg again. I was just out of sorts for a few minutes. I trust you, Fremont, and I know we will make it through this. I believe God meant us to see it through together."

"I haven't had a lot of time since I read the telegram to figure out what it means," he told her. "But I have prayed for wisdom about this."

"And what has God shown you?"

"I think that as soon as their accomplice telegraphed them we were headed for the railroad at Ogden they stopped thinking about Iron Springs. They knew they couldn't catch us. So they changed direction."

"To where?"

"If you wanted to make good time on horseback and try to get ahead of the train what route would you use?"

"I'm not sure." Zeph watched her brow wrinkle and the freckles gather tightly together around her small nose. "You can't ride through the Powder River Country. It's been closed to white travelers since the '68 treaty with Red Cloud."

"Are you sure?"

A flash of anger darkened Charlotte's eyes. "I'm the town librarian, remember? I read about these things all the time."

"What I meant was, do you think that treaty would keep Seraphim Raber and his crew off the Bozeman Trail?"

Her eyes widened. "But President Grant closed the forts along the Bozeman."

"All the better. No military patrols to slow them down."

"What about the tribes?"

"Raber and his men will move fast. Steal or buy fresh horses. Move by night as much as they can. I think Raber's more worried about the kids than he is the Indians."

The whistle blew. There was a jerk and a jolt, and Charlotte gripped Zeph's hands tightly. The train began to move forward. "We should get back to the children," she said, getting to her feet.

She linked her arm through his again. They came back through the smoking car. It was empty. They reached their seats just as Cody sprinkled water from a canteen over Cheyenne's hands. She looked up at Zeph and Charlotte and smiled.

"My fingers are pretty sticky. Sorry."

"That's fine," said Charlotte as she took her seat.

Zeph noticed right away it was a Union army canteen covered in blue cloth. Charlotte caught his look.

"I used it on the stage," she said.

"I guess I didn't see it too clearly in the dark."

"It was Ricky's. He always carried it."

"I remember it now. How do you keep it looking so new?"

"I wash the cloth regularly."

The train gathered speed. Cheyenne and Cody had the window seats and eagerly gazed in all directions. Cheyenne said, "Buffalo, Indians, cavalry, US Grant, buffalo, Indians, cavalry, US Grant," and Charlotte arched her eyebrows.

"That's quite a chant, Miss Wyoming."

"I like the rhythm. Cody taught me."

Cody looked embarrassed. "I didn't teach her to chant. I just told her that Cannonball would blow the whistle if he saw buffalo and that I hoped we'd see Plains Indians and cavalry, too."

She squeezed his hand. "That's all right. It might be nice to see all those things. Provided everyone comes in peace."

An hour passed. And another. Cody feel asleep with his head propped up on his hand and his elbow planted firmly on the windowsill. Cheyenne slumped into Charlotte's side. Charlotte placed her arm around the girl.

"Aren't they precious, Fremont?"

"They are. More precious than gold dust."

"That's a sweet way of putting it."

She stared out the window as the sun dropped lower and grew more golden. "Where do you think they'll show up?"

"They're going to keep riding the Bozeman and cutting a diagonal from west to east. They'll come out in Nebraska. We won't see a sign of them until well after Cheyenne."

"How long will that be?"

He shrugged. "Depends on where they want to make their move against us. They might wait until Omaha."

"You don't think that, do you?"

"No."

"How long, Fremont?"

"They'll want to put Fort Laramie well behind them. Catch us between Omaha and Cheyenne."

"You mean they'll try and stop the train?"

"There's six of them. Fewer men than that have held up trains."

Charlotte felt a shiver go through her like ice water. "Where are they going to block the tracks, Fremont?"

"The way I see it, they'll stick to the North Platte River after the Bozeman plays out and follow it right to the rail line. That'll put them far enough away from the law and the army to buy them some breathing room."

"Where and when, Fremont?"

"There's a little spot named Alkali that will suit them. Big Spring. O'Fallons. Maxwell. Any of them. Two days from here."

"Two days? Are you sure?"

"Less than two days."

She reached for his hand again. He held hers in both of his. The sun was beginning to set. The Rockies in the east were flames of crimson and bronze and made her cheeks shine.

"What will we do, Z?" she whispered.

He gave her a small smile and shook his head. "I don't know yet."

To himself he thought, *I can't say that I'll ever know, Charlotte.*

Chapter Twelve

Charlotte watched Zeph sleep.

They had enjoyed a fine supper the night before at the Green River Dining Halls in Green River, Wyoming. For the first time since she'd taken Cheyenne under her wing, the girl had taken a pencil to paper and tried to make a sketch of Castle Rock, a large hill in the vicinity. The sketch had been done so well it surprised Charlotte. Now they were through the high mountains and traveling across the plains.

The red light of dawn played over Zeph's eyelids and down over his mouth and the growth of beard that had begun in Virginia City, but he did not stir.

Somewhere in that head of his, she thought, *he is coming up with a plan to save us. Lord help him,* she prayed.

They had been so tired they hadn't bothered folding down their seats and making up their beds after Green River. All the others in their sleeper car had done so. Many of the temporary partitions that created a flimsy illusion of privacy were still in place. Charlotte yawned, with her arm over her mouth. They had all slept pretty well just the same. Perhaps tonight they might set things up so they could stretch out their legs and put their heads down onto soft white pillows.

Cody was up and whittling with the pocketknife Zeph had lent him. It looked to her as if a pretty good horse was emerging from the chunk of wood he'd picked off the ground in Green River. Cheyenne was still sleeping, nestled against Charlotte's side.

Charlotte gazed at the sky as it gradually turned blue like a fabric dipped in dye.

She opened a book in her lap and tried to read. "I remember that."

She flicked her eyes off the book and up at Zeph. "Remember what?"

"*Great Expectations*. I took it out once."

She smiled. "But did you read it?"

He smiled back, sleep still in his brown eyes. "You think I didn't?"

"I'd just like to know. You borrowed a number of books from Iron Springs Public Library. I've often wondered how many of them you finished."

"Often?"

"Often. Your titles were intriguing. Let's see, *Oliver Twist* and *Barnaby Rudge* by Dickens. *The Three Musketeers, Twenty Years After,* and *The Count of Monte Cristo* by Dumas. I think you read everything by James Fenimore Cooper."

"I kept hoping you'd call me Natty Bumppo."

"I recall you took out *The Deerslayer* more than once."

"My favorite."

"So you read it?"

"Three times. I even read *Pride and Prejudice* like you wanted."

"Like I wanted?"

"'Mister Parker, you will find some interesting male protagonists in her novels, as well as others not to be emulated.'"

She laughed and put a hand over her mouth, as there were still so many people around them sleeping. "I don't know if I should believe you."

"'It is a truth universally acknowledged, that a single man in possession of a good fortune must be in want of a wife,'" he said, reciting the opening line of *Pride and Prejudice*.

Her hand was still over her mouth. "'I strive to do right, here,'" he continued, only this time quoting from *The Deerslayer* by Cooper, "'as the surest means of keeping all right, hereafter. Hetty was oncommon, as all that know'd her must allow, and her soul was as fit to consart with angels the hour it left its body, as that of any saint in the Bible!'"

Charlotte dropped her hand and gave a squeal of surprise and delight. The heavy man in the white suit and gold paisley vest snorted in his sleep. She clapped her hand over her mouth again.

"Mister Wyoming," she said through her fingers, "how can you play with such a good woman so? Have you really read all those books after all? Have you truly memorized all of Natty Bumppo's lines in *The Deerslayer*? Every day you become a different man than the one I imagined you were. I don't think I can bear it. You make my head spin as if I were waltzing."

"'Lord, Judith, what a tongue you're mistress of!

Speech and looks go hand in hand, like, and what one can't do, the other is pretty sartain to perform! Such a gal, in a month, might spoil the stoutest warrior in the colony.'"

"Oh, stop! I completely misjudged you. I thought you were a good-hearted cowboy and Christian."

"That's all I am."

"I did not think you carried Shakespeare in your saddlebag."

"'Shall I compare thee to a summer's day? Thou art more lovely and more temperate.'"

She dropped her hand from her mouth, her lips curved upward in a permanent smile, and shook her head. "You are incorrigible. And all this time it was my belief you took those books out of the library just to see me."

Zeph nodded. "That's exactly why I did it."

"And that you chose authors I mentioned I liked just to please me."

"That is the only reason I chose them."

"But you read them!"

Zeph shrugged and squinted at the ball of fire that was the sun lifting off the prairie. "Well, at first I read them because I had all these ideas of going on long evening rides with you and quoting the books to you."

"So you did want to impress me." She felt happy inside at this thought.

"Sure I did. Just didn't realize I'd like the stories so much. Mom was a great reader, and we had a fair-size bookshelf in the house. I read books about King Arthur and William Tell and Robin of Sherwood. We had books bound in leather that put the plays of Shakespeare into story form, so I read *Macbeth* and *Hamlet* and *King Lear*. My favorite was *Henry V*: 'once more unto the breach, dear friends, once more…' I may dress cowboy and talk cowboy and act cowboy, but I have a first-class education in me, Missus Wyoming. I just like to hide it the way a Cheyenne brave hides himself in the buffalo grass."

"Why?"

"Because no one would understand."

She gazed at him. Zeph had already shown himself to be more of a man than she had ever dreamed he was during their flight from Iron Springs—the way he'd listened as she told about her Amish past, how he'd ridden after her and brought her horse to a halt, when he'd climbed out of the stage in a roaring storm and led the team of horses forward and saved them all. Now he was sitting in front of her and quoting lines from books and poems he'd memorized just so he could speak them to her on evening rides in the mountains at sunset. It was too much for her to take in, an answer to prayer beyond what she could ask or imagine. Yet the promise she had made to her brother bound her, and the binding must keep them apart. She felt a wetness slip down her cheek, but she did nothing to brush it away.

"Here now," he said softly and leaned across to wipe her face with a clean blue bandanna. He had the scent of apples and woodsmoke on him, as well as the pleasant smell of fresh soap that he'd washed up with at Green River.

"Z," she whispered.

"It's gonna be all right now. See? I'm talking like a cowpoke again."

She laughed and shook her head. "It's all so beautiful, and it's more than I ever dreamed. It's too good to be true. I just know something bad is going to happen to take you away from me like Daddy was taken and Ricky and my mother."

"Shh. Shh. It doesn't have to happen that way again just because it's happened that way before. Chapters have different endings. Not all books leave you feeling sad, do they? *Pride and Prejudice* has a good marriage to bring the story to a close. Two good marriages, as a matter of fact."

"Those are just books, Z. This is real life."

"Books are written by people who've lived real life, Char."

"That's the kind of thing a librarian like you should be telling me. What can a busted-up old cowpuncher really know about it?"

She laughed. "Some busted-up old cowpuncher."

The whistle suddenly shrieked four times in a row. Zeph and Charlotte jumped. People stirred all around them and asked what was going on in confused and belligerent voices. Partitions came down. Cody's eyes went wide in disbelief, and he pressed his face to the window.

"Buffalo!" he shouted. "Buffalo!"

Cheyenne woke up and looked out. Their seats were on the south side of the car, and the four of them could see the herd clearly.

"How many, Pa?" asked Cody.

Zeph was leaning over him to gaze out the window. "I'd say seven or eight hundred. Maybe a thousand. Isn't that something?"

"Did you ever see more than this?"

"Son, I've seem 'em so thick there was no grass for a hundred miles, just buffalo moving like a wide and muddy brown river, like some kind of prairie Mississippi of hair and horns."

Cannonball had slowed the train down so passengers could get a better look. The man in the white suit stooped in the aisle to get a look out their window.

"Amazing!" he said. "I thought there were only a few left."

"Mister," Zeph said, "compared to what there was twenty years ago, this is a few."

Charlotte found herself fascinated by a grand bull at the edge of the rolling herd. It seemed to be staring at her and at the locomotive with a grandeur and defiance that impressed her, as if the sturdy old bull were declaring, "You will not defeat me. I will endure. You may have your hour. But I will not be vanquished." Then he and the herd were gone, a dark shape moving slowly over the plains and raising a small haze of dust, not much, for there was some frost on the ground. Finally, there was only a black speck that could have been anything.

"What does buffalo taste like?" asked Cheyenne.

"Good," said Zeph, sitting back down, "it's very good."

"I'd like to try it someday."

"Well, my girl, we'll see what we can do."

Charlotte looked at the health in Cody's face and in Cheyenne's and thanked God. She also saw the sparkle in Zeph's eyes and realized how much he loved the West and the things that were part of it that few easterners understood. How would he feel being cooped up in Pennsylvania—the quietness of the land, the softness of the snow and winds, the lack of mountains and sharp peaks, and the impossibility of a chance glimpse of bison thundering over country that stretched for hundreds of miles without a building or a road or a sign?

If we get to Pennsylvania.

The fear fastened its teeth into her heart and mind, and she swiftly lost the peace and joy she had just been delighting in. Zeph was watching her face. She felt his gaze and looked over at him, not bothering to hide the cold, dark sensations that were paralyzing her thoughts and her happiness.

He understood. One hand went into the pocket of the coat she had sewn for him and came out with his brother's Bible. He opened it but did not bother to look down as he said, "'The Lord is my shepherd; I shall not want. Yea, though I walk through the valley of the shadow of death, I will fear no evil: for thou art with me… . Thou preparest a table before me in the presence of mine enemies: thou anointest my head with oil; my cup runneth over. Surely goodness and mercy shall follow me all the days of my life.'"

She sat and listened and waited. Suddenly she realized how much she liked his voice and how much it soothed her to have him read to her.

"Go on," she said.

"That's it in a nutshell, Conner." He smiled. "I'm getting used to that name. It's not half bad."

"Please go on."

"Only way to beat this fear is to face it. We can't keep running. We'll be running forever as long as Raber's alive: Wyoming, Nebraska, Illinois, Pennsylvania. He'd follow us all the way up into Canada or down into Comanche country. Probably cross the ocean to

England to corner us in a back alley in London. Only one thing we can do."

Charlotte felt goose bumps on her arms under the sleeves of her dress, as if she knew what he was going to say before he said it, as if the same words were in her mind, too.

"What is it?" she asked.

Zeph rubbed the beard on his jaw and looked away from her out at the miles of sunlit prairie glittering with morning frost.

"We're going to have to make sure he knows where we are and where we're going and when we'll be there. We're going to have to draw him out and then face him down. We're going to have to put the kids and ourselves right out there in the open as bait. Bait for a mad wolf named Seraphim Raber."

Chapter Thirteen

Zeph stood at the door to the telegraph office. He thought a moment and then pulled the badge from his pocket and pinned it on his coat. Then decided to remove his coat and broad-brimmed hat. Charlotte had plucked a spare from her luggage to replace the hat the winter storm had taken. He draped the hat and coat on a bench just outside the door, took the badge off the coat, and pinned it onto his shirt instead.

"Afternoon, deputy," said the elderly man at the counter.

Zeph nodded. "I'll need to send telegrams to the federal marshal in Iron Springs, Montana Territory, and another to the commander at Fort Laramie."

"Sure enough. Here's the pad."

Zeph hunched over the countertop with a stub of pencil and began to print.

Marshal Matthew Parker, We have had no trouble and are carrying on into Nebraska, kids are fine, will telegraph from Omaha, Deputy Marshal Zephaniah Parker.

* * *

He and Charlotte had decided to make sure Raber knew where they were headed and when. They counted on the accomplice, whoever it was, to get ahold of Raber and let him know what their plans were and that the children were with them.

Then he wrote another telegram out for Fort Laramie. Once again, he and Charlotte had talked it over. There was no guarantee the commander would do what Zeph asked. He only hoped the chance of nabbing Raber would make the fort commander cast all other plans to the wind. At the bottom he wrote, Zephaniah Truett Parker, Deputy US Marshal.

He put a few dollars on the counter, but the elderly man waved him off. "No charge, Deputy."

"Well, then, consider it a lawman's contribution to your retirement fund."

The man smiled. "Why, thank'ee kindly, Deputy."

Outside Zeph suddenly noticed the chill in the bright blue air and pulled his coat back on. With the large hat on his head and the badge in his pocket, he began to walk toward the shops on Main Street, no longer Deputy Marshal Zephaniah Parker, but Fremont Wyoming, farmer, father of two, and husband to one. He began to whistle a hymn without thinking, "Shall We Gather at the River."

He found Charlotte and the children in a general store, one he remembered from '73, the year he buried his father, except the shop was much larger now. Cody was staring at the six-guns locked under the glass countertop and Charlotte was saying, "Never mind those things, Cody, they're nothing but death and destruction. Let me buy you something sweet instead. What do you think of these candies? Wouldn't you like a big bag of them?"

Cody stared at the small colored objects in the jar. "What are they?"

"They call them jelly beans."

"What do they taste like?"

"Oh, they taste very good, son," said Zeph putting an arm around him. "First had some when I was in the army. A fellow named Schrafft used to have them sent down from Boston for the troops. The boys'd fight over these more than they'd fight over coffee. Yellow is lemon, red is raspberry or strawberry or cherry, black is licorice flavor. A big bag'd keep you smiling all the way through Nebraska."

"Excellent," Cody said with a grin.

"I'm happy to do it for you, dear," Charlotte replied. "What about you, Cheyenne? A Silverhair and the three-bears size of bag? One that's just right, not too big, not too small?"

"I'm too old for that." Cheyenne's eyes blazed up and then settled. "I'll be eleven in a few months."

Charlotte and Zeph glanced at one another.

"Well, then," said Charlotte, "what would you like?"

"Chocolate would suit me."

Charlotte snorted briefly. "I'm sure it would. Pick out what you'd like."

She pointed at a large bar of dark chocolate, and the shopkeeper took it, wrapped it, and placed it in a paper bag.

"Thanks," said Cheyenne to Charlotte.

"You're welcome, dear."

Cannonball had left them shortly after the buffalo sighting. Another engineer was running the US Grant into Nebraska. As they climbed back into their car, Zeph noticed familiar faces that were carrying on, as they were, for points farther east: there was a family of five who always smiled at Zeph and Charlotte and the children headed for Florida; a man and wife who bickered about returning to Liverpool, England, or taking a train back to Sacramento, California; and the portly man in the white suit and gold vest who always tipped his hat to Charlotte.

"Where you headed?" he asked them as they resumed their seats.

"As far as the rails will run," said Zeph.

"I see." The man nodded. "Henry Chase, by the way."

"Fremont Wyoming. My wife, Charlotte, and my two children, Cody and Cheyenne."

"How do you do?" said the man, standing up.

"A pleasure, Mister Chase," responded Charlotte, inclining her head.

Zeph knew his sudden good cheer came from having written out those two telegrams. Instead of running and hiding, he had a chance to fight back and protect Charlotte and the children. It made him feel better than he'd felt in a long time. If only the plan would work. If only Raber would take the bait.

He settled himself in his seat. He could see the length of the car and everyone coming in and out from the front of the train. Opening a package of Adams New York No. 1 chewing gum, he handed each of them a piece, though Cheyenne preferred her chocolate. Then he glanced out the windows on the north side of the train across the aisle and watched two cowboys, covered in dust, ride past the depot.

Suddenly a pang of fear stabbed him like a sharp knife. Suppose those two had just come off the Bozeman Trail? How would he know who were just ordinary cowpokes and who were Raber's gunmen? Just then a man stepped into the car. He was dressed in black from head to foot except for a few silver conchas on his hat and one on his holster. Tall and lean, strength coiled under his clothing. He glanced around, black carpetbag in his grip, met Zeph's gaze with a look like a gunsight, then took an empty seat halfway down the car, his back to Zeph. He pulled off his dark sheepskin jacket and rolled it up on the seat beside him, tipped his hat to an attractive young woman sitting opposite, and gazed out the window to his left at the same two cowboys Zeph had been watching. The cowboys had stopped and were sitting on their horses, staring at the train.

For the first time in over ten years, Zeph wished he'd gone heeled, wished he'd bought a small pistol at the general store and slipped it into his coat pocket. What would he do if the man in black was one of Raber's crew? If he came at them in the night with the train clicking through the wide open Nebraska miles? If the cowboys were there to back him up and they meant to make their move before the US Grant pulled out of the station?

There was nothing Zeph could do. Pinning on his badge would not stop them. If he made his way back to the baggage car to get the gun, he was pretty sure the car would be locked. And even if he got the conductor or one of his assistants to open it up and found his father's Remington, what good would that do when the cartridges that made it a threat to be reckoned with were rusting in the snow and mud on a road that ran north out of Iron Springs?

Charlotte read his face. "What's wrong?"

Zeph had stopped chewing his gum. "Too many strangers."

She glanced out the windows across the aisle. "Those two men on horseback?"

"They just sit and watch the train."

"No harm in that."

"They showed up the same time a man who looks like a gunslinger got into the car. He's sitting just ahead of us, and he's dressed to kill."

Charlotte looked over her shoulder and back at him. "They wouldn't do anything now."

"Why not?"

"The law in Cheyenne. They'd be caught."

"Char," he said in a low voice, "they'd gun down the law as quick as they'd gun down us."

They were silent a few moments. Cheyenne was taking bites of the bar of chocolate and sketching on a pad of paper. Zeph watched her scribbles turn into mountains and horses and buffalo. She was very good. He looked up at Charlotte.

"Even if we had a picture," he said softly, "and it was posted in every town and village and railroad crossing, it would make no difference. Raber would come for us anyway. Out of revenge."

The whistle blew. The car shuddered. The train began to move.

Zeph kept his eyes on the cowboys and on the man in black. The cowboys kept staring but made no attempt to follow the train. The man in black shifted his weight and pulled his hat down over his face and went to sleep. The train picked up speed.

Charlotte gave him a look that said, "You see? You're getting all worked up over nothing."

Zeph shook his head. "It can happen anytime," he whispered, "day or night, when we're asleep or awake. The man in black can make his play for us whenever he wants, and there's nothing I can do to protect you."

"Unless the plan works," she said quietly.

"*If* the plan works. If we even get to the only place in Nebraska where the plan has any chance of working at all."

"How long?"

"I'm not sure."

"How long, Z?"

Zeph shrugged. "We'll be out of Wyoming Territory in no time. There'll be some night travel. It won't be long. Well before noon tomorrow it'll be all over. One way or another."

"May I borrow your brother's Bible?" Zeph handed it over.

"I'm going to mark a place with this leather bookmark I have. Ricky brought it home from Denver. I'm tucking it in right here. Now tomorrow, when this is all over, I want you to take this Bible out of your pocket, open it to where I've placed the bookmark, and read the passage out loud to us. But I don't want you looking at it before that, promise?"

"I swear."

She gave it back to him, and he slipped it into one of his outer pockets. Then he narrowed his eyes and looked her over from bonnet to boots.

"What on earth are you doing?" she asked.

"It's not the same dress."

"No, it's not."

"It's a lighter shade of gray."

"Yes."

"When did you do that?"

"I changed at the last meal stop before Cheyenne. Glad you've finally noticed."

"It's very pretty."

"Really? It's supposed to be very plain."

"I'd like to know whatever would look plain on you. You'd make rags look like silk."

Charlotte smiled. "Why, that's quite a compliment, Mister Wyoming. I'm glad the gentleman rancher has returned. I thought I'd lost him."

Zeph looked at the children. Cheyenne had put aside her drawings and nodded off, and Cody had his head on his hand and his arm propped on the window ledge, snoring quietly into the glass. Zeph leaned over toward Charlotte.

"If they stop the train tomorrow," he said, "go with the kids back to the baggage car. I'll make sure it's open. Hide there. They may not think to check it or have the time. All right?"

"I'm not leaving you, Z."

"You will. For the children's sake. All right?"

Charlotte looked sadly out the window at the fields of snow and grass. "All right."

Zeph slid down in his seat and closed his eyes.

Lord, went the words through his head, *I'm not the kind of praying man Jude is, but You've got to help us out, You've got to bring things together, or we're not going to make it. Have mercy on us. Have mercy on the kids. May Your holy angels defeat the angel of death. In the name of Jesus.*

He felt the slightest bit better and the slightest bit calmer. Sleep began shutting him down. He heard the rustle of Charlotte's dress and caught a whiff of her perfume. Part of him thought of the man in black, but the larger part thought of Nebraska and the morning and Seraphim Raber. Then his mind was filled only with the rhythm of the train and the *click-click-click* of the iron wheels as they ran over the rails, taking them closer to the east and closer to Nebraska and closer to the day which the Lord had made, a day on which they might live or they might die.

Chapter Fourteen

When it happened, it happened so quickly Zeph barely had time to take it in.

That night they had turned their seats into beds and pulled another bed open above their heads. Cody had taken that one, Cheyenne was with Charlotte, Zeph slept on the outside close to the aisle. They had not set up the partition people often used for privacy because Zeph wanted to hear and see everything that was going on.

Something made him stir. He glanced out a window and saw a sign that said ALKALI roll past. Light was beginning to flood the east, and he wondered about a breakfast stop and why they hadn't pulled into the small town. Then he remembered the names Alkali, O'Fallons, and Maxwell. He sat up, fully awake, and looked for the man in black. Too many partitions were in the way. For all he knew, the man had changed seats to get even closer to them.

"Charlotte!" he whispered urgently.

"Mmm," she mumbled.

"Charlotte! Wake up! We're here!"

"Where?"

The car shook and squealed and slammed to a stop. People were thrown out of their beds and into the aisle. Partitions collapsed. A woman screamed, and several men began to shout for the conductor.

Charlotte was awake now, her hair in disarray, looking, Zeph could not help but notice, warm and child-like and wonderful; but when someone yelled, "There's men on horseback in masks; the train's being robbed," he thrust her sheepskin jacket at her and said, "Get the kids to the baggage car."

Shots were fired outside the window. Cody came sprawling out of his bed above them. Zeph put Cody's jacket over the boy's thin shoulders. "Go with your mother and sister to the baggage car behind us. It's two cars farther on. You lead the way. Go now."

"No!" Cody pushed away from Zeph with all the strength a burst of anger can give a twelve-year-old boy. "They killed my mother. They killed my father. I'm going to fight."

"Cody, you have to get to the baggage car."

"I'm not hiding anymore, and I'm not running. I will face them."

Zeph saw the blaze in the boy's eyes. He meant it. But Zeph didn't have time to argue this through. There were two more gunshots. He gripped Cody's shoulders.

"Who is going to protect Miss Spence? Who is going to protect Cheyenne? If they are in the baggage car and we are both here, who will save them if the gang breaks into their car first?"

The boy hesitated.

"Take them to safety," Zeph urged. "Fight for them."

"All right," Cody said.

Charlotte was on her feet, holding a sleepy Cheyenne by the hand, her face and eyes a strange mixture
of fear, anger, and defiance. "I am not happy about
leaving you," she said to Zeph.

"I'll be okay."

She looked at him in the half-light as the sun began
to slip over the rim of the prairie. People cried and
shrieked all around them.

Cody seized her hand and led her and Cheyenne to
the door. Then he turned.

"Is the baggage door open?" Cody asked.

"Yes," Zeph said. There was another gunshot. "I
got a steward to open it for me last night after you'd
all fallen asleep. Then I jimmied it, so he couldn't lock
it back up again. I saw some saddle blankets in there.
Maybe get under a bunch of them. Hurry now."

"Z!"

Charlotte's eyes were like twin fires in the dawn
light coming through the windows. "There's no man
like you, mister. No man ever."

And she was gone.

Zeph spun around and looked for the man in black.
He was sitting in the same seat, cool as ice, while pan-
demonium reigned left and right of him. The pretty
young woman, her face flushed, suddenly asked,
"What do we do? Where do we go?"

"Just sit tight," Zeph heard the man say in a deep
voice. "Give them your diamonds and pearls, and they
won't take anything more."

Zeph clenched his fists. Sure, easy for him to say; it
was his buddies that were going to board the train and
shove their gun barrels into innocent people's faces.
Maybe I should try and take him from behind. He took

a few steps forward and then looked out the windows on both sides of the train. Men with flour sacks for masks were riding up and down the line. There were four or five of them, and every few moments another one of them would fire into the air with a pistol or rifle.

Some children had begun crying. He saw the family that was bound for Florida huddled in tears at the front of the car. Zeph looked in vain on both sides of the railway for any sign of troopers from Fort Laramie. It looked like they were going to have to bluff their way out of this one. *Lord, the baggage car has to work. Help us.*

He saw a tall man ride up to their car and swing down from the saddle. He wore a long white duster that was covered in dirt and grime. The door at the front of the car banged open. The woman who couldn't make up her mind between Liverpool and Sacramento shrieked. The outlaw had a flour sack with two ragged holes cut in it for his eyes and a third for his mouth. A short-barreled pistol was in his left hand. In a voice like stones dropping in a bucket he said, "I'm lookin' for a man goes by the name Zephaniah Parker. Any of you folks know if he's in this car?"

No one spoke, but the sobbing and crying carried on. "How 'bout Charlotte Spence?"

Again, no one spoke up.

The man dug a small bag out of one of the pockets of his duster.

"Gold nuggets," he said. "It's yours if you point either of 'em out to me. And then I won't have to kill no one, neither."

Zeph was sure a number of people would have jumped at the chance if only they knew who he was.

One thing he couldn't figure out was why the man in black and the outlaw hadn't acknowledged each other, but he figured that when the time was right they'd hitch up and make their play. They were probably waiting to see if they could flush their prey first.

"There's two kids traveling with 'em. The man and woman abducted 'em. You'd be doing us all a favor if you pointed the kids out to me. I got to get 'em back to their rightful parents."

Who would buy that story? thought Zeph.

"The kids' names are Cody and Cheyenne Wyoming."

Fear ran through Zeph. How could the outlaw know that? The answer came quick as a peal of thunder—Raber's accomplice in Iron Springs.

To Zeph's dismay, the heavy man in the white suit and gold paisley vest, who'd introduced himself as Henry Chase, stood up, body shaking, and pointed a finger at him.

"There!" he squeaked in a high voice. "That's him! He goes by the name Fremont Wyoming! But he calls his children Cheyenne and Cody! He told them to hide in one of the other cars!"

"Is that a fact?"

The outlaw moved toward Zeph. "Well, Mister Parker, I got a bone to pick with you. Riding the Bozeman night and day ain't no Presbyterian picnic. Injuns killed my best horse. I've already taken a great dislike to you. So here's how it's gonna play out. I got questions; you got answers. The sooner you give me the kids the easier your pain's gonna be—"

A black leg shot out, and the outlaw tripped and fell on his face in the aisle. He was a tough one, though.

Zeph watched him twist like a snake and come up with his gun ready to fire. A black hand grabbed the outlaw's gun, so the hammer wouldn't go down, and clamped onto his wrist at the same time. The outlaw yelped. His gun fell to the floor. Another black hand swung at his head with a pistol butt. *Thunk.* It sounded to Zeph like a hammer hitting a stump. The outlaw lay still.

The man in black quickly put handcuffs on the unconscious gunman. Zeph heard him mutter, "One for the hangman," and then he stood up, tall, dark, and dangerous. He gave Henry Chase, quivering in his white suit, a piercing glance—"I want to have a word with you"—and came toward Zeph. Suddenly he smiled and touched the brim of his hat.

"Mister Parker, I am Marshal Michael James Austen. Your brother Matt thought I might find you on the train to Omaha, Nebraska."

Chapter Fifteen

The marshal shook Zeph's hand. Zeph was still trying to take it all in.

"My brother told you I'd be on this train?" he finally got out.

"He did. I work out of Cheyenne, and I got a telegram from him. Took me three cars, but I finally found you. Family of four. Handsome woman. He gave me a pretty good description of your face and build, though I have to say he got your clothes all wrong. Where are the others?"

"In the baggage car."

"It'll be chilly in there. Best get them out before the kids catch their death."

"But what about the rest of the gang?"

The marshal looked out the windows. "They don't know what's going on in here. Besides, they'll have their hands full shortly."

"What do you mean?"

"Do you have a pocket watch handy, Mister Parker?"

"Lost mine in a roundup last fall. Never got around to replacing it."

"Occupational hazard, I guess. I punched cows once."

He pulled a gleaming silver watch from his black vest pocket and flipped open the top. Glancing at the dial he said, "They're five minutes late. Anytime now. Maybe wait on the kids a little bit."

There was a flurry of gunfire just as he finished his sentence.

Somebody cheered. North of the tracks cavalry was pouring out of a gully and pounding down on the outlaws. Several were firing carbines as they rode. More gunfire from south of the train made him turn his head. Dozens of blue uniformed cavalrymen in brown buffalo coats were charging across the prairie at the outlaw gang from that side as well. Puffs of gun smoke erupted from their rifle and pistol barrels. A man cheered again, and soon the whole car was bursting with shouts and whistles. Zeph felt relief wash through him as if he'd just taken a large drink of cool water.

"Folks!" called the marshal. "You'd best get yourselves down on the floor! A stray bullet may come through one of the windows!"

When a bullet smashed one of the windows, Henry Chase almost pushed himself through the floorboards. Marshal Austen chuckled, and Zeph wondered if that hadn't been one of the reasons he wanted everyone on the floor to begin with. As for himself, the marshal remained standing and watching the action, so Zeph stood with him.

Horses raced back and forth, clods of frozen earth flew up into the air, smoke from the gunfire billowed and floated in the morning frost. One outlaw had been shot out of the saddle and stood with a hand clamped over his bleeding shoulder. The others had laid down a blistering fire, wounded several soldiers, and made a run for it on horseback. Gradually the shooting petered out. An officer shouted, "It's all over, folks, all over. You can rest easy now!"

Henry Chase slowly raised his head, like a turtle, Zeph thought. Marshal Austen had the satisfaction of glancing at Chase and seeing the grime and stains covering his white suit and gold vest. He nodded and smiled and went out the front door of the car. Turning his head, he called back to Zeph, "Now's the time to bring your family out." He stepped outside to speak with the officers from Fort Laramie.

Cody was right at the door when Zeph opened it and ready to brain him with an iron bar.

"Whoa, cowboy." Zeph held up his hands. "I'm one of the good guys."

Cody's eyes were like steel. "What happened?"

"They shot one. Caught another. The rest of the gang ran."

Cody brought Charlotte and Cheyenne out from under a stack of saddles, blankets, and harnesses. Charlotte gripped a pitchfork in her fists. Cheyenne held a steel currycomb and had the face of a cougar.

"I wouldn't want to tangle with you," he said.

"Where are they?" asked Cheyenne. "Are they right behind you?"

"They wounded one, the others ran, they caught two, the army has them."

Cody perked up. "The army?"

"That's right. Cavalry in blue uniforms and riding horses and blowing trumpets and everything. Go and take a look."

Cody flew out of the baggage car. Cheyenne ran after him, still holding the currycomb. Zeph and Charlotte had a moment alone in the dim light.

She anxiously studied his face. "Are you all right?"

"I am."

"Did any passengers get hurt?"

"Well, maybe Henry Chase's pride, but he'll live."

"What do you mean?"

Zeph explained how Chase had pointed him out and that the gunslinger-turned-marshal had taken great delight in watching Chase soil his white suit squirming about on the floor to avoid gunshots. Charlotte's face brightened with anger. "He told the murderer who you were and that Cody and Cheyenne were with you? What a despicable rattlesnake!"

"Go easy on him. He's just a frightened little man."

"Go easy on him!"

"You have that thunderstorm blue about you."

"What?"

"You know that dark blue of thunderclouds when they're coming at you full of wind and hail and fury? That's the color of your eyes right now."

"How can you tell what color my eyes are in here?"

"They glow."

Charlotte smiled. "Oh, yes?" Then she had a look of concern. "You're sure you didn't get hurt?"

"Well, the outlaw meant to give me a going over. But the man in black took him down."

"What's the marshal's name?"

"Austen. Michael James Austen."

"Your brother telegraphed him?"

"Yes, ma'am."

"'Yes, ma'am.'" She made a face that brought her

freckles tight around her nose. She kissed him on the mouth and then pulled away. He put one hand gently behind her head and brought her lips back to his. He expected the moment to be brief. But she slipped her arms about him and held him close. They kissed a second time.

"I was worried," she whispered.

"I know."

"Were you ever afraid?"

"Only that he might get past me."

"He'd never have gotten past you."

She gave him one more kiss and then stepped back and smoothed her gray dress. "The children will be wondering where we are."

Zeph felt light-headed. "After you."

When they got back to the car, three cavalrymen were talking with passengers, and Cody and Cheyenne were glued to one of them. They all wore buffalo coats over their uniforms. The unconscious outlaw had already been carried out. Marshal Austen touched his hat brim at Charlotte's entry and introduced himself and the officer standing with him. "This is First Lieutenant Robbie Hanson."

"Ma'am," said Hanson, giving a short tug on the brim of his cavalry Stetson. The number two stood out over the crossed sabers on his hat.

"Lieutenant. I see you're with the Second Cavalry. One of the best."

"Company K. *The* best I believe, Missus Wyoming. I hope I find you well after your ordeal?"

"Quite well, thank you. The greater part of my ordeal consisted of hiding under a musty saddle blanket and trying hard not to sneeze."

The men laughed.

"Well, ma'am," said the lieutenant, "I think I can safely say that your saddle blanket days are behind you. We have two of the gang in custody. The others are probably halfway to Mexico. We have already thanked your husband for relaying the information to us at Fort Laramie that permitted us to be at this location today to capture them. There was a score to settle."

"You gentlemen have done an admirable job. I thank you with all my heart for protecting us from these savages. I especially thank you for delivering the children from their hands."

"It was an honor, ma'am," replied the lieutenant.

"Very much so," responded Marshal Austen.

"Were any of your men hurt or wounded, Lieutenant Hanson?"

"Five, thank you for asking, ma'am. They will be all right."

"I am glad to hear it. Well, Lieutenant, what happens now?"

"Now, ma'am," said Lieutenant Hanson, "we will take our prisoners ahead to the depot at Maxwell where a special train that set out from Omaha yesterday will meet us. The train will take the prisoners and their guards to Cheyenne where they will be put on trial. Then there will be a public hanging."

Charlotte's face whitened. "A hanging? Both of them?"

"Yes, ma'am."

Charlotte recovered and patted him on the cheek. "I understand, Lieutenant Hanson. Thank you again for all you have done for us. I'll let you carry on with your duties."

"Thank you, ma'am. Will you be riding with us, Marshal Austen?"

Austen shook his head. "I'll take this train and go ahead to Maxwell. I'll meet you there when you arrive."

Lieutenant Hanson saluted and turned to leave the car, tapping his two men on the back as he did so. Cody and Cheyenne walked with their trooper to the door. He shook Cody's hand and gave Cheyenne a kiss on the cheek. Then, as he turned to go, he suddenly planted his Stetson on Cody's bare head and, whipping off his yellow scarf, tied it around Cheyenne's neck. Grinning, he climbed down from the car, swung up into the saddle, and galloped off with a wave of his hand and a shout.

Cody and Cheyenne came running back to Zeph and Charlotte.

"Look at this!" cried Cody. The Stetson had flopped down over his eyes.

"Very handsome," said Charlotte, "but you will have to let me put some paper under the sweatband, so it will fit."

"He gave me his scarf," said Cheyenne. "How does it look?"

"Wonderful. On windy days you could use it to keep your hair in place as well."

"No, it always needs to be around my neck." Cheyenne's face was set. "Just the way Trooper Johnny wore it."

"Trooper Johnny, is it? Suit yourself."

The whistle blew. People were tidying up their seats and putting away bedding. Charlotte began to do the same as the train lurched and started forward. Cavalrymen walked their horses on either side of the train. The two prisoners, unmasked, were escorted between them. Neither of the outlaws had boots. The breath of men and of horses hung like a white haze in the cold air.

Charlotte said to Zeph, "I can't see either of the outlaws' faces, only the backs of their heads. Did they catch Seraphim Raber?"

"I don't know."

"Did the others get away?"

"Yes."

The train left the cavalrymen and their prisoners behind. Marshal Austen watched the morning sun run over the prairie for a few moments, and then he said to Zeph in a low voice, "Your brother told me you don't go heeled."

"That's right."

"What would you have done with that outlaw if I hadn't been in the car?"

"I guess I would have tried to wrestle him to the ground if he got close enough."

"What if he kept his distance and just kept putting bullets into you?"

"He wouldn't have done that. He needed to know where the kids were at."

"He only had a couple more cars to search. He would've found the baggage car and gone through that, too. He didn't need you. If you'd told him where they were it would've made his job easier, that's all."

"I would never have told him."

"That's right. And once he'd put enough holes in you and realized that, he would've gone looking in the cars behind you and left you on the floor to bleed out."

"It's personal."

Austen nodded. "Most of us have our war stories,

Mister Parker. I wouldn't touch a firearm going on five years after Appomattox. Worked cattle in Texas and then ran a dry goods store in Missouri. Had a friend elected town sheriff nearby who swore off killing after Lee surrendered. Never wore a sidearm or carried a rifle or shotgun, though his deputies did. This all works out fine long as you've got outlaws that respect the code. There's many won't draw on an unarmed man. But the day comes you've got a gang that will. Perk was healthy up until a Sunday the Murfreesboro Gang were out hunting men that had been Union officers. Shot him full of holes and left him lying in the street. He lived. Lost all but one arm. Perk's not a lawman anymore. Can't take care of himself or his own family, let alone the citizens of a town that would be counting on him."

Charlotte stuffed paper inside the cavalry Stetson's sweatband Cody wanted to wear. "And what became of the dry goods merchant Michael James Austen?"

Austen fixed his gaze on her. "Why, missus, the same gang rode back into the neighborhood a month later when someone told them I'd been a Yankee colonel. They laughed when my wife pleaded that I didn't have a gun. Strung me up by my feet and covered me in flour and molasses. Said I wasn't but half a man, and they wouldn't even waste half a bullet on me."

Charlotte felt a sadness go through her. "At least they let you live."

"Did they, Miss Spence? They snatched up my wife and two children when they left. The kids are hollering, and I'm hanging upside down, choking on the molasses they poured into my mouth—I couldn't do a thing. Never saw them again. I hired Pinkerton's to track them down. Pinkerton's followed their trail as far as Arizona Territory. Then the gang vanished. I did some searching on my own. The story went that the gang had been wiped out by Mescalero Apache."

Chapter Sixteen

Charlotte did not know what to say. She wondered what Zeph would have done under similar circumstances. Neither of the children was listening. Cody had his hat on and was drawing cavalrymen on the pad of paper with strong, dark strokes, the man back to being a boy. Cheyenne was daydreaming and fingering the yellow scarf tied around her throat.

Austen coughed. "There's something you don't see every day."

Out the windows that looked south, a line of Indians on horseback were trotting single file.

"A war party!" cried Cody.

Austen shook his head. "No war paint. A hunting party. They're heading west. I expect they're following a herd of buffalo."

All the Indians were men, all were wrapped in buffalo robes or red point blankets, all had repeating rifles. A few wore eagle feathers in their hair. They did not look at the train. It was as if the railroad did not exist. There were about fifty of them. They stared straight ahead and their heads were erect.

"Lakota Sioux," said Zeph.

Austen nodded. "Allies of the Cheyenne. Looks like Oglala, some of the Kiyuksa band. I recognize a few of them. They're a ways south of the Black Hills."

"What will happen when they run into the Second Cavalry?" asked Cody.

"They'll ignore one another," said Austen. "The Sioux haven't been raiding, and Hanson has to get his prisoners to Wyoming."

"At least the gold rush in the Black Hills is over," said Zeph. "For now."

Austen tugged his pocket watch from his vest and consulted it. "We'll be into Maxwell shortly. It's only a half-hour run." From another vest pocket he brought out his badge. He smiled at Zeph. "I guess I've played a gunslinger on his way to points east long enough. I like black, but I like silver, too."

He stood up and pulled on his dark sheepskin coat. Then he clapped a hand to Zeph's shoulder. "No man can tell another man what to do. I admire your sand, Parker. And I wish you all the best. I pray to God it will be a clear run for you into Omaha and Chicago. If there's anything I can do, telegraph me at Cheyenne."

He began to walk up the aisle as the train slowed and the brakes squealed. Charlotte reached out and touched his arm.

"And are you a praying man, Marshal Austen?" she asked earnestly.

"On occasion."

"Then let's pray your family is alive. Isn't it possible the Mescalero have adopted your children and are raising them? And that your wife is with them in some Apache camp?"

He nodded. "It's possible."

He continued walking. When he reached his seat, he bent down and picked up his black carpetbag. The pretty young woman who'd sat across from him rose to say something with a most engaging smile. But he touched his hat brim and said, "I am a family man, miss," and carried on to the door. He stood there as the train came to a stop. Then he looked down the length of the car to Henry Chase. "Mister Chase."

The man looked up in surprise and a bit of fear. "Yes, sir?"

"You'd best be coming with me."

"But, sir—"

"Aiding an outlaw gang, Mister Chase. You and I need to talk."

"I need to get to—"

"Come along, Mister Chase."

He pulled aside his sheepskin coat just enough for Chase and everyone else to see the silver badge he'd pinned to his vest. Chase looked around him for support, but there was none. Reluctantly he got to his feet and walked in his stained suit and vest to the front of the car. Austen stepped to one side. "After you."

Chase climbed down the steps and Austen followed him. Then they walked back toward the baggage car. No one boarded the train. After a minute or two, the whistle shrieked and the US Grant began to pull out of the small town.

Zeph watched Marshal Austen—lean, tall, in black—standing beside Henry Chase—portly, short, in white—on the station platform with three gold carpetbags at Chase's feet. Then the train left them behind, and there was only a row of large bare-branched cottonwoods rolling past the windows.

"I feel alone," Charlotte said.

Zeph nodded. "I know. I trusted that man."

"It's chillier in here than it was yesterday."

"Mercury's dropped, I expect. Maybe put your sheepskin coat on. Here." Zeph brought a white blanket with colored stripes out from under his feet. "One of these'll help, too."

"Why, it looks new."

"I believe Marshal Austen left it for us."

"Marshal Austen?"

"Who else would have done it?"

"But we were both here—"

"He did it while we were in the baggage car, I expect. He left this also." Zeph held the silver pocket watch in his hand. "And this." A package of Black Jack chewing gum.

Tears sprang to Charlotte's eyes, and she took a handkerchief out of a pocket in her coat. "Of course a gunslinger in black would chew that kind of gum."

"Could I have some?" Cody has his eye on the package. Charlotte reached over, still sniffing, and plucked the Black Jack from Zeph's lap. "If the blanket was meant for me, and the watch was meant for your father, then I'm sure the chewing gum was meant for our two troopers from the Second Cavalry."

Zeph was examining the watch. "Don't know why he did that. It's a Waltham and it's engraved under the lid."

"To you?" Charlotte was surprised. "He didn't even know you before today."

He went silent as he read the entire inscription

on the watch lid. Then he blinked several times and snapped the lid shut.

"Well, what does it say?" asked Charlotte impatiently.

He handed her the watch. She looked at him a moment and then opened it up. The etching on the underside of the lid was very fine. She turned the pocket watch toward the sunlight. FOR CAPTAIN ZEPHANIAH TRUETT PARKER. WHO FOUGHT SLAVERY. AND WHO STILL FIGHTS FOR OUR FREEDOM. THE OPPRESSOR SHALL FEAR THEE AS LONG AS THE SUN AND MOON ENDURE. COLONEL MICHAEL JAMES AUSTEN. PSALM 72:3-5.

Charlotte looked up. Zeph was rubbing his eyes in a peculiar way.

"What's wrong?" she asked.

"Nothing. I'm just tired. I kind of had a rude awakening." He smiled.

"But this inscription is beautiful. Don't you think it's beautiful?"

"Sure."

"And he hardly knows you. But he's right, isn't he?"

Zeph did not answer. He leaned his head back and watched the prairie slip past. "They've got more snow here," he finally commented.

"Where's your brother's Bible?"

Zeph tugged the small Bible out of the pocket of the baggy coat she'd made him wear since Ogden. She took it from him and flipped pages. Then she read the passage inscribed on the watch: "The mountains shall bring peace to the people, and the hills, by righteousness. He shall judge the poor of the people, he shall save the children of the needy, and shall break in pieces the oppressor. They shall fear thee as long as the sun and moon endure, throughout all generations."

"My goodness," she said when she had finished, "He is paying you quite a compliment."

"For all his gunslinger looks, he is a kind man."

"And to say these things about someone he'd never met when he had the watch engraved."

"He was one of my commanding officers."

"Pardon me?"

"Look, I didn't want to bring it up. I had him pegged for a gunslinger at first. Then there was the holdup and all the excitement. I only figured out who he was a few minutes before he got up to leave. He had a beard back then—it was twelve years ago. I just wasn't sure."

"Obviously he was sure."

"Matt's doing, I expect. He sent the telegram asking Austen to help me. Likely mentioned I'd served in the war and wouldn't carry a gun now. The mention of the war would have jarred his memory, and then he would have made the connection with my name."

Charlotte's eyebrow arched. "Why? He must have known scads of soldiers."

Zeph was slow to answer. "Because of what happened. There was an incident he wouldn't have forgotten."

"What incident?"

"I don't want to talk about this, Charlotte."

She stared into his eyes. "Z. What incident? Tell me. Please."

"A night in Virginia. There'd been a clash. My boys had managed to free a dozen men, no, fourteen—it was fourteen men they freed from a Rebel company. They were freemen, African men, but they'd been captured when Lee invaded Pennsylvania, and the Rebs were taking them back to be slaves. There was a lot of that even though Lee forbade it and never kept slaves himself. We'd caught them out in the open, in a meadow; it was raining so hard the field was flooded. We could see the kind of men they had as prisoners, they weren't even soldiers. It was wrong.

"This was just after Gettysburg, and Lee was retreating. I guess he never stopped retreating from Gettysburg to Appomattox, and my boys were fed up with the whole Army of Northern Virginia and that attitude the Confederacy had about Africans and slavery. They went at the Rebs hand to hand—they wanted to make sure they didn't kill any of the freemen by mistake. It was after the fight I stood in front of Austen's tent in the rain with the Africans until he could see me. He had no idea yet of what had happened, but I brought two of the men with me into the tent once the orderly called my name. The orderly tried to stop me from bringing the Africans in. I just brushed him aside."

Zeph stopped, gazing out the window. "Please continue," Charlotte urged.

"Well. Austen was a lot younger then, of course, but just as slender, and he had a dark beard, like I said. One arm was in a sling from a wound. There was a lamp burning on his table and a Remington New Model Army revolver by his elbow. I noticed that because Dad had the same gun. Austen's uniform was buttoned right to the top."

Zeph stopped a second time, his thoughts far away.

Charlotte put a hand on one of Zeph's.

"Do you remember what you talked about?" she asked gently.

"It's funny.. You know how some things you've gone through come to mind again and again? You go over every word each time your memory calls those experiences up, and you can see every face? I haven't thought about that tent in twelve years—I haven't wanted to. I see the freemen; one was a lawyer, he's talking to Austen, Colonel Austen, and the other is waiting his turn. I don't remember anything Austen said. But he got the men into a couple of large tents, made sure they were served hot food and coffee, put them on horses at daybreak, gave them a mounted escort back to Pennsylvania."

"You can't recall even one sentence of what he said?"

"Have you got a piece of that black gum for me, Cody?"

"Yes, sir."

Zeph chewed slowly. "It's very good."

Charlotte was staring at him. The edge came into her voice. "Z."

He shook his head. "It's like I buried it." He chewed a little longer. "All I can bring back is Austen saying, 'You did the right thing, Captain. Your men are to be commended.'" Then Zeph's face clouded over. "He asked if we had taken any Rebel prisoners. I said we had not. He thanked me and dismissed me." Zeph looked over at Charlotte. "Not one."

"I see. So that explains the inscription and him having the watch ready for you. Not an incident a man is likely to forget, even in a war full of them."

"No."

There was silence between them. Around the car others talked and laughed, and Zeph heard a woman say a meal stop would be coming up soon. Charlotte was opening Jude's Bible to the spot where she had placed the bookmark. She held it out to him.

"Are you a praying man, Captain Parker?"

"I try."

"Then read this. Out loud. Remember, I marked this passage before the outlaws assailed our train."

Zeph took the Bible from her. "Which psalm?"

"Number one hundred twenty-four, please."

"'If it had not been the Lord who was on our side, when men rose up against us: then they had swallowed us up quick, when their wrath was kindled against us: then the waters had overwhelmed us, the stream had gone over our soul. Blessed be the Lord, who hath not given us as a prey to their teeth. Our soul is escaped as a bird out of the snare of the fowlers: the snare is broken, and we are escaped. Our help is in the name of the Lord, who made heaven and earth.'"

Charlotte leaned forward. "We prayed and the Lord rescued us, Z. Sending those telegrams, one to Fort Laramie and the other to Iron Springs, so Raber's accomplice would read it, that was the right thing to do. Now we're free." She took one of his big hands in both of hers. "I'm sorry about what happened in the war. About what happened to my father and what happened to you. For the killing that happened in that meadow in Virginia. But I'm not sorry you rescued those men from being taken down to Alabama or Mississippi and turned into slaves. You did the right thing. You fought to set them free, and that was the right thing to do. It's hard for me to admit, it's hard for me to accept, but if there was one good thing that came out of that terrible war, it was just that—some of you soldiers fought to end the enslavement of a whole race of men and women and children that God had created to be a blessing to the earth."

Zeph leaned back and closed his eyes, the Bible open in his hands. "Rich words, Miss Spence."

Zeph's jaw muscles tightened and then relaxed. He opened his eyes and tried to make light of the moment. "Pretty soon there won't be one secret of mine left hidden. I'll be an open book. Then I'll just be this dull person you know inside out and that you're bored to death with."

She smiled. "I doubt that."

"But what about all your secrets? Do I know any of them? Am I ever gonna know any of them?"

"Why, Mister Parker"—she fanned her face—"us girls have to keep our deepest secrets close to our hearts until the day we die."

Chapter Seventeen

Snowflakes were swirling down and mingling with the gray billows from the smokestack. Charlotte found the rolling plains a welcome relief after so many days of flat prairie. The farm buildings were also a pleasant sight, with their rows of windbreaks and their red barns and livestock. She was not sure Zeph would agree with her. Once the US Grant had pulled out of Omaha and crossed the Missouri River, he had groaned and said, "That's it. We've left the West."

They were halfway through Iowa, and she felt her apprehension growing with every mile. They had left the US Grant and the Union Pacific behind in Omaha and were traveling with the Chicago and Northwestern Railroad now. The train would pass over into Illinois in no time, and then they'd be buying tickets for a different one to take them from Chicago to Pittsburgh and Harrisburg. Before she knew it, she would be facing her old neighbors at Bird in Hand in Lancaster County, and she had no idea what she ought to say or do once she met them face-to-face. It was something she had pressed to the back of her mind because of the imminent danger from the Raber Gang. Now that the danger from the gang was past, other worries came crowding in to engulf her thoughts.

It was not just Bird in Hand. It was undoubtedly God's will that she deal with her past and confront the Amish community of her childhood and, it was hoped, learn to forgive and perhaps even love those men and women once again. What worried her far more than that was whether she could graciously give up Cheyenne and Cody to the Amish world and its ways—and whether that world would keep her darkest secrets hidden or bring them out into the open for all the world to see, including Zephaniah Parker.

She began to argue with herself.

Why not tell him those darkest secrets instead of waiting for the Amish church to break the news? It would come across much better that way to Zephaniah. It would build trust.

No, I can't; these are terrible things to tell someone. It would be better if they were left unsaid.

It is your Christian duty to tell him.

I don't care.

The Amish will tell him who you are if you don't.

I can't risk it.

Just by being silent you are risking it. You are risking everything.

The snow was falling more thickly and more swiftly now. Cody and Zeph were leaning against one another, practically head to head, breathing in and out through open mouths, fast asleep. Despite her anxiety and inner turmoil, Charlotte could not prevent herself from smiling. Oh, they looked so much like father and son. During the robbery, Cody had acted just like a fiery young

Zephaniah. How could she let Cody go? How, for that matter, could she let Zephaniah go?

Beside her, Cheyenne had been drawing all afternoon: cavalrymen and men being captured. Charlotte supposed it gave her a considerable amount of peace and freedom from fear, even some healing in her heart, to know the men who had killed her mother and father had been taken prisoner by the army and were never going to be able to harm her again. Yet, for some reason Charlotte could not yet fathom, Cheyenne's drawings were adding to the emotional stress she herself was experiencing.

The ten-year-old suddenly held up a full-page drawing of a man's face. Like all her work, it was well done. Charlotte could see Cheyenne had meant to portray someone friendly and kind.

"That's very good. Who is it?"

"His hat has a number two on it and swords. And here is his scarf."

"Your Johnny?"

"Yah." She smiled. "It was easier to draw his horse than to draw him."

"What else do you have?"

"I drew some of the wicked. Two of them had long beards and long hair. They looked like bears."

Charlotte glanced at the drawings and felt a chill. "Don't you find it icy in here today, Cheyenne? There must be a new draft coming in from one of the doors or windows." She took the white point blanket Marshal Austen had left with them and bundled herself in it. A corner was lifted for Cheyenne. "Do you want to get warmed up?"

"I'm fine."

She lifted up another drawing. "This one had red hair. It was very short. This other was fat and always yelling." She shuddered. "I was really scared of him."

"I'm sorry, honey. Maybe we should put the drawings away for now."

"They are all in jail. Or they've run to another country."

She pulled two more drawings from her pile. "These are the only other ones. This man was so skinny he made me think of a hoe. The others kept calling him Lunger."

"I see."

"And this was the leader. He told everyone what they should do. He shouted that he would kill us all." Her eyes narrowed. "Trooper Johnny said they had caught him and tied him up and put a gag in his mouth. He said they would hang him."

Ice went through Charlotte. "That's the leader?"

"Yes."

That's the Angel of Death, Charlotte thought. *That's the killer.* She kissed the girl. "You are very brave to make this picture, very brave. But if they've caught him, you don't need to think about him anymore, not at all. It's over, honey. So I really think this is enough. No more drawing, all right? See, you're trembling."

"I hate him. I hate him. I don't ever want to see him again."

"Shh, shh, you won't, not ever, not ever again. Put the pictures down and get under the blanket."

Cheyenne shook her head. But she allowed Charlotte to put her arms around her. Then she laughed.

"What is it?" asked Charlotte in surprise.

"Pa and Cody look so funny with their mouths hanging open."

Charlotte smiled. "I guess they do. If this was the summertime, a big old fly could buzz right in there."

"Yah, a lot of flies!"

Cheyenne slept in Charlotte's arms. Charlotte watched the snowfall, but after a while her eyes fell on the picture of the gang leader. Cheyenne had given him long hair past his shoulders and tried to make it look light colored. The eyes bulged a bit, and the twist of his mouth gave the drawing a nasty feeling. Down one side of his face Cheyenne had drawn a long line that started in his eye and ended somewhere under his jaw. At the bottom of the page she had neatly printed ANGEL.

Charlotte stared at the line that ran from eyeball to chin. So he had a long scar. From what? A knife? A sword? That would have made him easy to identify anytime he did not wear a mask. Well, it didn't matter now. That story was over. For a moment she indulged an image in her mind of a man standing on a scaffold with a black hood over his head and a thick rope around his neck. A minister who looked like Jude was reading the Bible to him. Then she made a noise as if something was caught in her throat and shook her head to shake off the picture in her imagination. It was finished. She and Zeph and the children were safe and on their way to Pennsylvania.

Yet once she thought of Pennsylvania and Lancaster County, a knot began tightening itself in her stomach again. *Lord, help me get free of these fears,* she prayed. It was not a very satisfying prayer, because she knew there were things she herself could do to rid herself of some of her anxiety. She blew out a breath. Then she picked up Zeph's Bible.

Don't be afraid. Don't be afraid. Her hands turned over page after page. *What am I looking for?* A part of her wanted to sleep. Another part felt her dreams would be stressful and unpleasant. A third part of her felt the right passage from holy scriptures would give her some measure of peace. *But which one? There were so many.*

Zeph had mentioned how Jude had used certain parts of his Bible so many times during the war it naturally fell open to several of these places. Now it happened to her. She was leafing through the New Testament when the book seemed to stop on its own and open where it wanted. The verse her eyes fell upon, 1 John 4:18, was underlined by sharp lines of black ink. "There is no fear in love; but perfect love casteth out fear: because fear hath torment. He that feareth is not made perfect in love."

Charlotte leaned her head back and closed her eyes. She listened to the *click-click-click* of the iron wheels over the rails. The sky darkened in the east, and the train moved into that darkness.

She knew what she had to do. But she did not think she had the courage to do it.

Chapter Eighteen

Once he'd told her it would take another two days to reach Harrisburg—"Well, just under"—she'd insisted on having a bath, even if it meant missing a connection. Which it did. Since there was no help for it, he and the kids had baths, too. Zeph even treated himself to a shave. "But not the whole beard," Charlotte had protested, "just the upper lip. That sort of beard goes with the clothes I made for you."

"You mean it makes me plain?"

"Yes. You will go over very well with the Amish in Lancaster County."

"Why does it matter if I go over very well with the Amish in Lancaster County?"

She'd patted his cheek. "Because, my dear, we have enough to overcome in Pennsylvania without having to worry about what the in-laws think of you. I want them to see that my Fremont is humble as well as handsome."

They had reverted to their Wyoming names again. He touched the broad flat brim of his hat. "As you wish, Conner." Clean as a whistle, upper lip shaved, the beard trimmed, he stood with Cody in their sheepskin coats and plain clothes and hats on one of Chicago's main thoroughfares and watched wagons, carriages, horse-drawn tramcars, and people stream past without ceasing. Steam and breath rose from the street like a fog. Zeph wanted to tilt his hat back on his head as he watched, but the hat Charlotte had given him did not work as well at this as a Stetson, so he was left with nothing to do except rub the beard on his jaw.

"It's like standing on the banks of a Mississippi chock-full of people and teams of horses," said Zeph. "Makes a fellow dizzy."

Cody had been to Chicago several times. "Pittsburgh is not so full. And Harrisburg has more trains than people."

"That so?"

"There was a great fire here four years ago. All of this has been rebuilt. And they're still building." Cody pointed down the street to where two steam cranes were hard at work and new buildings were rising into the cold winter sky.

"I guess you could say the mountains around here are man-made," mumbled Zeph. "I miss the real thing."

Cody nodded. "I do, too, but sometimes I like the excitement of the cities."

"Excitement! You call Chicago excitement?" Zeph lifted Cody's hat and rubbed his knuckles into the boy's hair. "Excitement is having a Sioux war party breathing down your neck and bullets and arrows making a colander of your clothes."

Cody laughed and fought back. "I wouldn't care. I hate these clothes."

"Me, too."

Two policemen in boots and belted overcoats with

brass buttons and large stars over their hearts approached them. They wore revolvers in holsters at their sides. One policeman touched the brim of his cap. "Everything all right here, sir?"

Zeph was confused and released Cody from a headlock. "Sure."

"You all right, lad?"

Cody's face was red. He put his hat back on his head.

"Everything is fine, Officer."

"Where are you two from?"

Zeph straightened up. "Just off the train from Omaha.

We'll be pulling out for Harrisburg in a few hours."

"That's a long trip."

Zeph nodded. "Three states. But not as long as coming all the way from the Montana Territory."

The other officer spoke up. "Did you?"

"Picked up the Union Pacific in Ogden, Utah."

The officer whistled. "We had a telegram about a wee bit of excitement down that way, was it yesterday or the day before that, Pete?"

The older man grunted. "They caught the Angel o' Death and that whole murderin', thievin' gang o' his."

"I'm glad to hear it," said Zeph.

"The noose is too good for 'em and all the savages like 'em," the older police officer went on. "Burn 'em at the stake would fix 'em. The Ind'ns understand that."

I know this accent, thought Zeph.

"You two sound like a man I was friends with back in the gold rush days of Iron Springs," he said. "Seamus O'Casey."

The older officer beamed. "A fine Irish name. Seems our people are everywhere, Pat."

The younger officer nodded. "Irish like to travel. And when they don't, someone always plants a boot in their pants and gets them moving." He laughed: "Oh, I think about going west someday. I have a cousin in Dakota. He joined the army. He's with that Custer."

"Fort Abraham Lincoln," said Zeph.

"I believe that's it. What's it like out there?"

"It's wide open and free, Officer. Everything's big. The prairies, the mountains, the rivers. Room to ride a hundred miles and never see another human being."

"Lots of outlaws?"

"A fair amount."

"Indians?"

"Plenty."

"Is there desperate need for lawmen in the West?" asked the younger officer.

"My brother's a federal marshal in the Montana Territory. He could use a fine young officer like yourself."

"What's his name, if you don't mind my asking?"

"Matthew Parker. You can always telegraph him at Iron Springs. Acres of train robbers and bandits for you to chase down and slap behind bars."

The older man snorted. "Ha! We got our own bandits and robbers thick as summer flies on a mule. We don't need to be chasing 'em all the way to the ends o' the earth in Utah and Montana."

The younger officer smiled. "Sure, Pete, but I get restless just the same. The Irish in me gets awful cramped in Chicago when the spring comes. I wasn't from Dublin or Cork like your kind, y'know; I grew up under the stars of Connemara."

The older man put his hands behind his back. "Suit yourself. I'd miss my baseball games. And the wife would miss her church teas."

The young officer put out his hand. "Pleasure to meet you."

Zeph gripped his hand and shook it. "If you ever make it out west, look me up in Iron Springs. Zephaniah Parker."

"I may just do that. Pat Cavanaugh."

The other officer nodded. "Pete Cassidy. A safe trip to Pennsylvania to you both. And"—he winked at Cody—"no more horseplay on the streets o' Chicago, if you don't mind. It looked to me like you were layin' an awful lickin' on your poor father here."

They all laughed.

"Come along and let's walk, Pat," said Pete. "It's getting nippy, and I want the blood moving in my veins to warm myself up."

Zeph and Cody watched them march away down the crowded sidewalk. Then Zeph dug the silver watch Austen had given him out of a pocket of his sheepskin coat. He opened the lid, looked at the time, whistled, and snapped the lid shut. "We'd better find our womenfolk and escort them to the evening train, pronto."

Charlotte and Cheyenne were in one of the shops down a block that Charlotte had indicated to Zeph earlier, dressed in matching navy blue dresses and bonnets with white lace, their arms full of bags and parcels.

"We were just coming," said Charlotte. "Here." She handed several brightly wrapped packages to Zeph.

"What is all this?" he demanded.

"Gifts for the Amish families in Pennsylvania."

"You mean peace offerings."

"Call them what you will. Cody, help your sister with her bags. What were you two gentlemen up to?"

"Just watching the locals."

They were walking briskly up a street toward the train station. Charlotte glanced over at Zeph. "Did you get a chance to get to the telegraph station?"

"There were no telegrams for us. Wrote Matt and told him we'd be in Harrisburg in two days—"

"I know we go left here," she interrupted.

"You're right. There's the Pennsy Station. I'd better make sure they've put our luggage on the right train. That's our locomotive there, I believe, Missus Wyoming, am I right?"

"Well, the number is correct. Unless they have two engines using exactly the same numerals."

"Do you have the tickets?"

"*You* have the tickets in your pocket, and you know it perfectly well."

"Here." He gave Charlotte the boxes he'd been holding. "Find us some good seats in one of the sleepers."

After talking with an official for the Pennsylvania Railroad who looked over a sheet of paper and nodded his head—"Harrisburg, the Wyomings"—Zeph made his way back to platform four. A young boy was selling the *Chicago Daily Tribune* and hollering at the top of his lungs, "Double hanging in Wyoming! Raber Gang plunged into eternity!"

The feds sure didn't waste any time, thought Zeph.

He bought a paper and opened it up. Above the fold were large black letters: HANGED! There was a photograph of two men hanging from ropes with black hoods over their heads. He kept walking toward the train as he read the story under the grim picture.

Charlotte was standing behind Cody and Cheyenne on the steps of one of the cars. Her arms were full of bags and parcels. She was rolling her eyes at a heavy woman who was taking her time making her way into the car. "Move ahead, Cody," she was saying, "move on ahead, son."

"I can't budge."

"Just push a bit, a little bit. Let them know we're behind them and that we need to get on board the train, too, before it leaves without us."

"Conner," said Zeph as he came up to the car.

"Oh, thank goodness. I thought you'd taken a horse back to the Montana Territory. Can you help me with these boxes again?"

"Conner, it's over."

Charlotte looked down at him from the steps. He held up the newspaper. She saw the headline and the picture. The blood ran out of her face. "Oh, my Lord Jesus," she said. Her eyes rolled back white, and she collapsed, falling down the steps onto the wooden boards of the station platform, cracking her head and lying still. Her bags and parcels tumbled out of her arms and over the toes of Zeph's boots. Five or six dropped down onto the tracks and lay under the wheels of the 5:17 to Harrisburg, Pennsylvania.

Chapter Nineteen

Zeph watched her sleep, listening anxiously for changes in breathing that might signal she was in some sort of distress.

He had not bothered to transform their seating area into beds, so Cody had rolled his sheepskin into a pillow and leaned his head against it and the window. Cheyenne was awake. She slowly and continuously stroked Charlotte's hair.

Lights flickered in the dark square of the window. Zeph supposed they would be coming into Fort Wayne soon. The morning would find them well into Ohio and through the Great Black Swamp. Travel would be a bit slower through the swamp, but vast sections of it had been drained for the railroad, and Zeph didn't think there would be much trouble. He smiled briefly when he remembered a story of how the Michigan and Ohio militias had tried to fight a war with each other over a boundary dispute, but each had gotten lost in the swamp and had a hard time finding one another. What if the Union and Confederate armies had kept missing each other on their marches north and south?

But there had been no Black Swamp between Virginia and Maryland to confuse them.

Gently he put one hand on Charlotte's wrist. Her pulse was not too weak, not too strong. On her forehead was a large bump with a plaster on it, a real goose egg. She would not be too pleased when she woke up and examined it in the mirror, but her anger would not chase it away. That would be difficult for her, not being able to rely on her strength and determination to deal with a problem. He smiled.

Take care of her Lord; she is one special lady.

A small crowd had gathered around Charlotte after she fell. An army surgeon had been among them, and he had Zeph hold her up while he administered smelling salts. She inhaled sharply, coughed and sneezed, and demanded to know who had struck her. When Zeph reminded her softly that she had fainted when he showed her the newspaper headline, her face had reddened. She told the people looking down at her, "I know those men were evil, but I have always found hangings brutal and upsetting. The mere mention of it causes me great distress."

She had rested there for about five minutes while the surgeon cleaned the cut on her forehead with alcohol and put a sticking plaster in place, then had leaned on Zeph and struggled to her feet. She almost fell a second time, and the people reacted with "oh no" and "keep a good grip on her," but with Zeph's help she regained her balance and thanked everyone for their concern.

"You have been most kind. But I fear I have delayed your travels long enough, and I am certain the engineer of this locomotive would like to have pulled into Pittsburgh Station ten minutes ago." The people had

laughed. "Please have a safe journey, and may God
bless you all."

Once Zeph had helped her into her seat in the car
she had groaned, "Oh, I made a perfect spectacle of
myself."

"Char—Conner, no one is going to remember this
incident a week from now," he'd soothed her, "except
maybe the army surgeon and four or five of the young
men who fell in love with you and wished I was your
brother."

"Oh, for heaven's sakes, Zeph—Fremont. The crazy
things you come up with."

"Well, I'm a man, and what they were feeling when
they looked at you, lying there unconscious in my
arms, was written all over their faces, plain as day.
Once the surgeon asked who I was and I told him I
was your husband, their faces went flat as pancakes."

"They did not."

"You bet they did."

"How can you know what's in another man's heart?"

"I'm a man, and it was in my heart, too."

"What was in your heart?"

"Your face so white and the blond hair falling over
your cheek and forehead, your hands so calm, your lips
quiet and pale, freckles sprinkled on your skin, your
soft breathing. There was a sweetness and a young-
ness. We could all see your beauty, and we could see
the sleeping child in your closed eyes and small hands."

Charlotte's face had taken on color for the first time
since she had fainted. "I doubt too many of the young
men you say fell in love with me while I lay prostrate
on platform four had those precise thoughts in their

head. You sound like a blend of William Shakespeare and James Fenimore Cooper."

"Maybe they couldn't have put it into those exact words, but that's just about where their thinking was at."

Charlotte had ducked her head and tried not to smile. "The notions you get in that mind of yours, Fremont."

"Would you like some fresh Chicago water?"

"Yes, thank you."

He'd handed her the Union army canteen. She had sipped at it, made a face, then sipped at it again.

"Well, it's not Montana mountain water." She'd handed the canteen back to Zeph. "Thank you, my dear."

"Are you feeling better?"

"Yes, yes, I'm so sorry about all that, Fremont."

"I'm the one who's sorry, Conner. What was I thinking? Flapping that photograph in front of your face. I apologize."

"There have been enough public hangings in Iron Springs and Virginia City. I shouldn't have been that squeamish."

"I'm sure you've attended exactly none of them."

"There were always better things to do. Not that I'm saying some of those men didn't deserve it. Especially that hoodlum Skipjack William, who shot the woman teller."

Zeph had nodded. "Hard to find room in your prayers for that man."

"Yes, and hard to find room for Seraphim Raber or any of his gang of beasts."

A spark of her old vehemence had flared. Zeph stared at the dark fire in her eyes. She had glanced out the window at an engine building up steam on another track.

"Though it is my Christian duty to pray for their black souls."

She had no sooner said this than a tear slipped down her cheek followed moments later by another. In a burst of anger, she struck at them with her hand. "Oh, stop it!" she snapped.

"Take it easy, Conner," Zeph said. "There's nothing to get upset at yourself about."

"How would you know? Or do you have total knowledge of my thoughts like you do of those young men?"

"I just meant it's not the time to get all worked up. Rest easy and get your strength back."

"I have plenty of strength, Fremont Wyoming."

"No one's denying that. Just like to see you with more."

"More?"

"You seem so fragile right now."

"Fragile?"

"Just joking, Conner. Anyone could see—"

"No one's ever used the word fragile to describe me in my entire life."

"You're building up a head of steam powerful enough you could roll over a buffalo herd. Don't want you to burst a boiler, that's all. Why don't you try and get some sleep?"

"What makes you think I'm tired?"

"Well, you got that knock on your head—"

"I'm perfectly fine. I don't feel a thing. I could waltz all night."

"I'm sure you could."

"Why hasn't this train left yet?"

"I don't know. Want me to walk up the track and give the engineer a dressing-down on your behalf?"

Cody had caught Zeph's eye. He raised his eyebrows. Zeph shrugged. Charlotte saw the interaction between them. Her eyes had narrowed.

"What are you men up to?"

Zeph had touched the brim of his hat. "Polite conversation, ma'am."

An hour after the train had left Chicago, Charlotte had fallen asleep. Over time the blow on her head had swollen while her breathing had relaxed and become deeper and more even.

Now he gazed at her pale face in the dark of the Indiana night and hoped when she woke up she'd be on the right side of heaven. His hand was still on her wrist. Thank goodness she was warming up. Cheyenne had stopped smoothing down Charlotte's hair and was asleep against her shoulder.

A lot of things didn't add up. He'd never known Charlotte Spence to faint over anything during all her years at Iron Springs. When he'd brought Ricky through the door that night, spitting blood, she'd scarcely blinked. She'd been thrown by broncs hard enough to knock the wind out of any ten men and swung right back into the saddle. Had cracked ribs once that she got Doc Brainerd to wrap tight, and Doc said she never dropped a tear or lost color in her face. So why had she fainted when he showed her the newspaper?

He blew out his breath suddenly and shook his head. He hoped she'd feel better after a couple of days' rest and a few decent meals. The train had a dining car and hot food on board.

"You're thinking about me, aren't you?"

He looked at her, surprised. "How long have you been awake?"

"Long enough."

He smiled crookedly. "I guess I'm hoping you feel a lot better by the morning, Conner."

"Conner."

He heard her sigh in the darkness. Her face was a pale smudge.

"I have so many names, don't I? Conner. Charlotte. Miss Spence. Missus Wyoming."

She was silent for a few moments. He could feel something building up in her, but she didn't speak. Finally, he heard the rustle of her dress and blanket, and she leaned forward in the dark. He felt her soft, warm hands on his.

"Z," she whispered, "I think you care a little bit for me."

"Char," he responded, "I care a lot more than a little."

"I've cherished the way you've treated me ever since we left the Sweet Blue. Your words, the gentle way you look at me, your kisses, your courage. I'm sure God has a special woman for you somewhere. I just don't think it can be me."

Zeph felt his heart drop and black dismay roar through his head. He opened his mouth, but felt her hand touch his lips. "Don't say anything. All the names you call me by, but you don't know who I am. The day you find out will be the day you turn your back on me forever."

Chapter Twenty

Another day and then a night and a morning and the train slowed as it came into Harrisburg, Pennsylvania. Cody and Cheyenne knew the city well and had their faces pressed eagerly to the windows.

"We are almost home," said Cody. "Soon I'll be able to introduce you to my aunt Rosa."

Zeph smiled. "I look forward to that."

"Her apple pies and cherry pies are excellent."

Zeph watched the buildings slip past as they slowly moved toward the train station. Charlotte looked at his face and eyes. Cheyenne was fastening a white bonnet.

"You have been to Harrisburg before," Charlotte said.

"My brothers and I were trained here," he responded.

"Camp Curtin. It would have been back there. They closed it in '65. The city's changed a fair bit."

"When are we home?" asked Cheyenne.

"Well," replied Charlotte, "there is one more train to take after we leave this one. But that will not be a long trip, less than two hours. Lancaster is only forty miles south and east of here."

"Then we will see everyone? All our old friends? My playmates?"

"Yes, darling, you will."

"Who will pick us up at the station? How will we get to Bird in Hand?"

Charlotte leaned over and kissed her on the forehead. "Remember when we stepped out for a walk in Pittsburgh and bought some ice cream? We telegraphed Aunt Rosa at the same time and told her which day we would be in Lancaster. She will watch the trains this morning and this afternoon."

"I want to show her my yellow scarf."

"Oh, no, dear, remember? Soldiers are not something Aunt Rosa and the others get very excited about."

"Why not? The soldiers saved us from the outlaws."

"I know they did. And we thank God they did. But soldiers and their guns and swords do not go down well with the church. You know that. I will keep the scarf and hat safe in my luggage, all right?"

Cheyenne sulked. "All right."

Charlotte smoothed down her own hair, placed a few more pins, then put on a white bonnet and asked Cheyenne if it was straight or crooked. The girl said glumly, "Straight."

"It will be fine, dear," soothed Charlotte, holding Cheyenne's hand. "I will keep your scarf safe, and one day we will show it to Aunt Rosa. You'll see."

"Why white all of a sudden?" asked Zeph, looking away from the window and seeing her bonnet.

She smiled. "That is the Amish way."

"How are you feeling today?"

"Here and there. Thank you for asking."

"It is not easy for you to come back to these people. They excommunicated your family. I pray for you day and night."

She touched his cheek with hers and whispered, "I know you do."

It seemed strange to Zeph to step off the train and stand on the platform and remember being a soldier here in 1862. He stretched in the cold sunlight and buttoned his sheepskin coat.

No warmer in Pennsylvania than it had been in Nebraska. He and Cody freshened up and got all the luggage on the train to Lancaster while Charlotte and Cheyenne were still using the restrooms. Then the four of them took a few minutes to stroll up and down the platforms and look at the different locomotives.

"How are we fixed for chewing gum?" Zeph asked.

"One stick of Black Jack left," said Charlotte.

"Well, I'd better take a quick hike into town and get some. What do you say, Code? Want to come with?"

"Sure."

"You ladies need anything?"

"No," said Charlotte, "we did our shopping in Chicago."

Zeph and Cody found a store that sold gum and candy.

They not only bought gum for themselves, but also for Cody's old friends and Cheyenne's, too.

"Who else do you think would like chewing gum at Bird in Hand?" asked Zeph. "I mean, among the grown-ups?"

"Oh, Augustine Yoder for sure, that is Aunt Rosa's

brother. And Martin Hooley, the farrier. And I think also Sarah Beachey, the schoolteacher."

They went back outside and shoved their hands in their pockets when an icy gust struck them.

"We should check the telegraph office before we go back," said Zeph.

"Sure," responded Cody.

They asked directions once or twice and made their way to the right building. Zeph fished his badge out of his pocket, unbuttoned the top of his jacket, pinned it on his shirt, winked at Cody, and then they both walked in the door.

"Deputy," greeted a man with no hair on top, but plenty on the sides and chin. "What can I do for you?"

He slid a pad over to them. Zeph considered sending Matt a note, but then decided against it. He didn't plan on being in Lancaster County more than a few days. There'd be time enough to telegraph his brother once he was on his way back west.

"Just checking to see if there are any telegrams," he said. "Name?"

"Fremont Wyoming. Zephaniah Parker."

"Which one are you?"

Zeph shrugged—they weren't on the run anymore. "Both."

The man grunted. "Well, I got something for Parker, so I guess that's one of you. Here you go."

"Thank you. Where from?"

"Omaha."

"Omaha?"

Zeph was puzzled. He picked up and read the telegram the clerk had placed on the counter.

PARKER
REVELATION 9:11 & 12
ANGEL

His head felt as if he'd swallowed ice water too fast—it went cold and numb. Without thinking, one hand reached inside his sheepskin jacket and pulled the small Bible out and the other hand worked with the eyes to find the passage. "And they had a king over them, which is the angel of the bottomless pit, whose name in the Hebrew tongue is Abaddon, but in the Greek tongue hath his name Apollyon. One woe is past; and, behold, there come two woes more hereafter."

"When did this come in?" Zeph asked the clerk.

"Oh, six, seven hours ago."

They left the office. Zeph walked swiftly with long strides.

Cody had to scramble to keep up.

"What's wrong?" he asked with a worried look on his face. "What was in the telegram?"

Zeph didn't answer. He continued to walk as quickly as he could to the train station. A part of him wanted to run.

There they were! *Thank You, Lord.* He hurried to Charlotte's side.

"We were beginning to wonder when you two were going to show up," said Charlotte. Then she saw his face. "You look like you've seen a ghost."

Zeph passed her the telegram.

She read the telegram. Her face went white. "I don't understand these words, *Abaddon* and *Apollyon.*"

"Jude talked about them during a sermon once,"

Zeph replied, his face grim. "Abaddon means 'The Place of Destruction.'"

He could see fear creeping back into her eyes. "What about Apollyon?"

Zeph did not flinch from her painful stare. "It means 'The Destroyer.'"

Chapter Twenty-One

Three buggies with matching dark horses were waiting at the train station in Lancaster. When Cody and Cheyenne stepped onto the platform, a short woman with a big smile climbed from the first buggy and came toward them, opening her arms. She was all in black—dark bonnet, long dark cloak with a cape at the shoulders, dark woolen shawl that fell down almost to the hem of her dark dress, and dark boots. The children ran into her arms, and there was laughter and a great deal of fast speech. The language was not English.

It was the first time Charlotte had smiled since she'd read the telegram from Omaha. "Pennsylvania Dutch," she said to Zeph.

Another woman, much younger and very tall and slender, approached from the second buggy. She came up to Charlotte, inclined her head, and began to speak in Pennsylvania Dutch as well. Zeph noticed that the only difference between her clothing and that of the older woman was that she wore a lighter colored bonnet.

Charlotte turned to Zeph. "This is Sarah Beachey,

the schoolteacher. I will be staying with their family. Her father is in the buggy."

"You mean we're splitting up?"

He said it as a joke, but Charlotte could see a flash of disappointment in his eyes. She gave a small smile and put her hand on his arm. "Yes, we are no longer Mister and Missus Fremont and Conner Wyoming. That journey is ended. Now I am Charlotte Spence again, and you are Zephaniah Parker. But I will never forget our short marriage. Don't worry, we will talk again in a few days."

Zeph was taken aback. "A few days?"

"I'm sorry. There are some things that have to be done. There will be meetings."

"And I can't be at the meetings?"

"You are not Amish."

Zeph felt a mixture of hurt and anger rising in him.

"So we go through all that trouble and hazard to get you and the kids here safe and sound, and the best these Amish can do is give me the boot?"

"They are not giving you the boot."

"I'll get your things. I take it the kids are going with Aunt Rosa, if that's her name?"

"Yes."

She sighed as Zeph stalked off to the baggage car.

A man climbed out of the third buggy in a black coat wearing a cape and a flat-crowned, broad-brimmed hat identical to Zeph's on his head. He was tall and massively built, with a beard that did not cover his upper lip. He followed Zeph to the baggage car.

Zeph was taking bags from the steward who was hauling them out of the car. The man reached forward and took two heavy carpetbags.

"Thanks," said Zeph curtly.

"I am happy to help. My name is Augustine Yoder. Rosa's brother. You know Rosa?"

"I've heard about her."

"I am the blacksmith. Also one of the ministers. Welcome."

"Thank you for bringing the children home safely."

Zeph grunted and took two more bags from the steward. "Miss Spence thought we might be here as long as four months."

Augustine gave him a puzzled look. "Miss Spence?" Then he shook his head. "Four months? I think she will be at Bird in Hand longer than that."

This was something Zeph did not want to hear. "I'll take these bags to her and come back for the others. Perhaps you could take those others to the children?"

"Of course. Did you notice you and I are wearing almost the same clothing? You might be one of us."

"Well, I'm not one of you."

"Where did you come by your clothing, if I may ask?"

"Miss Spence made it. Except the sheepskin jacket."

"This woman you call Miss Spence. Her mother was a wonder with the needle and thread. I see God has passed it down to the daughter as well."

"You knew her mother?"

"Yah. The father and brothers, too. A good family, you know, hardworking. But we had our differences."

Zeph carried four of Charlotte's carpetbags to the buggy where she stood with Sarah Beachey and her father. Aunt Rosa had also walked over with the children to speak with Charlotte. The Pennsylvania Dutch ceased once Zeph showed up.

Charlotte took Zeph by the arm. "Aunt Rosa, this is Zephaniah Truett Parker. He is the brave young man who saw us safely from the Montana Territory to Lancaster."

Aunt Rosa smiled a smile full of brown and white teeth and took one of Zeph's hands in both of hers. "Thank you, Mister Parker. We are so grateful. So much we wished to see the children again, Samuel and Elizabeth. And, you know, the last time I saw our girl she was only fifteen years old. Now look at her. A woman. A beauty."

Zeph found he had a hard time keeping his anger stoked with Aunt Rosa smiling up into his face and clasping his hand. He touched the brim of his flat-crowned hat with his free hand. "I believe she is God's masterwork, Aunt Rosa."

Charlotte flushed and Sarah Beachey dropped her eyes, but both Mister Beachey and Aunt Rosa laughed heartily. Mister Beachey climbed out of his buggy and stretched out his hand. "If God has a good eye then so do you, young man. *Velkommen.*"

Zeph shook the man's hand. "A pleasure to meet you, Mister Beachey."

"Moses."

To his surprise, Zeph found himself saying, "Thank you all, *danke schoen,* for finding homes for Miss Spence and the children. It has been a long and exhausting journey for them."

"Ah," said Moses Beachey, raising his eyebrows, "you know some of the language?"

"When I was a boy, there was a rancher in Cheyenne

by the name of Mueller. I listened to him talk the talk. His was not exactly the same as yours, but sometimes I remember a word or a phrase."

"Gute," said Aunt Rosa. "In no time you will be talking like one of us."

This rankled Zeph, but he covered it up with another touch to his hat brim. "I must get Charlotte's other bags. Excuse me."

Charlotte followed and stopped him a short distance from the others.

"Z, be patient with them. They are trying to be kind."

"I know it. I just don't like them always assuming you've come back to live here or that I'm anxious to become one of them."

"Who knows what will happen over the next few weeks?"

"Weeks?"

Zeph glanced over at the others. They were obviously listening. Without thinking, he began to speak to Charlotte in Spanish. "Señorita, what makes you think we have weeks? Have you forgotten the telegram?"

Charlotte's face clouded over. "No."

"It came from Omaha."

"The accomplice—"

"The accomplice is in Iron Springs. That's how Seraph Raber knew we would be in Harrisburg. How could the army or Colonel Austen have known if they had Seraph or not? The others wouldn't tell them he was one of the four who escaped. For all the army knew, he was one of the two they hung. Omaha, Charlotte. He's three days away. Four days, maybe, but that's stretching it. You think it will be hard for Seraph to locate a

man and a woman who just came into Bird in Hand
with two kids in tow from Montana?"

"What are you going to do?"

"At least I can tell them what Seraph looks like now.
We have Cheyenne's drawing. The army will know if
they hung him or not. If not, we'll know he's still at
large. I'll telegraph Colonel Austen. I'll telegraph Matt,
too. I'll try and throw some grit in that accomplice's
eyes. I'm going to tell Matt we're pushing on to Philadelphia because the kids have relatives there."

"Aren't we going to tell the Amish that Seraph Raber
is hunting us?"

"What can they do? Throw stones? Why, they
wouldn't even do that. No need to get them and the
kids all worked up. You know we can't stay here after
three days, not if they haven't caught Raber. We'll have
to run."

"No."

"To save others' lives. You know he won't care who
he murders to get to us."

"No."

Zeph stared at her and the blazing lights in her blue
winter eyes. "I guess I've run out of Spanish," he said
in English.

"Where did you pick it up?" she asked, also in
English.

"Same place as you. Ricky hired on that Vicente
when you were still a girl, didn't he? You've been
learning Mexican since you were a kid on the Sweet
Blue. Well, Dad brought in a hired hand to help on our
place in Wyoming when I was no bigger than a cricket.
I learned from him, same as you. Pablo was his name.
A great man. A true vaquero."

"I was fifteen when Ricky brought me to the Montana Territory. Hardly someone you'd call a kid, señor."

He smiled. "I'll get your other bags. Adiós."

She gave his hand a squeeze. *"Vaya con Dios."*

In another ten minutes the three buggies were rattling east over the rutted road and slush to Bird in Hand. The long fields were sheeted with snow. Zeph sat next to Augustine Yoder in his buggy. There was only one carpetbag, a bedroll, and a pair of saddlebags for luggage.

"It is not far," said Augustine. "My house and smithy are on the edge of town and closer to Lancaster. You will want to lie down, I think, and get some rest. Long journeys can be tiring."

"Mister Yoder—"

"Augustine."

"The last thing I want to do, believe me, is lie down. Back home I ride the land every day. I felt like a fox locked in a coop on that train trip. I want to use my muscles. You're going to put in an afternoon at the anvil, aren't you?"

He nodded. "That I am. I must put some iron rims on several wagon wheels."

"Can I give you a hand?"

"Have you worked with a blacksmith before?"

"Not much. But it's always fascinated me."

"So. No food? Straight into the shop?"

"Bitte."

Augustine smiled at Zeph's use of the German word.

"And Mister—Augustine—thank you for taking the time to come to Lancaster and fetch us. And for giving me a few minutes at the telegraph office. I'm very much obliged. *Danke*."

"*Bitteschon*."

After Augustine had turned the buggy onto his property, Zeph jumped down and led the horse toward the large, gray barn. Augustine took Zeph's belongings.

"Shall I remove his harness and rub him down?" asked Zeph.

"Yah. There are stables at the back of the barn and hooks for the tack. Please give the gelding some oats. The buggy stays in the barn as well."

Augustine watched Zeph gently begin unhitching the horse, smiled, and nodded. Then he went to his house—white, plain, sturdy, two stories. At the door he leaned in and called to his wife in Pennsylvania Dutch. He put Zeph's carpetbag, bedroll, and saddlebags in the hall and shut the door. Then he jerked his head toward a small building which stood about a hundred feet behind the house. "You will meet Rebecca at supper."

Chapter Twenty-Two

Augustine showed Zeph how to work the bellows to keep the furnace red-hot. "My boys used to do this. But now they are grown. One has a dairy herd; the other is a carpenter. And my daughter, my Katie, she is married to Amos Zook—he is the honey man, he has the beeyard, what do the English call it?"

"Apiary?"

"Yah. Big word. Why not just say hives?"

They set to work, Zeph pumping, Augustine hammering the strips of hot iron into hoops. In no time Zeph's sheepskin jacket was on a peg, soon followed by the black coat Charlotte had made for him. Augustine looked at his clothing and pointed with his smoking tongs. "Who you call Charlotte?"

"Yes."

"She has made for you a perfect *mutze*, a dress coat, do you know that? The vest, the broadfall pants, all from our people. Comfortable, eh?"

"Sure, but a little loose."

"Your shirt, no collar, just like mine. You see that?" Augustine had stripped down to his shirt before he'd struck his first blow with the hammer. "But you need suspenders. Your pants want to sit around your knees." He barked a laugh. "How did she miss that?"

"By not having to wear them herself."

"Yah, but you are plain, very plain, *alle ist gute*."

Sweat made their faces shine, the heat and wood coals made their skin glow crimson and bronze. Zeph helped Augustine fit one, two, three, four, five wheels. Then the big man sat and mopped his brow with a towel before tossing it to Zeph to do the same.

"Do you have a watch, Zephaniah?"

"Mm." Zeph walked over and pulled the watch from a pocket in his vest, which was hanging from a hook. The silver gleamed in the light from the furnace. "Five thirty."

"Not so plain."

"A gift."

Augustine grunted. "Enough for today. At six, Rebecca will be wondering if we mean to make a night of it. Come, I'll show you where to wash up."

When they stepped outside the shop, the cold made Zeph suck in his breath.

Augustine grinned. "I have a good trade for the wintertime, eh?"

"Your smithy is as warm as California."

"But in the summertime, I am always drinking water, gallons of it, and lemonade. It's a different matter then. I feel like a ham dangling in a smokehouse."

After he had cleaned up and changed into another shirt, equally as plain as the one he'd taken off, Zeph came to the table. Augustine and his wife were waiting patiently for him. They rose, the wife coming around the table to greet him and take one of his hands in hers.

"Velkommen," she beamed. "Our home is your home as long as you remain under our roof. My name is Rebecca."

She was short and slender, and dark red hair gleamed under the dark mesh covering on her head.

Zeph lifted his hand to touch the brim of his hat, but it was hanging on a peg in the hall. He touched his forehead anyway and smiled. *"Danke*, Missus Yoder. I feel very much at home already."

"We will pray and then sit," said Augustine. "Everything is cooling off."

Rebecca laughed. "Just because the food does not smoke like your blacksmith shop, you think it will turn to ice in a few minutes."

"Still, we'll pray."

Zeph bowed his head as Augustine prayed in Pennsylvania Dutch. At his "amen," Zeph added his own and sat down with them to the meal: chicken, dumplings, a soup.

"This looks much better than train food, Missus Yoder."

"Rebecca. Well, I am glad to hear it, but it is only a small supper."

"She means there are only three of us," said Augustine. "She is happiest when she is cooking for our sons and our daughter and their families. Or for the whole church."

"Well, once you have put the pot on the stove it is as easy to cook for fifty as it is for five."

"Start with the sauerkraut soup," suggested Augustine. "Do you have sauerkraut out west? Very good. Cabbage that is pickled. Great flavor. And the chicken and dumplings, go ahead, fill your plate, taste one of the dumplings, very good—"

"Augustine, for heaven's sake," Rebecca said with a laugh, "leave the poor boy alone. It sounds like you are trying to sell him something you have made with your hammer and tongs."

"Let him eat what he eats. Would you like some coffee with your meal, Zephaniah?"

"Why, thank you, Rebecca, I would like that very much."

"You're right, Mister Yoder, the soup is full of flavor."

"Ah, you see, Rebecca. Now a dumpling—"

"Augustine, enough. Zephaniah, how was your trip?"

"Well, the children saw buffalo and a Sioux hunting party, and they met some cavalrymen from Fort Laramie, so I guess for them it was pretty eventful."

"It is a lonely land, they tell me."

Zeph ate and swallowed and then spoke.

"Well, there are vast stretches of open country with not a building or a person in sight, Missus Yoder, but some folk like it that way, and I have to admit I'm one of them. The wind and rain are fresh out of the Lord's kitchen, and you can see the rims of heaven and earth, sitting astride your saddle in the tall mountains."

"I am told your Charlotte has a property out there."

"That's true. Her brother Ricky made the purchase, but she has been running it since his death."

"Dairy cattle?"

"Beef."

"How long since her brother passed away?"

"Only a few years, ma'am."

"I remember Ricky well," said Augustine. "A fine boy. Very loyal to his father. That is why he left us."

"Zephaniah, will you have some snitz pie?" asked Rebecca, changing the subject. "It is a pie made with plenty of dried apples and brown sugar and butter."

"I'd like a slice very much."

"And perhaps some of our vanilla and mint ice cream with that? Augustine makes it."

"Thank you."

She placed the pie and ice cream before him and waited like a mother waits for a favorite child to eat hearty.

"Is it to your liking?"

"I haven't tasted a better pie in years, Missus Yoder."

"Now you are making a joke."

"Ma'am, I am a bachelor, and I am telling you the plain truth."

"But don't you meet with your Charlotte socially? Surely she would bake a good Amish pie for you now and then."

"At the church picnic I generally have a good feed. But no, ma'am, Charlotte and I do not see one another socially. Until this train trip east, I guess I haven't spoken more than two dozen words to her in the past year."

Rebecca frowned, her eyebrows coming together. "Why is that?"

"Well, I suppose we are both very busy. I have a ranch and she has a bigger one. It takes a lot of hard work, dawn to dusk."

"Is it common for a woman out west to run a ranch and a household?"

"No, Missus Yoder, not common, but Charlotte is

very good at it. And her spread is no small enterprise. She has ten men working for her."

A sudden chill descended on the table. Zeph felt it at once and looked up from what was left of his pie and ice cream. Rebecca and Augustine were looking at each other with the kind of expression on their faces that Zeph would have translated as, "You see what becomes of our women when they leave the church?"

Augustine pushed his chair back. "Will you walk with me to the barn, Zephaniah? I want to check on the horses. It will give my Rebecca time to clean up in here and also to prepare your bedroom."

Augustine tugged on his overcoat with the cape and Zeph his brown sheepskin jacket. The stars were glittering in the cold night sky like broken glass. Augustine carried a lantern to the barn and looked carefully at all three of his horses, each in its own stable. He rubbed their ears and spoke to them soothingly.

"Shall I pitch them some hay, Mister Yoder?"

"Yah. How many horses do you keep at your farm, Zephaniah?"

Zeph located the pitchfork and set to work. "Well, if I have a good spring, I hope to have eleven."

"Eleven? Yah? And what about your Charlotte? How many horses will she have this spring?"

"Well, if she has a decent spring, my guess is she will have around ninety-five or so."

"What? So many? Is it true?"

"Some of the spreads down around Texas have remudas that number in the hundreds."

"Remuda?"

"Spanish for a change of horses. It's the horse herd the hired hands get their remounts from. We do as much as we can with our horses out west, Mister Yoder. There's friends of mine who think if you can't do a job from the back of a horse it ain't worth doing."

Augustine barked his laugh. "So you care very much for your horses in Montana and Texas?"

"A man that doesn't care for his horse is a fool, Mister Yoder. They are the difference between life and death when you're out on the prairie."

They walked from the barn to the blacksmith shop. Augustine wanted to make sure the coals were well banked and there would be no danger of a spark starting a fire.

"You did not mind working with me today, Zephaniah?"

"I enjoyed it very much, sir."

"You would do it again?"

"I would."

"Well, I have meetings in the morning, but I hope to be back in the smithy after lunch. How does that suit you?"

"I'll meet you there."

"Or at lunch. Rebecca will certainly be expecting you at our table."

"All right."

Augustine glanced up at the February stars. "I never tire of God's handiwork. In my own poor way, I try to do what I can to emulate him in my shop. I try to make everything come together just so."

"I know what you mean. But when I look at the Rockies it puts me in my place, Mister Yoder. On moonlit nights, with the peaks glowing with snow, you kind of feel you've died and gone to heaven. I do the best I can with my hands, but it'll never be like the work of the Master."

Augustine looked at him. "You think about such things?"

"When you spend whole days in the saddle, you get to think about a lot of things."

Inside the house, Rebecca was waiting with an armful of towels. "Zephaniah, I have your room ready. Here are some towels when you wish to wash up."

"Thank you, ma'am."

"Now just follow me."

He walked after her down a short hall to an open door that looked to be about three inches thick. Inside was a bed; chair; desk; washstand with basin and jug; and a freestanding, full-length mirror. A candle burned beside the bed.

"Well, that looks mighty cozy, Missus Yoder."

"Rebecca. It was our Daniel's right up until the day he was married. This room has many good memories for Augustine and me."

"Thank you for fixing up such a special place for me, ma'am. I could've made do in the barn."

"The barn!" she snorted and then said something in Pennsylvania Dutch. "You are not a cow."

"I sure admire that quilt you put on the bed."

"It is the lone star. Those are log cabin blocks around it."

"My Rebecca made this only last winter," Augustine spoke up. "Many hours, many fine stitches sitting by the fire."

"Hush, Father, there is no need to say all that."

"It will keep me plenty warm, I can see that, just as if I'd made my bed in the stove."

Rebecca smiled. "Well, good night then. If you need anything, we are upstairs."

"I'll be fine, Missus Yoder. Good night."

"God bless."

When they had left, Zeph shut the heavy door and sat on the edge of the bed. The mattress felt pretty firm, and he was glad for that. He watched the candle burn and let what thoughts he had been holding back for a quiet moment come tumbling into his head. He was pleased that the first ones were images of Charlotte— her blue eyes, her golden hair down around her shoulders and uncombed, her lips, her smile.

What was she doing right now? What would she be doing tomorrow? When would he get a chance to see her again?

He lay back on the bed, his feet still planted on the floor.

No way around it. This was her childhood home. Shunned or not, she was an insider; he was an outsider. She fit in; he was like a donkey kicking up its heels among palominos.

It's Thursday night, another part of his mind cut in, *so that gives you the weekend, and then you'd better be gone.*

"I know it," he said out loud. But gone where?

He thought about the passage from Revelation again. Raber calling himself the Destroyer made sense enough, but what was the Place of Destruction? The first woe was past—the holdup at the train? But what were the second two woes? Especially if Raber only meant to see them one more time and then kill them.

The Place of Destruction. The two woes. Zeph felt there was a message from Raber for him in those phrases, but he couldn't figure it out. There was a knock on the door, and he almost jumped.

"Mister Parker." It was Augustine's voice. "I am sorry to disturb you. Could you please come to the front door? There is someone here to see you, and it is urgent."

Zeph sprang to his feet. Had something happened to Charlotte or Cheyenne or Cody? He came out of his bedroom. Augustine was gone. The house seemed deserted. He made his way to the front door and stepped outside. A person was standing by the road.

"Who's there?" he asked.

The person did not answer. Zeph walked up to them in his shirtsleeves. A woman in a bonnet turned to face him.

"Charlotte." He wanted to hug her, but her face was like rock, and he hung back. "I thought I wouldn't see you for days. What's wrong?"

She reached out and took one of his hands in hers. Her fingers were like ice, and her eyes like dark pits.

"I thought I could keep my secrets forever. But I realize it cannot be done. God will not have it."

Fear tore down the track of his heart like a wild horse. "Charlotte. What is it?"

"You call me Charlotte. No one else here does, do they? Why is that, Zephaniah?"

"I thought it was because they know you by another name, a childhood name."

"Oh, yes. They know me by another name." She reached a hand to his cheek. "Thank you for all your gallantry and kindness. And now it is finished between us."

"What are you talking about? What have I done?"

"No, it is nothing you have done. It is I. My hair should be sheared in shame. You know me by the name Charlotte Spence. But that is not who I am. I have another name I thought I could leave buried in Pennsylvania, but I find I cannot. Now everything in my life has caught up with me, and you will see I am nothing more than one great lie."

"Charlotte—"

She put her fingers to his mouth. "Hush. No more of that. My real name is Lynndae Raber. The Angel of Death is my brother."

Chapter Twenty-Three

Lynndae finished buttoning her sky-blue dress and then put the long light-blue apron over it, fastening the apron at the back with pins. She looked in the mirror and placed the white prayer covering on her head—her blond hair had been pinned up as tightly as she could manage. *Perhaps too tightly,* she thought, *I am going to get a headache.*

The tabby with the coffee-colored fur on her tummy rubbed against Lynndae's legs, purring like some sort of small train engine. She smiled, bent down, picked the cat up, and cuddled her.

"*Guten morgan,* Snitz," she cooed. "It would be nice if they would let you into the meeting with me." The cat pushed her head against Lynndae's face.

There was a tap at the door. "Lynndae, the pastors are ready."

"Thank you. I will be right out."

Lord, please be with me at this hour. Help me to be honest with them and also with myself.

She opened the door with the cat still in her arms. Mary Beachey, Sarah's mother, smiled. She took the cat from Lynndae and handed it off to her daughter, who stood nearby. "Sarah, please take care of our little Princess Snitz."

"Yes, but she will be on the loose once I leave to teach school, Mama."

Mary came with Lynndae into the room where four men were waiting, closed the door, and sat beside Lynndae in the center of the room. Augustine Yoder nodded and stood up. He prayed for several minutes and then sat down again.

"Do you know all the pastors, Miss Raber?" he asked in Pennsylvania Dutch. "Here to my right is David Lapp. On my left, Malachi Kauffman. And Moses Beachey you know."

Lynndae inclined her head.

"We wanted first of all to offer thanks to you for bringing Samuel Troyer and Elizabeth Kauffman back to us. It is our understanding that your journey was not without its hazards. We are grateful God's hand of protection was upon you."

"Thank you, Pastor Yoder, but I must tell you that God worked through the person of Mister Zephaniah Parker in a very great way—"

Augustine held up a hand. "We will speak of your young man later, Miss Raber."

"Pastor Yoder, I would not call him 'my' young man, but I would be happy to speak about him later and at great length."

Mary Beachey squeezed Lynndae's hand as a warning, but did not look at her.

Augustine looked to Moses Beachey. The older man spread his hands. "Miss Raber, let us come right to the heart of the matter. Your family was asked to leave the church because your father and brothers insisted on going to war. Some of our people do not think it is right that the sins of the father were visited upon his womenfolk. Nevertheless, we must ask you, do you support your father's actions, or are you opposed to them?"

Lynndae looked calmly at Moses. "I respect my father, as God has taught all children to respect their parents. But I look at that war, and I see only pain and bloodshed and the loss of life. I hate war, Pastor Beachey. I hate what it does, and I hate what it takes away from God's earth. My father and brothers were wrong to take up arms."

"So you are opposed to your father's actions?"

"Yes."

"You are opposed to his defiance of the Ordnung and his dismissal of the teachings of our pastors and bishops?"

"Yes."

"We must also ask about your brother; I am sorry."

"I understand perfectly, Pastor Beachey. It is a necessary question."

"Bishop Schrock wished to be absolutely clear on this and on the matter of the children. He is on a business trip to Philadelphia and New York. Otherwise, he would have been here this morning."

"What about the children?"

"First we must discuss your brother Seraphim."

"No, first we must discuss the children."

Mary Beachey hissed under her breath, but Lynndae was in no mood to listen to her warnings.

Moses considered Lynndae for a few long moments. "Very well. It is only that with their parents dead, we feel it is best Samuel and Elizabeth remain here with their relatives and their church. Bishop Schrock was quite determined about that. As are all of us. We know they have grown attached to you. But if you choose to return to the Montana Territory, we want you to understand we believe they belong with us."

"Perhaps if you had not excommunicated their parents, we would not need to be discussing their fate this morning."

"They violated the Ordnung. They were warned on several occasions. The matter was handled properly. It is none of your concern."

"Excuse me, Pastor Beachey, but it is my duty, my Christian duty, to be concerned. You punished my mother and sister and me, as well as my youngest brother, for something our father did, not us. Then you punished Ricky and me for something our brother continued to do. Has it occurred to any of you that there might not have ever been an Angel of Death if you had shown love to my family instead of judgment?"

"We are a church who love one another."

"Yes, you love those who are like you. Everyone does that. You do not need Jesus Christ to help you do that."

"We do not need to be lectured by you, Miss Raber," Malachi Kauffman spoke up. "Take care."

Lynndae turned on him. "Those were your own relatives you sent to their deaths, Pastor Kauffman."

Malachi reddened. "It was their choice to travel west. I did not want them to do that."

"What did you expect them to do? You shunned them to such an extent they could not live here anymore. Where would they be able to find land where they could afford to start over again except by going into the Territories? The terrible irony is, they were ex-communicated Amish who were murdered by another Amish man who had been excommunicated. All from the same community and the same church."

"That is enough, Miss Raber," said David Lapp softly. "You sit and speak of judgment and shunning so calmly and easily, even though many have died due to your decisions. I wonder what you will do when God faces each of you on your own day of judgment and passes sentence on your lives? What will you do if He has as little pity on your souls as you have had on the souls of others?"

Mary had her head down and her eyes closed, but Lynndae could see that her lips were moving. Across from her the men were stone-faced and silent. Then Augustine cleared his throat. "Miss Raber, still we must clear up the matter of your brother Seraphim."

"Pastor Yoder, with all due respect, what do you expect me to say? That Ricky and I believed in what Seraph has done for the past ten years? You must know we have never condoned any of the terrible killings he has participated in."

"Seraphim Raber was ushered into the presence of his Maker only last week. There he will receive a just judgment for the deeds he committed while in the flesh. But we must hear from your own lips how you felt about those deeds."

"I have told you how I feel."

"Did you ever encourage or assist him in his activities?"

"How can you ask this?"

"Do you know about John Wesley Hardin?" said David Lapp.

Lynndae felt confused. "The outlaw from Texas?"

"We read in the New York and Philadelphia papers about the men he has killed, more than forty, and this despite the fact his father is a Methodist preacher and that he was named after the founder of Methodism, John Wesley, a God-fearing minister."

Lynndae waited.

Malachi Kauffman spoke. "We read how his brother helped him, how even his father, a Christian man and a minister, assisted him in eluding the law. Time after time family and relatives kept him out of jail and hid him, and time after time he killed more men because of this. Today he is still on the loose and will destroy more lives. So we ask, did you or Ricky assist your brother Seraph in his crimes?"

Lynndae sensed a tightening in her throat and a burning in her eyes. "No, never."

"Did you ever help him to elude the law?"

"No."

"Did you ever go to the police or the sheriff and tell him what you knew of his whereabouts or his plans?"

Lynndae bent her head and felt the streaks of warm tears on her cheeks. Mary's hand rested gently on her arm. "We never knew of his whereabouts or his plans. He never wrote, and he never came to our house. I tried, Ricky tried, several times, to get messages to his camp, asking him to stop the raids and turn himself in, but we never knew where to send them. Sometimes the messengers found Seraph and sometimes they didn't. Two or three times, a reply made its way back to us, months later. They always said the same thing—as far as he was concerned, the war was not over, the war would continue until the day God told him to stop."

Augustine held up his hand. "I am sorry. It is our duty to ask these questions. Why did you not make a sketch of him for the police?"

"For the same reason you didn't, Pastor Yoder," moaned Lynndae. "I did not know what he looked like. The last time I saw him was the last time you saw him—a tall boy, too tall for his age, skinny as a stalk of wheat; yes, just a boy with a pet dog and a pet raccoon, you remember, only twelve. What could I give to the police? A drawing of a young boy, when it was a man who was leading the raids, a man whose face was no longer that of a youth's, who may have gained weight, grown a beard, perhaps lost one of his eyes in battle and might now be wearing a patch? My memory of a child would have served the law no good purpose. That is why I did not go to them. And that is why no one in Bird in Hand went to them. None of us knew him anymore."

"Calm yourself," whispered Mary in her ear.

"I do not mean to be disrespectful. I am still tired from the journey and the danger, but that does not excuse my tongue. None of you passed judgment on my family in 1861, none of you were pastors at that time, and I know that not everyone agreed with the shunning, the *streng meidung*. I am told several families left the church because of the decision to excommunicate my family and because of the judgment passed on other families. I came back to talk these things over with the church, and so many words have just come tumbling out. I accept that the children must stay. I only ask that you consider the circumstances of my life when you come to make your decision about whether I may come back into the church or not. I do not know whether I will stay or go. I myself have not been able to make up my own mind, but I ask that you consider what my brother Ricky and I went through and how we had no other choice but to leave and start again in the West."

Lynndae cried with a down-turned face. Moses nodded and got to his feet.

"We will talk alone now, Miss Raber. My Mary will stay with you. When we are done we will ask for you."

Mary and Lynndae put on long dark *mandlies*, the woolen cape coats the Amish women wore in the winter season, and thick bonnets and walked out into the road. They held each other's arms.

"I am sorry, Mary," Lynndae said.

"Hush."

"I spoke too much. I cried too much."

"Hush. None of us have ever been through what you have experienced all these years. None of us have had such a train journey as you had this past week. Hush now. We will not talk. We will walk and pray in our hearts. They are good men; they have wisdom among them. And Moses and I want you to know, we did not agree to the shunning of your family, nor to the shunning of the Kauffmans, Troyers, and Millers. Moses only drew the short straw to be a pastor last month. God have mercy on us all."

It began to snow gently from a sky that was both blue and the color of woodsmoke. Lynndae hoped they might see Zeph or Samuel or Elizabeth, but the muddy track was deserted. Over their heads, now and then, a few crows flew back and forth. Gradually the snowflakes covered up the mud and ice like a clean blanket.

When they returned to the house in an hour, the ministers were still meeting behind a tightly closed door. Yet no sooner had Mary and Lynndae sat down to coffee, Snitz happy in Lynndae's lap, than Moses came out to the kitchen.

"Yes, we are ready for you now," he said.

Chapter Twenty-Four

Once the two women had sat in their chairs, Augustine stood up and prayed again before they began. Then he sat and nodded at David Lapp.

"Miss Raber," said David, "we understand the young man Zephaniah Parker was instrumental in seeing you safely to Bird in Hand."

"Yes, Pastor Lapp. God alone knows, but I do not think we would have arrived here in good health were it not for Mister Parker."

"Is it true the Raber Gang stopped a train you were on?"

"Yes. The Union Pacific between Cheyenne and Omaha."

"They wanted Samuel and Elizabeth because the children had seen their faces."

"How did you escape?"

"Zephaniah told us to hide in the baggage car. When outlaws boarded the train, he refused to tell them where we were."

"Did he shoot them?"

"Zephaniah does not carry a gun, Pastor Lapp."

"Yet he sometimes wears a badge, the children tell us."

"He was deputized by his brother before we left the Montana Territory. If he needed to ask for help from government officials, he put the badge on. Being deputized was not his idea. But his brother insisted on it."

"His brother is?"

"A federal marshal. His other brother is pastor for the church in Iron Springs."

David nodded slowly. "Why does he not carry a gun when so many other English do?"

"The war."

"So it is not a religious conviction?"

"I cannot say it is or isn't, Pastor Lapp. You must speak with him."

"Have you never discussed it?"

"Not at length, no."

"Yet you were on a train together for so many days."

"We read the Bible together a good deal, spoke with the children, looked at herds of buffalo. We slept. No, we did not spend any amount of time discussing firearms and killing people."

Another squeeze from Mary Beachey's hand.

"Tell us, what do you think, can you see yourselves as a married couple, raising children, starting a farm?"

"I have thought about it a little. But he has never declared such intentions to me in so many words."

"If you remained here and were welcomed back into the church, what do you think, would he wish to remain behind and marry you? Would he willingly take up our ways and ask for baptism?"

"Oh, I cannot answer that. He knows so little about

our ways. He would need more time to think it over than a day or two."

"But would he stay behind for you?"

Lynndae felt her face growing warm. "I hope if he stayed behind it would be for God as much as it would be for me, Pastor Lapp. But I cannot say I matter to him anymore. He did not know my real name until last night. He did not know I was Seraph Raber's sister. Now I have told him, and I do not know if he can love me or forgive me."

"What did he say when you told him?"

"He looked at me in disbelief. 'Why did you hide the truth from me?' he asked. 'You were not the killer, were you? Why could you not trust me after all we have been through?' Then he turned and walked back into the house."

"He is a farmer in the Territories?"

"Beef cattle. A rancher. As I am."

"Yes. As you are. You have many men working under you, we are given to understand."

"I have ten hired men and a cook."

"And a cook?"

"I am often out and about on horseback, Pastor Lapp."

"Yet you found time to sew plain clothing for the children and for Mister Parker."

"I did."

"You own a good deal of land out there among the English?"

"Ricky bought it. It is in my name, yes."

"Can you give it up?"

"Pardon me?"

"If it were God's will for you to remain here and

marry and raise a family, could you give up the land in the Territories? Could you give up being a boss— *der chef*—out in the west and be here a mother to your children and a helpmeet to your husband?"

"That is something I am praying about."

"Well, keep praying. I am sure the answer is not difficult to find, Miss Raber, not for an Amish woman baptized into the church as you are."

Lynndae sensed a fire rising up inside her, but she bowed her head, so the men would not spot it in her eyes.

Moses Beachey spoke. "You are not sure yet and neither are we. We hold nothing against you from your past, not from your father's decision to be a soldier or from your brother's decision to be an outlaw. What we are uncertain about is whether you can submit to a Christian life that sees you in the home instead of telling ten hired men what to do. It does not sound as if you are certain you can see yourself in that Amish home yet, either. So we must proceed slowly. There is plenty of time. We hope you can remain here indefinitely—or at least until a decision is made on your part."

Augustine Yoder coughed. "It is something you must come to terms with in your own time and through your own prayers. Of course, we will be praying with you. But it must be your decision. If you can be that Amish wife in an Amish home, we will bring you back into the church. Meanwhile, the ban is lifted. There will be no more shunning directed toward you from anyone in the community. This Sunday the church gathers for worship and teaching at Amos Zook's house. You are welcome to join us; the door is open to you. It is also open to your young man. He is welcome to attend. We owe him a great deal. It would be good for him to see how we come to God and good to have him worship alongside us. Though it will be in our heavenly tongue and not the tongue of the English—or the Spanish."

The men laughed.

"Thank you all for being patient and gracious towards me," said Lynndae. "It means a great deal to feel I have been heard, forgiven, and embraced by my childhood friends and neighbors and Christians."

"There is so little to forgive," said Malachi Kauffman softly. "But there is much to give thanks for in heaven this day. Personally, I must thank you, from my heart, especially for young Bess's safe return. She lights up our home like a hundred lamps."

"I grew to love her very much. It was a privilege to bring her home to you, Pastor Kauffman. I hope I will see her again very soon?"

Malachi nodded. "We have told her she will see you on Sunday. We will make sure it is a long and wonderful day spent with God and with one another."

Moses stood up. "So we will conclude." He prayed and then the meeting was over.

After a quiet lunch with Moses and Mary and a short walk to the barn to look at the dairy cows, Lynndae took the cat with her into the bedroom that the Beacheys had set aside for her use. She lay back on a quilt with a brown and navy mariner's compass design, Snitz purring and licking herself. Lynndae had borrowed a Bible and was leafing through it, thinking about reading some of the Psalms and the Gospel of John.

She found she missed the days on the train when, for the better part of a week, she had been wife and mother in a family of four. Every day she had spoken with Zeph. Every day she had laughed with Samuel and Bess. Now she felt lonely without them. She drew a circle over and over again on the quilt with her finger. At first the cat was interested in this movement, but after several minutes without any variation on the part of the circling finger, Snitz chose to tuck her tail around herself and doze off.

Lynndae found herself wondering if the kisses in the baggage car had been real. Had Z meant them, or was it just the relief they both felt once the gang had been captured? They had said so many wild and crazy things to one another on that trip, all the way back to Virginia City and the days on the stagecoach—did any of them matter now? Zeph felt so far away from her, it was as if he didn't exist.

Lynndae propped her head up on one hand and gazed out the window. It was snowing heavily now, like salt pouring out of a shaker. She had a view of the barn and the sloping land behind it. A lovely place. But then, so was the Sweet Blue a lovely place. Could she leave her cattle and horses behind, her mountains and rivers, the heart-stirring bugle of the elk, and the chilling night moan of the wolf?

What about Z? How was he feeling about her now that he knew who she really was? Did he hate her? Could he forgive her? The woman he had cared about was the sister of a monster. Did that make her a monster in his eyes as well? Was he willing to wake up every morning and look in her eyes and see Seraphim Raber? How could he forget she shared blood ties with a cold-blooded killer?

She stood up and began to pace, squeezing her hands together.

A killer who still hunted them. She felt no fear. Yet she had experienced moments of great fear on the journey from Iron Springs to Bird in Hand. Was it this place, with all its prayers and faith and open Bibles and absence of violence, that calmed her spirit? She glanced down at the Gospel of John and picked the Bible up. It was chapter 14 and verse 27 that caught her eye, underlined as it was with a neat black line of ink and marked with a date in equally neat and precise handwriting, August 17, 1863, probably by Mary Beachey: "'Peace I leave with you, my peace I give unto you: not as the world giveth, give I unto you. Let not your heart be troubled, neither let it be afraid.'"

She laid her head back on the pillow and watched the snowflakes pelt against the window and the frozen earth. Her fingers stroked Snitz's fur.

Please protect Mary and Moses, Lord. Bless and protect Samuel and Bess as You have already done. Watch over these homes and these families. Watch over Zephaniah—and grant this peace You speak of to all.

Chapter Twenty-Five

Even with the bellows making the forge roar and Augustine hammering a section of an iron plow on his largest anvil, Zeph could still hear the horse walking carefully up the icy track to the Yoder shop. Was there some sixth sense of his that had come back into operation since they'd ridden out of Iron Springs in the middle of the night? He'd had that feeling for things during the war, but had been determined to bury it once the fighting stopped. Yet there it was, back again. He could see that Augustine didn't realize a horse and rider were coming. He tapped him on the shoulder, and the big man looked up, face and beard dripping sweat. Zeph indicated the visitor with a jerk of his chin.

Augustine stared at the man on the tall chestnut horse and said something in Pennsylvania Dutch. Then he spoke in English for Zeph's benefit. "Big R. What brings him out?"

"Hello, the smithy!" called the man. "A good Saturday morning to one and all in the Yoder family."

"Velkommen, wie geht es dir?"

"Gute." The man swung down from the saddle. He

was taller than Zeph or Augustine by half a foot. He squinted up at the February sun as it pulled free from a cloud bank and made the snow and ice dance. Then he took off his dark-brown Stetson and ran a gloved hand over his iron-gray hair—it was cut close to his scalp, Zeph noticed. Under his earth-brown duster he wore a lighter brown, three-piece suit. A star glinted on its lapel.

"Always the Lewis Tweed," complained Augustine with a smile.

"Not plain enough for you?"

"The pattern—"

"Houndstooth? I have seen your women wear calico that makes my tweed look Amish enough for the bishop."

"Only the young, maybe you've seen."

"Depends what you call young, August. Well, the day you strap on a six-gun and clean up Lancaster County is the day I wear Amish black. How are you?"

He and Augustine shook hands. "The Lord is good," said Augustine.

"I feel the same way."

"Is there something wrong that you are up and about on your best horse?"

"Shotgun and I are just doing our duty, August, working hard to keep you Amish out of trouble."

The man turned to Zeph. "Mister Parker? I asked for you at the house. Sheriff Friesen. Lancaster County is my jurisdiction."

Zeph took his hand. "Sheriff."

"Folks call me Rusty. Or Big R. Take your pick."

"Rusty?"

"No, it's not too red anymore, is it? Someone sticks

a handle on you when you're young, and it's yours for life."

"He came to us with the news of what had happened in your Territory," said Augustine, looking somber.

The sheriff nodded. "I had to find out who the kids' relatives were. August, we're going to walk a bit, is that all right with you?"

"Sure, sure, I'll go inside for a coffee; take your time."

"Danke."

Sheriff Friesen led his horse back toward the main road, and Zeph walked with him. Augustine suddenly clapped Zeph on the shoulder, and he turned around. The blacksmith put his cape overcoat in Zeph's hands.

"One of you must be plain," he said.

Zeph shrugged it on and immediately felt warmer in the cool winter air. He caught up to the sheriff. They went a ways in silence.

The sheriff didn't appear to be armed. Zeph wondered if that was because he harbored the same sentiments about guns and violence the Amish did.

As if sensing his thoughts, the sheriff spoke up. "I go heeled, Mister Parker. But it doesn't seem right to aggravate these good folk unnecessarily. I have a Smith & Wesson Schofield snug in a holster that's sewn into my suit jacket, just inside on the left, and unseen. It's the Wells Fargo model, barrel cut to five inches and the whole revolver refinished in nickel. I favor a cross draw; I believe it's faster. Only had to use it twice in Lancaster County. Which makes my parents happy. I am of Mennonite stock, and a good many of them hold to the same opinion of guns and shooting our fine Amish friends do. I appreciate my parents' point of view, but considering the evil I've seen men do, I beg to differ on what's best needed to quell some of that wickedness. The lawful authorities have the power of the sword, and sometimes we need to use it. How does the Bible put it?"

There was a long pause. Zeph decided to quote the verses he felt Sheriff Friesen had in mind. "'For rulers are not a terror to good works, but to the evil. For he is the minister of God to thee for good. But if thou do that which is evil, be afraid; for he beareth not the sword in vain: for he is the minister of God, a revenger to execute wrath upon him that doeth evil.' Romans, chapter thirteen, part of verse three and all of verse four."

Sheriff Friesen chuckled and glanced over at him. "That's pretty good. You go to Sunday school?"

Zeph laughed. "Yeah, my brother Matt's Sunday school. He's drilled that passage into me ever since he became a lawman back in the '60s. My other brother's a clergyman, and Matt always tells him he's a minister of God, too, the Reverend B. A'Fraid."

Friesen laughed along with Zeph and nodded. "Well, it's God's truth, even my Mennonite relatives admit that. They question whether a Christian man ought to be caught up in it; that's the issue they have. I say to them, 'Would you rather have outlaws pinning on sheriff's badges and enforcing God's laws for you?' That's usually when they tell me to take a second helping of chicken and dumplings to shut me up."

They walked a little farther, and then the sheriff spoke again. "I had a telegram from a Marshal Austen in Cheyenne, Wyoming. It seems we are about to have some unwelcome visitors in Lancaster County."

"I contacted Marshal Michael James Austen from

Lancaster. Seraph Raber wasn't hung, sheriff. He slipped through K Company's fingers the day they caught two members of the gang."

"Mm."

"Raber knows we're in Lancaster County. I told my brother in Iron Springs, Montana, we'd be pushing on to Philadelphia. Raber has an accomplice in Iron Springs. He will pass on the news to the gang."

Sheriff Friesen shook his head. "Raber won't buy it. You tricked him at the railroad. He'll come here."

"What do you plan to do?"

"Well, if I thought it was just Raber, I'd sleep a lot easier. No, he's got the rest of his men with him, the ones that got away after they held up the train."

They reached the road and stopped.

"Raber telegraphed you from Omaha on Thursday, is that right?" asked the sheriff.

"Him. Or someone else. He could have already been far up the line in Chicago."

"Well, let's hope it was him and that he really was in Omaha. He could be here Monday if that's the case. What am I looking for?"

"He has a cut that runs from his eye to his chin."

"Which side?"

"I can't tell you that. I've never seen him. The girl did a drawing of his face and put it in. The left side maybe."

"Mm."

"He could have covered it with a beard by now."

"Or a woman's makeup."

"Sheriff, if he knows I'm not here, he won't stop in Lancaster. The information about his scar is going to be right across the country after a couple more days.

Killing the kids won't change anything now. But he has a score to settle with me. Two of his gang were hung. I helped the army trap them. He wants me. I've got to be bait again."

"I told you. He's not likely to go for it a second time."

"If I pick a spot he can check out before he makes his play, a spot that will make him confident, I believe he may go for it. He has to prove to whoever's left in his gang that the people who cross Seraph Raber die hard deaths. He'll build another gang around that reputation."

"How do you expect us to protect you if you go someplace where he can see gophers and wood ticks for a thousand miles?"

"I don't."

"What are your intentions? To be a holy sacrifice?"

"He murdered Amish in Iron Springs. I don't intend to let him do more of the same here in Lancaster County. If he wants me, I'll make sure he knows where to find me."

"Have you got a place in mind?"

"Not yet."

"And you won't tell me when you do anyhow."

"No, sir. I'd rather have you keeping an eye out for the good people of Bird in Hand. In case I get it wrong and he comes here to work mischief, regardless of where I'm holed up."

The sheriff swung up on his horse. "I'll have some deputies riding the roads hereabouts. And I'll have men watching that railroad station the way a hawk watches a pigeon. Raber doesn't get by with anything in Lancaster County, not without a fight. To quote that verse, I don't bear the sword in vain."

Friesen rested his hands on the pommel of his saddle and looked at the snow-covered landscape. "I always hoped the James-Younger gang would try to take the bank in Lancaster some fine day, but it's never happened yet. Things are so quiet here among the Germans it gets a lawman hungering for action, even the most hazardous kind. I may never get Jesse James, but the Lord has so arranged matters that I may just get the Angel of Death instead." He smiled down at Zeph. "I need to go tell my good wife, May, what's going on. She'll be fussing with our horses and dairy herd. Mister Parker, I wish you all the luck in the world." Then he spoke to Shotgun, and the big chestnut began to trot along the road back to Lancaster.

Zeph walked back to the smithy. Augustine called to him from the front door of the house, his hands in his pockets.

"How about some coffee?"

"Sure, I'd like that."

At the kitchen table Augustine worked a toothpick back and forth in his mouth. "So? Did you have a talk with Mister Friesen?"

Zeph smiled. "How does Romans thirteen, verses three and four suit you?"

Augustine paused and thought. Then he shook his head and growled, "Yah, yah, *flammenschwert*." Then he barked his laugh and slapped the table and shook his head again. "Ach, we need more coffee."

"Zephaniah," he said, when he had poured both of them another cup, "tomorrow we have worship at our Katie's home, at Amos Zook's. We would like you to join us. It will also give you an opportunity to see Samuel and Elizabeth. And Lynndae Raber, if you are interested."

"I'd be happy to join you."

Augustine stared at him. "How do you feel about the woman now?"

"I don't know."

"She did not do what her brother did."

"I didn't know who she was all those years. I don't know who she is now. She made a fool of all of us. She made a fool of me."

Augustine sipped at his coffee.

"This afternoon, the wife and I will take the buggy into town to buy some things she needs for baking. I also have a few items I must look at. Do you wish to join us?"

"What about the plow you have been working on this week?"

"The plow? Spring is months away. Smucker has time. I have time. Everyone will bring their plow for repairs and sharpening in March. There will be plows from here until spring planting."

Zeph hitched Matchbox up to the buggy, and the three of them went into Lancaster. After stopping in a few shops, Zeph excused himself and walked over several streets to the telegraph office. When he was given the pad of paper to write on, he leaned against the counter and thought as hard as he'd thought about anything in his life.

What will flush Raber? What will make him risk coming out into the open?

Getting his hands on Zephaniah Parker, of course.

But where? Where will Raber feel safe enough to

show himself? Zeph went over the verse from Revelation in his head. Again and again he came back to Abaddon, the Place of Destruction. Did Raber have such a place in mind? Or was he going to create such a place, maybe turn Bird in Hand into a location fixed for slaughter and devastation? How could he get Raber and his killers away from Lancaster County and spare these people's lives?

Lord, I need Your help with this, one way or the other. I don't care if I make it through. But I care if Lynndae and the kids and all these decent folk do.

After several minutes, images began to form in his mind, images of death and suffering he had worked hard at suppressing for more than ten years. Soon his head was flooded with them. He could hear the *crack-crack-crack* of thousands of muskets and the roar of cannon, and he could smell the stink of smoke and sulphur and blood. He almost gasped, the memories were so raw and overpowering. The telegraph clerk glanced his way once or twice. Finally Zeph leaned over and wrote a message on the pad.

Raber

    I will come alone to the Place of Destruction. It is only forty miles south of Lancaster. You know the location I am talking about.

    If you have the courage, meet me there.
Parker

"Send this to the office of the federal marshal in Iron Springs, Montana Territory," Zeph said to the clerk. "Matthew Parker."

"Very well, sir."

Zeph paid him and left. Then he walked quickly to the station and purchased a ticket for the Sunday evening train to Gettysburg, Pennsylvania.

Chapter Twenty-Six

Several dozen buggies were already lined up outside the Zook house when Augustine and Rebecca Yoder and Zephaniah came down the road, Matchbox trotting cheerfully through the sparkling frost and blue sky of a Lancaster winter morning. Rebecca carried in several snitz pies, and Augustine walked carefully, with a large container of bean soup. Zephaniah came through the doorway balancing several loaves of heavy brown bread and a massive pot of beef and cabbage, still warm, against his chest.

Zeph had risen early, bathed in a large wooden tub with water heated on the stove, trimmed his beard, and shaved his upper lip clean. Put on a fresh shirt. Used the suspenders Augustine had lent him to hold his pants up. Brushed his dress coat and pulled it on over a plain Amish vest Augustine had also lent him. Wiped muck off his black boots and polished them to a gloss. Exchanged the hat Lynndae had purchased for him in Ogden for a hat the Yoders' son Daniel had left behind. Rebecca Yoder called it a piker. It had a crease in its crown that gave it, Zeph thought, a bit of dash. He placed his silver watch in a vest pocket.

"How do I look?" he asked Rebecca.

She had smiled and nodded. "Very plain. A good Amish." When Zeph entered the Zook house with the food, there were people everywhere, talking in Pennsylvania Dutch, at least a hundred of them, he figured, probably more. He noticed when he glanced out a window that a number of boys had gathered near the barn. Some of the older horses were being stabled there. Women were rushing about in the kitchen organizing the food. Several men were carrying benches into the house. Elizabeth found him and wrapped her arms around him. He kissed her on the top of her head.

"Hello, Mister Parker."

"Hello, Miss Kauffman. Are you well?"

"Very well. But I miss our train rides."

"I do, too. Where is Master Troyer?"

"With the other boys at the barn."

"And Miss Raber?"

"Oh, I saw her outside walking with Sarah Beachey and Rachel Otto. But then Aunt Rosa called them into the kitchen to help."

"I didn't notice her there."

"Well, she is dressed very plain and is in and out of the pantry with things."

Zeph looked toward the door of the large kitchen and thought about invading the Amish women's domain on some sort of pretext. But he didn't know if he was even halfway ready to make peace with Lynndae Raber. Maybe he never would be. A hand fell heavily on his shoulder. He turned around and it was Augustine.

"Mister Yoder," he said by way of greeting.

"Come. I have some men I would like you to meet."

He was introduced to the pastors, David Lapp and Malachi Kauffman. Moses Beachey he had already met at the train station. Then in swift succession, he met a number of Zooks, Hooleys, Umbles, Petershwims, and Planks, until he could no longer match faces with names.

"I am James Lambright," said one thin man, taking Zeph's hand in a tight grip.

"A pleasure."

"They tell me you are from the West."

"Montana Territory."

"Do you farm there?"

"I raise horses and graze beef cattle."

"Who do you sell them to?"

"Some of my horses I sell to officers in the army. The beef goes east to feed people in New York and Boston."

"What about Indians?"

"All is quiet, sir. I am hoping we may have found a way to live at peace with one another, something that will last."

"I pray so, I pray so."

Another man came up with glasses and red hair and pale skin.

"I am Jonathan Glick. All praise to God."

"Yes."

"I hear you have become quite a blacksmith, yah?"

"Oh, I wouldn't say that. So far, all I have done is pump the bellows."

"Do you like to work?"

"I do."

"A smithy is a wonderful place on a cold day."

"It is."

"I have been cutting and storing ice for the summer. Chills you to the bone."

"It would."

"Do you do that out west?"

"We cut the ice from lakes and rivers, yes."

"Store them in sawdust and straw?"

"Please, everyone, it is time to meet with God." This was said in Pennsylvania Dutch, but as people began to move toward the benches, Zeph followed them. His pocket watch read eight o'clock. He caught a glimpse of Lynndae and felt an unpleasant darkness inside himself. She saw his glance, but he looked away and bowed his head. She looked so Amish in her dress and head covering, Zeph would not have been able to tell her apart from any of the other young Amish women.

He felt a sting in his heart. Lynndae was one of them. She had returned to her home, and this was where she belonged and where she was going to stay. All her years in Iron Springs she had been one of them, but he had never known it. He shook his head. There couldn't be any future for them as man and wife. All the things he would have done for Charlotte Spence, he could not do for Lynndae Raber, the sister of a heartless killer, a woman who had lived so many different lies he no longer knew who she really was. The only thing he was sure of anymore was that he had a date with her brother in Gettysburg.

People continued to find places to sit all around him, but he scarcely noticed. His thoughts had made their way to Gettysburg. Monday night could find him buried with Union soldiers in southern Pennsylvania. Strangely, the thought of that had not yet frightened him. Still, now that it had surfaced, he was glad to be in a place of worship where he could hand everything over to God among a people of faith and goodwill. "The men sit together," said Augustine, who was suddenly at his side. "Here, sit with my son-in-law, Amos. I must join the pastors in another room during the singing. We need to decide which of us will preach today."

Zeph sat next to a tall, straw-blond, young man who smiled and shook his hand.

"Amos Zook."

"Zephaniah Parker."

"The cowboy?"

"Yes. And you are the honey man?"

"For sure."

A young man came and stood by them, uncertain of his welcome. It was Samuel. "Good morning, Mister Parker."

Zeph shook his offered hand. "Why, good morning Master Troyer. You're looking very well. Where have you been hiding these past couple of days?"

"I have been with my friend Nathaniel Mast and his family, Mister Parker. I hope I may introduce you to him at lunch if that is all right with you?"

"I'd be glad to meet your pal, Samuel—"

"Shh," came a woman's voice behind them.

Zeph shrugged off his cape overcoat. Hymnals were passed down the rows. They were thick and heavy. When Zeph opened his, he saw that it was in German, but he left it open in his lap anyway. A man began to sing. All around him men and women and children joined in. There were no fancy notes, Zeph noticed, no harmonizing or polished transitions, just a simple strong melody that was carried by earnest voices far beyond their hearts or the roof of the house. No piano played, neither was there an organ in the room. He closed his eyes, listened, worshipped, and prayed.

After about half an hour, Moses Beachey came into the room with the other pastors and began to preach. He had a lilting way of talking, almost like chanting, and Zeph watched, fascinated, as he wandered about the room and then disappeared into other parts of the house where people were seated, still preaching. It was as if his voice were floating far away in a cave or catacomb. Then he returned. It seemed as if he was pleading with them. A man groaned out loud and sunk his head into his large hands. A woman nearby began to cry openly. Next to him Amos Zook was nodding his head, mesmerized, and biting his lower lip.

Lord, I am not used to this, prayed Zeph.

Moses sat down. There was the sound of sniffling and amens for a few moments, and then Amos stood up and began to read from his black Bible. Once he had finished, another man's voice came from a room Zeph could not see. He presumed the man was reading scripture as well, his tone rich and deep. Then everyone went to their knees and Zeph did likewise. A man prayed out loud, then another. When Amos rose, so did Zeph.

Augustine Yoder was preaching now. He, too, moved from room to room, his voice now booming, now scarcely more than a whisper. He began to cry, tears rolling down his broad cheeks and into his dark beard. Again and again, Zeph caught the words, *Jesu Christi am kreuz,* and he realized Augustine was talking about Jesus Christ on the cross. Women and men began to weep. This went on for more than an hour. It was as if the hearts and souls of the congregation were suspended in the air of the house and God was personally touching each one as He walked among them. Zeph understood nothing—yet, it seemed to him, he understood everything, far more than he might have understood in a calmer worship service in an English church.

When Augustine sat down, David Lapp got to his feet and seemed to Zeph to be addressing himself to various points Augustine had raised. Malachi Kauffman got up and did the same. Then everyone went to their knees to pray again, and after that the hymnals were opened and there was more singing. Once they began to clear the rooms to set up tables for lunch, Zeph felt he needed to be alone with God and not sitting and talking with the men again, as good-natured as they were. So in the moving of the benches and the setting out of breads and jams and soups and meat dishes, he slipped out the back door of the kitchen and walked off across the fields of snow without the long overcoat Augustine had lent him.

He did not mind the chill. The presence of so many people had made the house very warm. It had been quite an experience. Zeph sensed God was trying to say something important to him through it all.

Jesu Christi am kreuz.

Jesus on the cross—for Zeph, for Augustine, for Sheriff Friesen, for Colonel Austen. For Lynndae Raber. Yes, even for Seraphim Raber. The Angel of Death had heard sermons like this. In some corner of his heart, they were still lodged there. He had chosen to ignore them.

Jesu Christi am kreuz.

Was it possible? Could God be expecting him to say

something about this to Raber when they met? Would Raber be in any kind of mood to hear it? What if Raber just shot him or hanged him before he had a chance to open his mouth?

There was a cluster of barren winter trees, heavy branches outstretched, and Zeph found a patch of dry earth and sat in their midst. He looked back at the house. It was perhaps two hundred yards away. He could see some people moving about in the snow, crossing between the barn and the outhouses.

Lord, he prayed, *if there is something You want me to say to Seraphim Raber, then please give me the words. Yes, bring us together and give me the words. May Your hand of mercy be upon him, may it be upon me, may it be upon all the people of Lancaster and Bird in Hand, may it be upon the woman I care for more than anyone else in the world even though I myself must release her.*

He changed position so he could look out over the fields and sky rather than watch the smoke rising from the house chimney. His thoughts wandered back to Montana, back to the long train trip, back to the moment he put his lips to Lynndae's in the baggage car of the train. Maybe he was just meant to get Lynndae and the children safely to Pennsylvania, and that's all there was to it. It felt like there should be more when he turned everything over in his mind and remembered the feelings that had poured through him, but maybe that was the whole story. It hurt a bit, but a man got used to hurts or he died young. After all, she had never trusted or loved him enough to tell him the truth about herself—that she was Amish, that she was the Angel of Death's sister. A darkness settled deeper inside him as he turned this bitter pill over in his mouth. No, there was nothing between them now. It was over.

Zeph checked his watch. Two o'clock. His mutze dress coat was no longer proof against the cold. Nor did he want to appear as if he had disliked the worship service. He started back through the snow to the white, two-story house.

He had only been walking for a minute when he noticed a figure coming over the fields toward him. It moved lightly and smoothly. His heart quickened— Lynndae Raber.

She stopped and looked at him in her white prayer covering and black dress with its gray apron. The sun brushed against her cheek and lit up her blue eyes.

"I have come to ask on this Lord's Day," she said, "if you can forgive me and we can start again."

And she stretched a hand toward him.

Chapter Twenty-Seven

The feeling in him was to take the hand. He fought it. Dark feelings and sensations of light whirled around in his head and heart. She watched the struggle but did not drop her hand. It remained suspended in the cold afternoon air, fair, ungloved, lovely. Finally, Zeph realized he wanted her and wanted to forgive her more than anything else in the world. He stopped resisting and reached for her hand. In taking it, he drew her closer to himself.

She squinted up at him and at the sun that rode his shoulder. "Are you forgiving me?"

He nodded. "You had your reasons. It's not like I was your husband or lover. I'm sorry I've been so harsh."

"Thank you, Zephaniah." She touched his cheek with her free hand. "Everyone was asking about you."

"I found the worship service to be a powerful experience. I just had no appetite for talk or food afterwards. I needed to be alone with the Lord. So I came out here to pray and think myself clear. Listen, we haven't got a whole lot of time."

"Z, we have all the time we need. The Amish like things to happen at a slow pace."

"I'm leaving on a train in a few hours, Lynndae. I've got to go alone. You can't come with me. Though I do pray to God you'll let me take you with me in my heart."

Her stomach went cold. "Are you heading back west?"

"No."

"Then where are you going? And why are you going?"

"I can't tell you everything. But I need your prayers. If all goes well, there's no reason I won't see you in a day or two."

"A day or two?" She studied his eyes and every line in his face. "It's something to do with my brother, isn't it?"

"Yes, it is. Lynndae, I can't have him coming in here like he meant to do at Iron Springs and shoot everyone on sight and burn every house to the ground."

"He won't do that—"

"He will do that. He wants revenge for the men that were hung, and he wants revenge against the people who shunned him and his family for taking up arms for the Union. He will come here and set houses and haystacks ablaze. Unless I draw him off."

"You?"

"He doesn't want the kids anymore. I telegraphed his description to Colonel Austen and my brother. He knows the information will be right across the country and through all the Territories over the next couple of days. No, he wants the man who set him up at Alkali and had troopers ready to gun down his men or take them west to Cheyenne for a hanging. He wants me more than anyone else I guess he can think of right now. If I get him away from here, the people will be safe."

"Z, I don't want you to do this."

"If I don't, the Mary Beacheys and Aunt Rosas and Augustine Yoders are going to die."

"They have Sheriff Friesen."

"A good man, but he's not enough, nowhere near enough to take on a killer like Seraph Raber."

"And you are? Unarmed? Alone?"

"He wants me—Z. He'll come after me. And he knows where I'm going."

"But I don't."

"You can't. You might be crazy enough to follow me."

"I have things to say to my brother that have been left unsaid for too long."

"Yeah, well, that's exactly the way I feel about you and me."

"Pardon me?"

"It was no game for me on that train, Lynndae. I never had to act one moment since we became Mister and Missus Fremont and Conner Wyoming. For me, it was all for real."

One hand touched her chin and lifted her face toward his. "I love you, Charlotte. I love you, Conner. I love you, Lynndae. I forgive you. Just as Christ on the cross has forgiven me. I want you to be my wife. I want to marry you and take sunset rides in the Rocky Mountains. I want to fill you with God's happiness. I want to raise a family with you and have a house full of good words and good laughter and good loving.

"That's all I want." He paused.

She looked straight into his eyes. "Z, do you really mean all that you're saying?"

"I mean it. But you can't give me your answer yet. I know you've got your Amish ties to think about. Your home on the Sweet Blue. I guess, in a way, I've got no right to be saying these things to you when I might not be alive a day from now. But if I never said them today I might not ever get another chance. If things don't work out the way I've planned, well, I want you to know that this cowboy really did love you, Lynndae. I love you more than heaven and earth."

She touched his lips. "You're a crazy fool, Zephaniah T. Parker. Do you think I'm going to wait another day to tell you how I feel when I've been waiting so long to hear you say the words you said to me just now? Amish are slow, but we're not that slow. I'm not waiting another moment."

She threw her arms around him with a strength that made him gasp. "I love you, I love you, yes, yes, yes, a thousand times yes. Marry me, take me back to our Rocky Mountain sunsets, and let's ride until we find a stream where we can toss down our bedrolls and sleep under the stars and thank God for everything."

Her face was close to his, and he could see the light dancing in her blue eyes like sunlight sparkling on water. "I guess I'm kind of confused right now, Lynndae Raber."

"Why's that?"

"I'm not sure how to kiss in Amish."

She laughed. "Slow, and you take a long time at it."

Zeph did as he was told. He had stopped feeling the cold of the afternoon air ever since she'd walked out to meet him. Now he felt heat roar through his lips and head and heart. Once he'd started, he had no idea of stopping and neither did she. He tasted her sweetness and her love, and there was nothing like it on the face of God's good earth, nothing.

"Who needs breath?" he finally asked her. "That's why God gave us noses."

A long time later they walked back to the house. Many of the buggies had left. By common consent, they did not touch or hold hands, nor did they have any intention of telling anyone anything yet. A hundred feet from the house he stopped, and she turned to look at him.

"I've got to go to the station now," he told her.

She held his gaze and her eyes were violet. "You've given me the happiest hour in my life, Z. The hours to come will be the longest and the hardest."

"But you understand, don't you?"

"I do understand, my love. And I'm proud of you."

"You'll pray for me?"

"How can you ask that? I'll be praying without ceasing." Then she placed a hand on his heart. "Listen. Long ago, in Montana, I made a promise to my brother on his deathbed. The promise was that I'd never marry outside the family, never split up our ranch or join it to another's, never let a marriage contract threaten the land. Never."

A chill swept through him. "I'm no cousin of yours."

"I've fought with Ricky's words for years. Should I keep the promise, should I break the promise. Why do you think I never let you get close to me? Why do you think I never responded to your warmth and friendliness in a way a woman who adored you would? I made a promise to my dying brother."

He was confused. "Didn't you just say you'd marry me?"

"Yes, I did. And I meant it. But I need some time to make peace with Ricky. I need time for his spirit to understand. I want to go ahead and have a life with you. But please don't ask for the wedding ceremony to be tonight or before you get on that train. I need time to work this through with him and God."

Moses Beachey came around the corner of the house. He smiled. "There you are, Lynndae. We are just about to head home."

She dropped her hand from Zephaniah's heart but held his gaze. Neither she nor Zephaniah were smiling. "Yes. All right. I'm coming."

"Mister Parker," said Moses. "I have not seen you since the morning worship."

"I found it a very moving and very meaningful time, Mister Beachey. Please convey that to the others. I don't want my absence to be misunderstood. Those hours of worship and preaching meant more to me than many a church service has in a long time. I needed to be alone to pray and think over what I had heard taught and sung and prayed."

Moses looked surprised. "But you do not have the language."

"Today I understood the language of God's Spirit, Mister Beachey, and that was all that was needed."

Moses nodded and looked at Zeph for several moments, thinking. Then he said, "I sense God will bless you in the days to come."

"Why, thank you for that, Mister Beachey."

Zeph walked out to the buggy with the two of them and touched the brim of his piker hat. "Miss Raber, I wish you every goodness Christ has to offer those He loves."

She inclined her head. "The Lord be with you, Mister Parker, night and day, day and night."

Their eyes locked for a brief instant, and then Moses shook the reins. The buggy moved off down the rutted track of snow and mud. Zeph stood watching.

A hand came to rest on his shoulder. It was Augustine. "So it was a good day for you?"

"It was a holy day, Mister Yoder. Thank you for your sermon."

"What? You understood some of it?"

"Jesu Christi am kreuz."

Augustine had been working a toothpick around in his mouth. He stopped. "I saw you under the trees. I thought the morning had disappointed you."

"No. I was greatly blessed. I needed a place to pray."

Augustine grunted. "So, what did prayer help you to figure out?"

"I would be much obliged if you took me to the station after we've dropped off Missus Yoder and I've picked up my luggage."

Augustine looked hurt. "You are going back west so soon?"

"I'm not going west."

Augustine narrowed his eyes. His toothpick began to move around again. "All right. We should go."

At the Yoder house, Zeph said good-bye to Rebecca and picked up his carpetbag, bedroll, sheepskin jacket, and the saddlebags, which he had stacked just inside the front door. She remained at the roadside while the buggy rolled over the mud and water to Lancaster.

"I hope to be back Monday or Tuesday," said Zeph as Augustine hunched over the reins and stared straight ahead.

Augustine flicked the reins and sat back, appearing to relax a bit. "*Gute.* For Rebecca it is like having one of the boys back in the house again."

"Mister Yoder, I am grateful for your hospitality and the kindness of the Amish community. Thank you for allowing me to worship with you this morning. My few days here have been very pleasant and invigorating. Now I must tell you something you will not want to hear. Seraph Raber is still alive."

Augustine glanced at him in astonishment. "No, he was hanged with the other outlaw—"

"They didn't catch him. He's still at large. I am going to meet him."

"What are you saying?"

"He is angry with me for trapping his men at the train last week. I am going to meet him and talk. But that does not mean he will not send some of his gang here after the children or to seek revenge against the Amish for shunning his family. You must get everyone to a safe place."

Augustine considered this and worked at his toothpick. "He has no gang left."

"Sheriff Friesen thinks he has a few that weren't captured at the train. I believe he's right. They did not vanish across the Mexican border. They may come here."

"You want us to gather in one place?"

"Maybe not one place. It would be better if you used

three or four houses. All at the same location. That way Sheriff Friesen will be able to keep an eye on all of you. You will need to tell him where you are."

"When should we do this?"

"Now. Tonight. As soon as I've left on the train."

"There are animals to take care of."

"Let the men do that and then join their families in the houses."

"In the morning also there are chores—"

"The gang may come at daybreak."

"We have our farms and livelihood, Zephaniah."

Zeph reached over and gripped Augustine's broad shoulder as tightly as he could. Augustine looked at him in surprise.

"Mister Yoder. Seraph Raber has killed people past counting. He murdered the Kauffmans, Troyers, and Millers at Iron Springs. All that for no more reason than wanting to hurt and destroy. Now his men have been shot and hung. So he has a bigger reason. How much worse do you think he can be when real fury is in his heart?"

Lancaster was in sight. Matchbox quickened his pace. Augustine worked at his toothpick and flicked the reins to keep the horse moving smartly.

"You think Raber will meet you?"

"I'm counting on it."

"Where?"

"South. A place I swore I'd never go back to."

"He will want to kill you, Zephaniah."

"That's why I'm sure he'll be there."

"This is something for the rulers God has appointed over us. You do not carry a weapon."

"Not since the war. Another thing I swore I'd never go back to."

"What can you do against his hate but remain among us and pray?"

"If I remain among you and pray, he will come right to where I am and cut through all of Bird in Hand to get to me—every man, woman, and child."

"No, Zephaniah, this is not something you can do; this is for the law."

"Mister Yoder, I am the law." He brought the badge out of a pocket in his mutze and pinned it on his vest. "I swore an oath on the Bible I would protect people like you from people like him."

"We do not swear oaths."

"But I did."

They were at the station. Zeph stepped down and pulled his luggage out of the buggy.

"Thank you, Mister Yoder. God bless you."

Augustine sat in the buggy and looked down at him. His toothpick had stopped once again. "I will tell the pastors what you have said. We will move everyone before sunset."

"That sounds right."

"We will see you Monday or Tuesday."

"I look forward to it."

"Don't forget your coat." Augustine tossed him the overcoat he had left on the bench at the Zook house. "It is best to dress plain among the English."

Zeph smiled and touched the brim of his piker hat.

The sun was an orange and purple blaze only a little ways above the horizon. Zeph walked into the station holding his gear. A clerk nodded at him and said the train south for York and Gettysburg would be along in forty-five minutes. Zeph thanked him and went into a restroom, where he uncinched one of his saddlebags and drew out his father's Remington revolver. He turned it over in his hand. It was empty, and no stores were open on a Sunday where he could purchase ammunition. But maybe it would slow down Seraphim Raber just enough if he saw its butt sticking out of the waistband of Zeph's pants. Which is where he put it, the long barrel grazing the inside of his thigh. Then he walked back to his seat in the station, checked his watch, and waited.

If he had glanced east out of one of the windows, he would have seen that Augustine Yoder had not yet left. What he had done was climb out of his buggy and kneel by its side in the snow and ice and pray for God to spare the life of the young man from the Montana Territory. He stayed on his knees in the cold for at least ten minutes. Then he rose and got back into the buggy. Matchbox stamped his front left hoof, but Augustine did nothing. He waited until the train arrived and Zephaniah boarded. Not until the black smoke of the locomotive was a distant pillar in a sky rapidly losing its light did he flick the reins, turn the buggy around, and set Matchbox on a fast trot for the village of Bird in Hand.

Chapter Twenty-Eight

He came to the cemetery at night after he stepped off the train. Stars were white and sharp and pointed in the chill air of the February night. He walked through the tall brick arch of the cemetery's gatehouse. Sometime ago back in the Montana Territory, he had read in a paper about the project, how the Union dead had been moved from other locations on the vast battlefield and reburied here, state by state, over three thousand of them. The moon rose like a bonfire and lit the white headstones, row upon row, and they suddenly gleamed like candles. Zeph put down his gear and moved among them like a spirit.

He read the names. *I know none of them,* he thought, *yet I fought beside them all.* Up and down the rows he went. *We fell here and there like sacks of corn, all jumbled up with one another and with dead Rebs, yet now we lie in straight lines without a hint of confusion or messiness.* Zeph touched a headstone. He let the cold work its way up his fingers to his arm and shoulder and heart, so he could remember this place was about death, not order and decency.

No Confederate soldiers were buried here. They had been unearthed and removed to cities like Charleston and Savannah. He kept walking through the snow. At one point he stopped and began to look past the naked branches of trees to the fields and hills that were white as open bone. It looked different from those hot July days, yet it seemed right to him that he should be here in the season that allowed no growth or green or lushness.

He strained his eyes.

Where was the wheat field and Emmitsburg Road? The McPherson Woods? Devil's Den and Little Round Top? The peach orchard? The clamor of battle and the cries of dying men assailed him. Zeph groaned and put his hands to his face. Wednesday, Thursday, and Friday. The only respite at night when lamps floated over the carnage as men looked for missing friends and wounded comrades.

Why couldn't Raber let the war go? Hadn't once been enough? What could possess a man, any man, that he would want to relive the battles and the horrors, the death of companions, and the slaughter of boys no older than fourteen, fifteen, or sixteen, their young faces motionless against the tall hay and moist summer earth?

They had almost lost Jude in the orchard. And Matt at Cemetery Ridge—he had taken a ball in his leg and come close to bleeding out. Three, four, five times over the three-day battle Zeph was certain he himself was in a fix he could not get out of and that he was finished. It was a miracle he had survived. Yet here he was at the battlefield again, and it was not clear at all whether he would walk away unscathed a second time.

He had no idea what he would say to Raber or if Raber would even give him a chance to speak. Well, as long as the hope of getting his hands on Zeph drew Raber out of hiding and away from Bird in Hand, that's what mattered. He was not interested in dying only hours after the most beautiful woman in the world had said she would marry him, but he was even less interested in seeing her and twenty or thirty men, women, and children die along with him. Gettysburg was where he had to be. If only Raber felt the same way.

Zeph cleared away a patch of snow and laid his sheepskin coat down over the frozen soil. Then he untied his bedroll and spread it out, placing the Amish overcoat on top of it for extra warmth. Raber or no Raber, he was cold and tired. He removed his boots and climbed into his bedroll, tugging his father's pistol free and holding it in his hand under the blankets. Then he put his head on his bent arm and lay down to sleep among the Union dead.

When he woke, he could not remember having dreamed. The morning chill had woken him. The piker hat had fallen off, and the cold had gnawed at his skull. He sat up, found the hat, and crammed it back on his head. Then he put the revolver inside the top of his pants just near one of the suspenders. Tiny snowflakes melted against his forehead and cheeks. The first proper thought that came into his mind was a verse from Psalm 23: *Yea, though I walk through the valley of the shadow of death, I will fear no evil: for thou art with me.*

He heard a footstep in the snow. A heavy coil of

rope landed on his legs with a thump. At one end of it was a hangman's noose.

"Good morning, Captain Parker."

Zeph looked up. A tall man stood over him in a long sheepskin coat and Union slouch hat that reminded Zeph of Samuel's cavalry Stetson. Sideburns curled down both sides of his face.

The man smiled. "Looks like you could use more sleep. Well, I believe I can help you with that. Give me a few minutes, and I'll see what I can do to help you find that long, deep rest you seem to need."

The man looked out over the fields and slopes covered in white. "I was here the whole three days. You?"

"Wednesday, Thursday, Friday."

"Lee always felt he would have won if he'd had Stonewall the Presbyterian. What do you think?"

"I think if we'd had Grant the war would have been over on July fourth."

The man snorted. "Is that what you believe? The war ain't over for me yet." He looked around. "Thank you for being a man of your word. This will be an honorable exit, even if it is at the end of a rope. We spent an hour scoping this place before we came down. Been here for a day, truth be told, keeping an eye on things. No cavalry, no lawmen, just you and your piker hat. Get up and let me take a look at you."

Zeph climbed out of the bedroll in his bare feet. He and the man were about the same height. Just under the sideburn on the left side of the man's face Zeph could see the trace of a scar it covered up.

"Raber," he said.

"I am. Sideburns grow faster than a beard. You'll recall it was a Union general who started the fashion."

A man stood a few feet behind Raber. He held a pistol in his hand and wore a long woolen coat and slouch hat like Raber's, though it was quite a bit more battered and stained. Raber indicated him with a flick of his head. "Major Spunk Early of Illinois. I have two more of my boys watching the approach to the cemetery with sniper rifles. Billy and Wyatt are death at half a mile."

"There won't be anyone coming."

"After the railroad I take precautions." Raber glanced about. "Is there a tree you favor, Captain? I don't want to prolong this."

"I'd like to take the train back to Lancaster. It was slow coming down by horse. I have work to finish in a timely fashion."

"What work?"

"Oh, rape, pillage, and plunder, I reckon, the same as we did on our immortal march through Georgia. You killed a couple of my men, Parker. There's a debt to pay."

"Those Amish are more your people than they are mine."

Raber exploded with rage. "They are not my people! They haven't been my people since the day they threw us out of their church and killed my mother and my sister Mary! I hope they will take a picture of their bodies swaying in the breeze just as pretty as the one that graced the front page of the *Chicago Daily Tribune*!"

He glared at Zeph. "Get the rope, Major Early."

"Yes, sir."

"I know you came here on your own to draw me away from Bird in Hand, Captain, and you must understand I admire that. You're a man of substantial courage. I salute you. It did the Amish no good, they will die anyway, but no one can say you did not make the most valiant effort. So I offer you a final opportunity—is there a view you'd like to see one last time while you're swinging from your neck? Little Round Top? The peach orchard? McPherson Ridge?"

"Someone coming!" yelled a man by the cemetery gatehouse. Raber looked at Zeph. "Just one?"

Zeph shook his head. "I swear, I have no idea—"

"You swear, do you? On a stack of Bibles?"

"It's a woman! No one else! Just a woman in them funny clothes!"

Raber drew a revolver from a holster under his sheepskin coat. "Let's go take a look. After you, Captain. Put on your overcoat first. I wouldn't want you to catch your death and cheat the hangman."

Zeph threw on the cape overcoat and slogged through the snow to the gatehouse. Two men in blue were using it for cover. The woman was about a hundred yards away, head bent, doggedly marching through the snowdrifts. A white bonnet, a long cape coat, very plain.

"Amish," said Zeph.

"She your cavalry this time around?" Raber reholstered his pistol. "Didn't think you'd get a woman to do your fighting for you."

"I don't know who it is, Raber."

"Major General Raber."

"I didn't tell anyone where I was going."

"Well, then I guess a little sparrow told her."

As Zeph watched her come toward them, his heart began to sink. He had seen that very walk only the day before as he sat under a cluster of trees on the Zook farm and waited while a person made her way across the snow toward him. He hoped he was wrong. But the closer she got the more certain he became.

Oh, Lord.

As she approached the gatehouse, Raber swept off his slouch hat. "Good morning, ma'am. Where have you come from?"

"Good day to you, sir. I have just stepped off the early train from Philadelphia, Lancaster, and York."

"Perhaps you have come by to place some flowers on a brave soldier's grave, even at this chill winter hour?"

Her head was still down. She kept her eyes on the steps she took through the snow and ice. "Not entirely. Although I have come to find and speak with a brave soldier if one may be found."

Raber smiled broadly. "Look no further then, ma'am, you have found what you seek."

"Why, a brave man, sir?"

"None braver."

"And a soldier?"

"All my adult life and most, I may confess, of my youth."

"I am glad to hear it. Because then we may actually be able to hold a Christian conversation and you can explain to me where that brave soldier has been hiding these ten years. You have certainly not been him, and he has most certainly not been you."

A frown covered Raber's face. The woman lifted her face defiantly and let him stare at her in astonishment.

"Good morning, brother. It has been a long time since our good-bye in the summer of 1861, when you snuck out of the house to enlist in the Federal Army."

Raber looked as if he had been bayoneted. "Little L," he finally whispered.

"Seraphim." Her blue eyes crackled with fire.

"What are you doing here?"

"Well, since you have made up your mind to hang my husband, I thought I should at least come along to pay him my last respects. Isn't that what a good Northern woman would do, Major General Raber?"

"Him?"

"He declared his love for me only yesterday, brother, and I accepted. It was he who protected me and the children all the way from Iron Springs. Don't you know my name? Charlotte Spence, the woman you threatened to kill in the Montana Territory."

Raber stood rooted, taking it all in like a boxer standing stunned and still absorbing fresh blow after fresh blow.

Lynndae stepped closer to him so that they were only inches apart. "My brother. The boy I played with. The boy I read to. The boy with a dog named Sparkles and a raccoon named Jingles. The boy who became a man amidst the horror of war and led his men, Ricky said, like King Arthur leading the knights of the Round Table—brave, gallant, chivalrous, merciful to the defeated, courteous to the prisoner, noble, unconquerable, the very flower of manhood. What happened to that officer and gentleman, brother? Who stole his soul out of your body and replaced it with the spirit of a demon?"

She drew back and slapped him across the face with all the force she could muster, which, Zeph knew, was not inconsiderable. Blood sprayed from Raber's lips. Still he did not move or speak. His men looked alarmed, and Spunk Early took a step toward Lynndae.

"Child killer!" she spat. "Woman killer! Thief! Murderer! Is this how you honor our father? Would he be proud to stand up among the saints in heaven and have them look toward earth with him? 'There is my youngest boy, Angel. There is my pride and joy. There is my heart and soul, my righteous and holy Christian son?' Do you remember nothing of the prayers he prayed over you or the Bible stories he read to us by the fire at night? Have you forgotten your own baptism or the day you knelt before us all and said Jesus was your Savior and Lord?"

Raber continued to stare at her, his face white, blood trickling from the cut on his mouth.

"What about our mother? They say there are no tears in heaven—oh, Seraph, how could she have no tears when she looks down on the babies you have murdered and the mothers you have slaughtered and the fathers you have put in early graves—unarmed, unwilling to fight, innocent—yet you butchered them like cattle and hogs, no remorse, no conscience, not a drop of pity in your heart. Oh, stop it, stop it, put away your guns and ask God's forgiveness and give yourself up. End this bloodshed, and even if you find death in this world for your sins, you will find eternal life in the next in the presence of God. Angel, I beg you, don't go into eternity an unrepentant killer—"

"Shut up, you devil!" shouted Early.

Raber turned to him. "No, Spunk, don't—"

But Early's gun swung up on Lynndae, and his face was a mask of hate. "I'll close that mouth forever and thank the good Lord in heaven I did it!"

Chapter Twenty-Nine

Early was going to shoot. Lynndae didn't even notice him; she was still looking up at her brother's face, tears springing into her eyes, her gloved hands on his chest.

The snow was pouring down. Raber drew his revolver as he turned toward Early. But Early caught the movement of Raber's hand and flicked the barrel away from Lynndae. He fired and Raber went down. Lynndae cried out and knelt over her brother. Early shifted his pistol back to her.

Zeph pulled his father's gun free from under his vest and overcoat. He knew there were no bullets in it, but there was nothing else he could think of to do that might save the life of the woman he loved. He hoped Early would see him draw the revolver and swing his weapon away from Lynndae a second time. But Early ignored him, yelling as he aimed his pistol to fire. Zeph squeezed the trigger of the six-gun. A roar filled his ears, and the bullet caught Early high up on the shoulder of his gun hand. He flew backward into the snow, and his pistol went spinning into the air.

Dad loaded six chambers, Zeph thought in astonishment as the gun smoke burned his nostrils.

But now the two men at the gatehouse had decided
to shoot.

"I got him!" shouted one, aiming his rifle at Zeph.
"I got the woman!" shouted the other.

Zeph ran at Lynndae and drove her backward with
the weight of his body. Something like a hot knife went
through his clothing and into his arm. The force of the
blow spun him around and hurled him onto his back.
Snow stabbed at his neck and made him wince.

Lying in the snow, he thought he could hear cannon
fire, the shouts of men charging, the crack of muskets,
and the whiz of minié balls as they scorched the air
over his head. He glanced to his right and saw Raber
push himself up on an elbow, his revolver flashing.
All of earth and heaven seemed to be roaring, seemed
to be on fire.

Where was Lynndae?

He struggled to sit up. One of the men at the gatehouse was lying in the snow. He was not moving. The
other was wounded in his leg and leaning against the
brick of the arch and fumbling to reload his rifle. Finally he tossed it to one side in frustration and dug a
small pistol out of a coat pocket. Zeph watched him
aim it at Raber and fire twice. Then he pointed it at
Lynndae, whom Zeph saw was only a few feet to his
left. She was struggling to get to her feet, bracing both
hands against the snow and frozen earth. All he could
think to do was roll. In a sudden swift movement, he
came at her. Again, he felt heat cut through his clothing and sting his flesh. This time it was the back of his
leg. She fell as he smacked into her.

"Stay down!" he hissed.

There was still firing. Snow and dirt spat into his face from a near miss. A ricochet whined nearby. He lifted his head and saw that Spunk Early had climbed back to his feet and was trying to cock a revolver with his one good hand. Early ignored Raber and Zeph. He was clearly interested only in getting a shot off at Lynndae. Zeph squirmed through the snow and placed his body between Lynndae and the gunman. A bullet smacked into his boot, but he felt only a short stab of pain. Early fired again, and Zeph heard it go past his ear like a wasp.

Zeph glanced at Raber, who had pulled another pistol from a holster under his arm and was aiming it at Early. Zeph saw him shoot three times. Then an invisible hand seemed to lift Raber off the ground, shake him, and drop him into the snow. He fired a final shot in the direction of the gatehouse and then lay still, snowflakes covering his face and hands so rapidly that soon all his flesh had vanished.

The roaring stopped.

Zeph was on his stomach. One arm would not work, so he used the other to push himself up. The man at the gatehouse had slid to the ground with his pistol in his hand, and his eyes were closed. He could see Early sprawled on his face and the snowfall burying him as it came down thicker and thicker. Zeph tried to reach out to Lynndae with a hand that would not respond to his commands.

"Are you all right?" he asked.

She looked at him. "There's blood on your coat."

"No matter."

He turned and began to crawl toward Raber, propelling himself with his good arm and leg. When he reached Raber's side, he collapsed.

"That you, Captain?" asked Raber in a raspy voice.

"Sure is, General."

"How're we doing?"

"Lynndae's fine. You saved her life."

"I saved her life? I recall as you were the one who pulled a pistol out from under all those Amish clothes and stopped Early from shooting her."

"The same way you stopped those two sharpshooters at the gate from killing all of us."

"It's strange the things a man will do for family, Captain."

"I know it. Are you hurt bad, General?"

"No, no. Early always was a poor shot, and Billy and Wyatt were only reliable if the target was a thousand yards away."

"Never thought I'd have to come all the way back here to Pennsylvania just to get a proper wound."

Raber laughed and coughed up blood. "Ain't it the truth? The ways of God are past finding out."

Lynndae was at their sides. "Oh, no, oh, no no no, my Angel, my Z," and she began tearing at the hem of her dress to make bandages even though both Zeph and her brother protested. She moved swiftly to staunch the flow of blood from her brother's two leg wounds, and then she bandaged Zeph's shoulder, leg, and foot. Turning back to her brother, she whipped the bonnet off her head and pressed it down over a large wound in his chest. But he firmly placed a hand on her arm to stop her from doing anything more.

"What I really need, Little L," he whispered, "is someone to pray with me."

"There are three or four other wounds—"

"Let it be. I've only got time enough for one good confession and one good prayer, so pay attention to my words and not my wounds. The holes in my spirit are bigger, and you need to tend to them first."

He reached up a hand to her face. "I haven't felt shame in more years than I can count, but I felt shame today when you spoke to me like you did. It's as if your talk snapped me out of some kind of spell. Seems I haven't been able to see straight or think straight for a long time. I fooled myself into believing God approved of what I did because He never meant for the war to end until all slavery was vanquished. Now here I'm about to meet Him, and my hands are smothered in blood. I can't undo the wickedness I've done. I can't stop what my men are doing right now at Bird in Hand. All I got to offer up in place of all my murders is saving your life today. That's a big thing to my way of thinking, but big as it is, I know it's not near enough. Little L, can God forgive me?"

She kissed the hand against her face. "Oh, Angel, if you are sorry for all the killing you've done—"

"I believe I am."

"—and you know you've committed terrible sins—"

"That I am certain of."

"—and you repent of all the crimes and blood-shed—"

"I do, I do repent. When you spoke to me, I wished again and again I had laid down my sword at Appomattox."

"—then the Lord has promised to forgive you and cleanse you. Jesus has died for your sins on the cross. You know that, Angel, you know that."

His whisper grew harder and harder to hear. "Sure, I know that. I just needed to hear it again coming from Little L."

He turned his head. His eyes were almost colorless. "Captain?"

"Yes, sir," responded Zeph.

"Pleasure to soldier with you, Captain."

"Pleasure to soldier with you, General."

"They say we're all of us Americans now, Captain. What do you say?"

"I believe that's so, General."

"Then you take good care of my sister and you raise a good American family, y'all hear?"

"I will do that."

"Got any names picked out? For the first one?"

"How's Angel suit?"

Raber smiled and closed his eyes. "Works for a boy or a girl." He drew a deep breath. "Lord Jesus, have mercy on my soul, have mercy on me a sinner." His breath came back out in one long sigh, and he was gone.

As Lynndae cradled her brother's body in her arms and wept, Zeph looked on and felt a great sadness well up inside him. Here was the man they had been fleeing, who had sworn to kill the children, who had left a trail of innocent blood behind him all of his adult life, and now Zeph wished, like Jesus with Lazarus, he could bring the man back to life. He groped for one of Raber's hands with his good hand and held it tightly. A verse passed through his mind: *And the publican, standing afar off, would not lift up so much as his eyes unto heaven, but smote upon his breast, saying, God be merciful to me a sinner. I tell you, this man went down to his house justified.* Zeph felt a pounding in the frozen earth he was lying upon.

Horses. There was nothing he could do if this meant more of Raber's men. He could scarcely move. Turning his eyes to the left, he saw three men ride up through the snowstorm and dismount, each of them bristling with guns. They stood over Lynndae and him, and he could tell one of them was surveying all the bodies and trying to figure out what had just happened. "What in the world? Did you folks have a need to refight the battle or something? Can either of you explain to me just what went on here?"

Zeph looked up into a face with a chin beard and a mustache that drooped around the corners of the mouth. "Who are you?"

The man pulled aside the flap of his winter jacket so Zeph could see the star. "Sheriff Buck Levy. Gettysburg township. Adams County. Elected, genuine and official. These are my full-time deputies, Mister Flint Mitton and Mister Josh Nikkels. Our citizens heard the gunfire and became concerned that Lee and Meade were going at it again."

"These men are the last remnants of the gang that Seraph Raber led."

"Is that a fact?"

"I am Zephaniah Parker, Deputy US Marshal. This woman has just lost her brother. He died defending us."

The man stooped over Zeph and flipped both the front of the overcoat and the mutze open and found the badge on his vest. He grunted. "Kind of a funny occupation for an Amish man like yourself, isn't it, Mister Parker?"

"I'm not Amish, though this woman is. It was simply a way for me to travel unnoticed in these parts."

"That so? Maybe you can explain to me how your travels brought you to my battlefield cemetery and involved the deaths of four men."

"That's a long story, Sheriff, and I'm not sure I'm up to telling it right about now."

"Maybe not. But I need some kind of explanation to take back to the town fathers."

For the first time, Lynndae pulled herself away from her brother, laying him gently back on the ground, and turned her grief-stricken face toward the sheriff and his deputies. Her features were so distraught and broken that all three men took off their hats and bared their heads to the snowstorm.

"Sorry for your loss, ma'am," mumbled Mitton. Snow had already made his red beard white.

Lynndae stood to her feet, snowflakes catching in her pinned-up hair and eyelashes. "Deputy Parker came from Lancaster to Gettysburg to apprehend these members of the Raber Gang, Sheriff. They were supposed to talk, but the gang members chose to ambush him. I traveled down on my own to see if I could be of assistance. I can assure you, the first shots were fired by the gang members and my brother, and Mister Parker returned fire only in self-defense."

"I'm sure that's the case, ma'am, but we do have to check the facts. Flint, Josh, make sure all those bodies are armed and that their weapons have been discharged."

The deputies placed their hats back on their heads and made their way through the blowing snow to the bodies by the gatehouse and to Early. Sheriff Levy returned his hat to its rightful place as well.

"Sorry, ma'am, I realize this is a bad time to question someone who has lost a loved one under such circumstances—"

"Do your duty, Sheriff," replied Lynndae coolly.

"But what brought your brother into this fracas? You make no mention of him being a lawman or being deputized by Mister Parker here. Was he your escort?"

"No, I escorted myself from Lancaster."

"Very well."

"My brother was in the company of the gang itself, Sheriff, but it was his express desire that he disentangle himself from his involvement with notorious criminals and take that opportunity to live an honest Christian life."

"That so?"

"His dying wish, Sheriff."

"And the point of your traveling from Lancaster County to Adams County unescorted was perhaps to coax your brother to initiate this disengagement from the remnants of the Raber Gang?"

"Quite so."

Levy scratched the scrap of beard on his chin. "Maybe this will all come together for me if I start with your name."

"I am Lynndae Raber."

Sheriff Levy stared at her through the shower of snowflakes. "And your brother?"

"Seraphim Raber."

"The Angel of Death himself."

"So the newspapers called him. At the end, if anything, he was an Angel of Life."

Levy shook his head. "This has to be some story you're spinning me, Miss Raber, and I'm not exactly sure why, unless it's meant to cover up the murder of these four men—"

"This is no cover-up, Sheriff, I assure you."

"Seraphim Raber and his whole crew were hung by the neck until dead in Cheyenne, Wyoming, a week ago. You must've missed that little bit of news before you concocted this yarn of yours."

Even through the snowfall Zeph could see Lynndae's eyes turning to blue ice. "I haven't missed a thing, Sheriff, and you'll look the fool when you speak with Sheriff Friesen of Lancaster County or Colonel Austen, a federal marshal out of Cheyenne, or the commander of K Company, Second Cavalry, at Fort Laramie. I think you'd be better off taking my story to heart just as I've told it to you."

Levy nodded. "I'm sure you think so. But the way I look at it, I'd be better off getting you and Mister Parker down to my humble accommodations in town while I send out a few telegrams to the sort of people who can offer me a yea or nay on all this stuff you've been selling. If you're on the money, I'll know about it in a few hours and, by way of apology and redress, I'll buy you steak and eggs for dinner. If you're not on the money, well, you'll have to settle for whatever's on the jailhouse menu for Monday night."

"All of them had guns," said Flint Mitton, walking back through the snow, "and all of them have been fired recently."

"Well, that's something," grunted Levy.

"Something else. Josh noticed the two guys who had

rifles, well, they're for sniping, Federal Army issue, the sort of guns Raber's men'd be toting."

The sheriff wasn't impressed. "Maybe."

"They're Sharps rifles and they fire a big cartridge. We pull a bullet like that out of one of these two, it'll go a long way to making their case for self-defense."

"Hm."

Zeph saw the sheriff look down at him, but it seemed like Levy was at the end of a long hallway with white walls, a hallway that was getting longer all the time. It came off as comical to him when the sheriff's face took on a sudden look of concern.

"How many times was he hit?" he heard the sheriff ask Lynndae.

"I bandaged three bullet wounds."

"Three! Flint, you get this man over your saddle and in to Doc Murphy as fast as you possibly can. We're standing here yapping and the man's losing blood. Look at him—you can see how much blood he's lost. Josh!"

"Yes, sir."

"Help Flint get him over the saddle. Then you go in and get a wagon for these others. You understand? Pick up the horses they staked out yonder. And that bedroll and those saddlebags."

"Yes, Sheriff."

"Come on now, get him up, get him up. This ain't no Presbyterian picnic, get moving."

Far away Zeph heard Lynndae asking, "Is he going to be all right?"

The last thing he could make out was the sheriff's response: "I hope so, ma'am, I hope so, but I had no idea he was losing so much blood."

Chapter Thirty

The feeling came over her that she liked least of almost any feeling she had to deal with, including grief—the feeling of being utterly and unbearably alone.

She was sitting in a straight-backed wooden chair outside one of the rooms in the doctor's three-story brick home, which also served as his surgery. Across from her was Flint Mitton, an apologetic look on his face, left by Sheriff Buck Levy as her guard. The fingers of her hands kept knotting and unknotting. Behind the closed door, Doctor Clyde Murphy was working feverishly, along with his wife and an assistant, to save Zephaniah Parker's life.

Lynndae could not stop condemning herself for putting Zephaniah in this situation. She had been so stricken by her brother's death she had sat crying and rocking him when she knew with every fiber of her being his body was only an empty shell and that his spirit had left to be with God. Yet while she wept over Angel's body, the man who was to be her husband was bleeding to death in the snow. How could be she be so thoughtless?

To make matters worse, she had then proceeded to argue with Sheriff Levy, too proud to back down, too headstrong to wait for the truth to come out later, stubborn to the point of stupidity. Ten minutes or more lost for no good purpose other than to satisfy her own vanity, wanting the final word, while Z continued to lie cold and bloodless, snow covering his body like a winding sheet.

Oh, Lord, forgive me. Spare his life, oh, please, spare his life.

Do not pile sorrow upon sorrow.

She wiped away tears quickly, not wanting the deputy's sympathy.

The door opened and the doctor came out of the room, his shirt red with blood. His young face was lined with sweat and worry. He was holding a pan in which several small objects rolled back and forth.

"The bullets are out," he said.

She was not interested in the bullets, instead looking at him with fear and hope for news about Zephaniah, so he handed the pan to the deputy. Flint Mitton fished out the larger of the three bullets and looked at it closely.

"That's no 44," he said. "It's like Josh was talking. One of the men at the gatehouse got him with a Sharps."

"That came out of his shoulder," the doctor told him.

Flint eyed the other two bullets. "That woman's brother was using a 45 and these are both 44 caliber. Had to come from their pistols and not his. The evidence is backing her story more and more."

"Where is Sheriff Levy?"

"Getting Lance to take care of the bodies. Sending

and receiving telegrams." He flicked open the lid on his watch. "It's half past five. He'll be by shortly, I expect."

The doctor turned to Lynndae. "Miss Raber. We are doing the best we can. His blood loss is acute." She felt a sting in her heart as Zephaniah's bleeding was brought up before her yet again. "We may be able to save his arm and leg; it's too early to tell."

"Oh, please try, doctor."

"There's massive tissue damage to his left shoulder and the back of his right leg. I may have to remove the limbs to avoid gangrene. I'm going to get some coffee, and then I'll take another look. My wife and Tommy are cleaning his wounds as thoroughly as they can right now. Deputy, we need more ice to keep the fever down."

Flint Mitton looked confused. "I have to watch Miss Raber here."

"I need the ice. Either you go or she goes or you both go together."

"For heaven's sake," cried Lynndae, "where do you think I am going to run to when the man I hope to marry is fighting for his life in the next room?"

She saw Mitton glance at her empty ring finger and said, "He only asked for my hand yesterday afternoon. There hasn't been time for any of the formalities yet. In fact," she added, her eyes meeting those of Mitton and the doctor, "you are the first people to know. We never told a single soul, everything happened too fast."

The doctor nodded. "Congratulations. Flint, I'll be responsible for Miss Raber. Go get that ice. We have a wedding to look forward to."

The deputy got to his feet and placed his hat on his head. "Sorry, ma'am, I'll go get the ice."

Suddenly there was a knocking on the front door. The doctor shook his head. "I need to coffee up and get back into the surgery. Miss Raber, could you see who that is?" He vanished into another room.

Lynndae stood up, and she and Flint Mitton walked down a hall to the front of the house. Before they could get there, the door burst open and Aunt Rosa rushed in, followed by Augustine Yoder. Behind them were Sheriff Rusty Friesen from Lancaster County and Sheriff Buck Levy, who looked like he'd been kicked in the stomach by a horse.

Lynndae and Aunt Rosa flew into each other's arms.

"Oh, Rosa," cried Lynndae, a little girl again, allowing the tears to streak down her face, "he's in the surgery. He covered my body with his. Oh, Rosa, he took the bullets meant for me." She sobbed in the older woman's arms.

"Hush, hush," Aunt Rosa soothed, patting Lynndae on the back, "everything will be all right. That is why the train brought us. We are in this place to pray with you; God will hear."

"He took the bullets meant for me."

"Hush, hush." But tears sprang into Aunt Rosa's eyes as well.

Augustine Yoder was pale, watching the two women hold one another with large liquid eyes. Snow melted on his hat and overcoat.

Flint Mitton looked at Sheriff Levy. "I was just going out to get some ice. The man has a bad fever."

Levy nodded. "Go quick and get it." As Flint stepped around him, Levy took him by the arm. "I got telegrams back from everyone and their horse. Seems I heard from every person in the country but President Grant. Her story checks out. This is Sheriff Friesen from Lancaster. He confirms those were the last of Raber's gang."

Lynndae broke away from Aunt Rosa. "What happened? Was anyone hurt?"

Mitton hung back to hear the news, but Levy fixed him with a glare. "We caused enough heartache for these folk, Mister Mitton, what with doubting their story and leaving a good man to bleed out in the snow." He looked down at the floor, disgusted with himself, and muttered, "While we argued for points like some Harvard debating society playing to the gallery." He glanced up at Mitton and growled, "Get."

Flint rushed out the door into the swirl of snow.

Sheriff Levy removed his hat. "Miss Raber, I apologize for the way I acted early this morning. I confess I was bewildered by the scene we came upon, but it would have been better to have helped you out first and asked for your story later. I hope I will be able to make amends to you and Mister Parker over the course of the next few days. It's my prayer he will pull through as fine as sunshine."

"Thank you, Sheriff," Lynndae responded. "I admit I had my back up pretty quickly, and I don't think that helped you any. I appreciate your concern, and I believe both Mister Parker and I will be able to take you up on your offer of assistance before the week is out."

The doctor came down the hall with a fresh shirt on. "Miss Raber, I am going back in now. Are you folk in some need of medical assistance?"

"We are here for Miss Raber," explained Augustine Yoder.

"If you need extra chairs, there are plenty in the front room."

Aunt Rosa spoke up. "We will pray for you, doctor."

He smiled. "Why, thank you, ma'am, I am grateful. My father is a Presbyterian minister. He would be glad to hear you offering me that sort of divine aid."

As he strode off, Lynndae turned back to Sheriff Friesen. "What happened at Bird in Hand this morning?"

Friesen removed his hat and knocked snow off with the flat of his hand. "Miss Raber, is there some place we can sit? The doctor mentioned the front room."

"Right through here," said Sheriff Levy, making a gesture with his hat.

They went down a short hall into a room that looked out over the street. A fire was in danger of going out in the fireplace. Levy began to stir the ashes with a poker and place on more logs. Aunt Rosa found a coatrack and began to peel a wet, black shawl from her shoulders.

"Come, Father," she said to Augustine, "don't drip over the doctor's nice wood floor."

The men removed their coats and hung them on the rack while the fire burst into life. When everyone was seated, Lynndae leaned forward anxiously.

"Please tell me what happened," she asked again.

"Lynndae," said Aunt Rosa, "you must first tell us how Zephaniah is doing. I am sorry, but we cannot go on and talk about anything else until we know that."

Sheriff Friesen nodded. "I agree."

Lynndae passed a hand over her eyes as the tears welled up again. "The doctor doesn't know. It's too soon to tell. There was so much blood loss. So much damage from the bullets to his arm and leg. They may have to amputate."

She broke down. Aunt Rosa left her seat to put her arms around Lynndae. "Yes, yes, that is why God told us to come here. We are going to pray. We do not leave until everything is all right, even if it takes days or weeks. You will not be alone."

"That is so," agreed Augustine.

"My brother defended us," blurted Lynndae.

Surprise crossed Friesen's face. "What?"

"At first he was going to—going to hang Z. But when I walked down from the station, one of his men took exception to the things I said to Angel—things about his life of crime, his murders, his sins—and this man pulled his gun out to shoot—to shoot me, but Angel tried to stop him. And he shot Angel. Then the man aimed at me again, and Z had his father's old revolver. He fired and the bullet knocked the man down. Then the other men from the gang, there were two of them, tried to shoot Z and me, but Angel began to fire at them from where he had fallen to the ground when he had been shot. Oh, there was so much gunfire back and forth—it was like a small war. That was when Z covered me with his body to keep the bullets from hitting me. Angel stopped the men of his gang from killing us, but he died from his wounds—not before he confessed his sins and repented and asked God's forgiveness in the name of, the name of Jesus—"

Lynndae could not continue. Aunt Rosa held her and shook her head at the others. "Hush now, that is enough, your Angel is with God. That is enough, do not speak anymore. We have heard you." Then she prayed, "Lord, spare young Zephaniah's life. You know him.

He was Your chosen instrument to bring Lynndae and her brother together again and to help save Lynndae from death and her brother from damnation. Restore him to us, dear Lord; give him many more years among those he loves. Guide the doctor's hands; bless his healing work done in Your holy name. Oh, You who healed in Galilee, will You not heal this night in Pennsylvania as well?"

No one spoke for several minutes, then Lynndae lifted her head from Rosa's shoulder, her eyes crimson and swollen. "I must know. Did Z's sacrifice change anything? Did it matter that he brought my brother here, my brother and his three gunmen? Did it make any difference at all, or was it just wasted effort? Sheriff? Augustine?"

Augustine and Sheriff Friesen glanced at one another. Augustine nodded at the sheriff to go ahead. Friesen leaned forward in his houndstooth suit, brown Stetson in his hands. "Miss Raber," he said earnestly, "I'll give it to you straight.

"If Raber, your brother, if he had come up to Bird in Hand leading the men that were left of his crew, and he was the Raber who shot, murdered, and maimed, not the one who repented, there wouldn't be a stick of Bird in Hand left standing tonight. They'd have burned every house in the village to the ground. They'd have killed us all."

Chapter Thirty-One

Lynndae sat holding Aunt Rosa's hands.

"I had found out from Mister Simpson at the station that Zephaniah's ticket was for Gettysburg," she told her. "I left well before six. There was a train from Philadelphia that was heading to York with connections to Gettysburg and Baltimore."

Friesen nodded and looked at Aunt Rosa. "It was still dark, and one of my deputies escorted the buggy Mister Beachey used to take Lynndae to Lancaster."

Lynndae protested. "I did not want Mister Beachey to take me. I was afraid of putting him in harm's way."

"But he insisted," said the sheriff.

Lynndae smiled weakly. "Many of the good people of Bird in Hand insist on things."

"My deputy saw him back safely."

"You had men all around the depot." Lynndae leaned forward. "Surely you stopped some of the gang members when they came off the train?"

"I'm afraid not, Miss Raber."

"Why on earth not?"

"For the simple reason that none of the gang members came by rail. They came by horseback."

"Oh—"

"Now that doesn't mean they didn't take a train part of the way. For all I know, they might have been lying in wait a day or two in advance. Two came up the road from the east, from White Horse and Intercourse, and two came up from the south, by way of Paradise and Gordonville. Not a shot was fired. So we didn't know there was trouble until a house went up. I saw the flames and hurried some of my deputies in that direction.

"This would be about a half hour after your train left for York, Miss Raber. I had five men at the station, and they might just as well have not existed for all the good they were to us. I couldn't spare a rider to get a message to them. So I hoped they'd see that a house was burning and make for Bird in Hand to help us. But they never did. They were afraid to leave the station unguarded in case more outlaws came in by rail. I honestly can't fault them for that line of thinking. That's why I had them there, armed to the teeth. In retrospect, I should have given them more leeway in making decisions to stay or go. The mistake rests on my shoulders. I was convinced Raber's men would come in by means of the Lancaster train."

Lynndae felt her anxiety grow as the story unfolded. "What houses were burned?"

"The Ottos' went first. That was done by the two that rode up from Paradise. We were no sooner trying to deal with the Otto place when another house went up in flames from the direction of Intercourse. I had seven men in all—there would have been twelve of us if the boys from the station had ridden in—but I'd already sent a couple south to the Otto house. So I ordered three toward the new fire, and that left just me and Joseph Sheridan to keep an eye on the two homes that had fifty people crammed into them. You can imagine how difficult it would have been for us if all the families had remained on their own properties. Your Zephaniah's idea to get the people into one spot saved lives."

Lynndae felt a surge of pride, but the feeling was quickly lost as she remembered the danger Zeph was in. Aunt Rosa squeezed her hands. A part of Lynndae did not want to hear the rest of what Sheriff Friesen had to say for fear the story of the raid on Bird in Hand might get worse. But she steeled herself and said, "Please continue, Sheriff."

"The Bender house was burning east of us, the Otto's to the south. Joe and I stayed put. If there'd been another bunch of Raber's men coming at us from the west or north, say those three at Gettysburg and Raber himself, we'd have been done for. There was nothing more we could do. My men ran off the two that had set the houses on fire to the east, but my two boys that had gone south were ambushed."

Fear hit Lynndae again like an icy gust of wind. "Are they all right?"

"One died in the saddle. That's how we found him. The other was wounded. But he fought back from behind a clump of trees. He dropped one before the other rode off and left him." Friesen stopped and his eyes took on a haunted look. "I thank God your brother wasn't there to lead them, Miss Raber, and I thank God that was as far as they got." Lynndae waited.

"I don't know what idea they had in their heads. That no one would be armed? That they'd only be fighting Amish and the Amish wouldn't fight back? Maybe they didn't have a plan, I don't know. But they sure didn't take us as seriously as they should have, that's for sure.

"They had expected there to be people in the houses, of course, and some of them out doing their morning chores. But by the second house, they could see they were torching empty homes, and with the sun up now, they could see there wasn't a soul for miles, not on the roadways, not in the lanes, not in the fields. There weren't even any animals out; we had them all locked up tight in the barns.

"So they didn't know what to do. It seemed as if they didn't even have a leader of any kind. They hit on racing from property to property, hootin' and hollerin', shooting their guns in the air, hoping, I guess, to stir something up, bring the people out of hiding, frighten some animals out into the open. I don't know exactly what they had a notion of doing. But they paid my deputies and me no mind. Maybe it was just that they only saw me and Joe sitting there on our horses and thought that was it. Maybe they could see we were too far away to do them any damage. I don't know. They kept on riding back and forth like madmen, doing their yell as if Sheridan and I didn't exist. As if doing the devil's business was all the protection they needed.

"Well, in the clear light of day, galloping or not, they made fine targets, and although they might have felt they were out of range, Joe and I jerked our Sharps carbines clear of their scabbards and proceeded to target the three of them, one after another. The Sharps can send a bullet a long way, Miss Raber, even the shorter barreled carbine's a shooter, and Joe's been handy with one since the war. Long story short, two of them went down, and the last one lit out towards Intercourse and ran into my three deputies, who saw him coming. They all cheated the hangman, Miss Raber, but none of them will hurt innocent people anymore."

"No one else was hurt except for your deputy?"

"I had another man wounded, but he's doing fine."

"The man who died, was he a family man?"

"No ma'am, Frank wasn't the marrying kind."

"What about the houses?"

"We get spring and a spell of dry weather, I believe the Amish will be having a couple of house raisings."

Augustine nodded. "Everyone has a place to go. Each family is moving in with another family. It will be all right. They did not touch the barns. The children are safe. We thank God. The killing we do not like, but we are grateful for the lives spared."

Lynndae's head was in turmoil. "I wish there never were such men."

"So do I, Miss Raber," said Sheriff Friesen quietly.

"I wish we did not have to fight. I wish there were no fighting at all."

"I understand. But you know as well as any of us here that this is a sinful world where people are permitted to follow the devil's ways if they choose. In matters like this, Miss Raber, lawful authorities must bear the sword and protect the righteous and the innocent. That is what we have done. My deputies and I were, as the Bible puts it, ministers of God, revengers 'to execute wrath upon him that doeth evil.'"

"I know, Sheriff, I know," sighed Lynndae, "and I'm

thankful you saved the lives of so many good people. I suppose I am just wishing it was a different sort of world altogether, one where the swords are beaten into plowshares and the spears into pruning hooks."

"Ma'am, the Lord hasten that day when it is true for the entire earth."

"Amen," said Rosa and Augustine together.

Sheriff Levy had left the room to look for his deputy, Flint Mitton. He walked back into the room with Mitton in tow. It looked like the deputy had something to say.

"Go ahead," urged Levy.

Flint held his hat in his hands, turning it over and over in his nervousness. Again, Lynndae endured the cold blast of fright. She got to her feet.

"What is it, Deputy?" she asked, a bit more harshly than she intended.

"Ma'am," Flint finally got out, "I came back with the ice about ten minutes after I left. Had to get some from the hotel a few blocks over. Doc Murphy asked me to help in his surgery. He gave me an apron to wear over my duds. He was—he was going to use his saw."

Lynndae felt her legs grow weak, but she was determined to remain standing and take the news Flint had come to give her. "Thank you, Deputy. May I ask why the doctor isn't out here giving me this news himself?"

"Why, I guess he would be, except that he's still busy in there, what with your husband, that is, your fiancé—"

Lynndae had a momentary image of Zeph with an empty sleeve pinned to his shoulder and a wooden leg replacing the one of flesh the doctor had cut free of the bone. Blood roared through her head. She felt Aunt Rosa's firm arm steady her. "I understand, Deputy. There's no need to speak any further—"

"—sitting up all of a sudden and talking, well, pretty much of a whisper, I would say, but I could understand him. He was asking about you and asking for water in about the same breath, said the ice felt good against his skin. Well, Doc wanted you to come right quick while he's awake so's you might say hello—"

Lynndae ran from the room and down the halls to the surgery door. Behind her she heard Aunt Rosa say, "Oh, thank You, Lord." When she entered the surgery, the assistant, Tommy, was holding up Zeph's head with one hand and a glass of water for him with the other.

"Z!" she called to him, unable to contain her excitement.

The doctor and his wife were washing their hands at a corner sink. She looked up and smiled at Lynndae. "I am so happy for you, dear. We are so pleased he pulled through."

The doctor nodded. "He is a strong man, Miss Raber. He wanted to come back. If you work in medicine long enough, they tell me, you see everything. Well, his recovery is nothing less than a miracle, and I haven't seen anything like it. This man was definitely meant to live."

"And his arm and—"

Murphy shook his head. "The way he's coming around, I wouldn't touch them."

She rushed to Zeph's side and said to Tommy, "Thank you so much; I'll do that," and put her arm under Zeph's head and shoulders.

He smiled up at her weakly. "Hey, I know that face," he whispered.

"You gave us quite a fright," she said softly.

"I wanted to stay awake and help you handle that ornery sheriff with the rug on his chin—"

"Shh. He turned out all right. Got his deputy to fetch you extra ice."

"Well, good for him. Good to know a leopard can change its spots." He held her gaze. "I am sorry about Seraphim, honey. He saved us."

It was all too much—Zeph dying and now sitting there alive, her brother fighting to protect her and now silent in a pine box. Tears filled Lynndae's eyes. "He is coming home with us to Lancaster County. The mortician has taken good care of him, and Seraphim will be ready anytime you are able to board a train."

"That won't be for a few days, I'm afraid," the doctor spoke up, "but as soon as he is able to handle a short train journey, he'll be all yours."

"I need to lie back," said Zeph, so Lynndae gently put his head down. "Now stay with me, Conner, and hold my hand awhile."

"You like that name, don't you?"

"I like all your names."

She kissed him on the forehead. "Choose whichever you like."

"Can I make one up? Like a nickname?"

"That would be sweet. My brothers always had nicknames for me."

"What about your oath to Ricky?"

"My big brother is looking down from heaven and saying to me, 'Lynndae Sharlayne, what the heck is the matter with you? That promise was never meant to keep you from the arms of a good man like Zephaniah Truett Parker. Have you abandoned all the common sense I raised you with in the Montana Territory?'"

Zeph tried to laugh and choked out, "Is that a fact?"

"It is."

"In that case, if there's a cloth handy, and your brother has cottoned to me, I'd be grateful if you would bathe my forehead with cool water."

"Of course."

Lynndae reached across a small table next to the bed. She noticed that a tall, broad figure had filled the doorway.

It was Augustine. His large eyes seemed to sparkle in the lamplight from the surgery. A toothpick was going back and forth in his mouth.

"So, so, so," he said, "I have come here in the hopes that someone will introduce me to the bride and groom. The doctor made a point of telling me that Gettysburg has a pair and that they are both dressed very plain."

Chapter Thirty-Two

Four days later Zeph hobbled on board a train bound for York, Lancaster, and Philadelphia, one arm in a sling, a leg in a leather brace, and a wooden crutch to lean on. Augustine helped him to his seat while Aunt Rosa stayed by Lynndae, who was making sure the pine coffin that contained her brother's body was securely stored in a freight car. Sheriff Friesen had returned to Lancaster the morning after his visit to Gettysburg, but Sheriff Levy promised to provide an escort in his stead. He saw Aunt Rosa and Lynndae safely to their seats with the men before settling back with his 1873 Winchester and a dime western with the title *The Blazing Guns of Texas, A Kid Comanche Adventure*.

At the Yoder house, Levy enjoyed three bowls of sauerkraut soup and several thick slices of smoked ham before heading back on an evening train with connections to Gettysburg and Baltimore. As he left the house to ride to the station in the Yoder's buggy, he touched the brim of his hat to Lynndae.

"I hope you will fare well," he said, "and that your

marriage will be everything a young woman like you dreams of."

"Thank you, Sheriff. I'm grateful for all your help."

Zeph was placed back in his old room at the Yoders', and Lynndae was set up in the room Katie had grown up in. For the first few days, Zeph slept off and on around the clock as his body worked to heal itself. Rebecca and Lynndae cooked pots of chicken and beef broth and fussed at him to eat bowl after bowl from morning to night. Lynndae often sat at his bedside and read James Fenimore Cooper out loud. "Where'd you get those books?" he asked. "Were they in your three months' of luggage along with everything else?"

She smiled. "If I'd known when I packed that I was traveling with the Yale professor of early American literature, yes, I would have found room for some of the Leatherstocking Tales. As it is, now that I know you better than I did in Iron Springs, way back when I thought you were just a cowboy with sweet eyes—"

"I am a cowboy."

"—I took the liberty of borrowing these from the Lancaster Library. Do you know who started the library in Lancaster? William Penn's daughter-in-law, Juliana. She gave books and money. They showed me her Bible while I was there. Two volumes. I opened the first one, and where do you suppose I found myself?"

"The wedding feast in Cana?" Lynndae gently hit him with the book in her hand, *The Last of the Mohicans.* "You think you're funny? I was in the Old Testament. The book of Ruth."

"So?"

"Oh, for heaven's sake, I thought you were a literary scholar."

"I am. Jude's the Bible scholar."

"Don't you remember Ruth's words? 'Intreat me not to leave thee, or to return from following after thee: for whither thou goest, I will go; and where thou lodgest, I will lodge: thy people shall be my people, and thy God my God.'"

"I have heard that."

"I want to use those words in my wedding vows."

"I've no objection, as long as the words are spoken to me."

Lynndae found the Cooper book useful for another swat at Zeph's healthy arm.

The Tuesday after their return to Bird in Hand, while Zeph slept, Lynndae sat in a rocker in a corner of his bedroom writing a letter with a steel nib pen and using a lap desk to support the sheets of paper, ink bottle, and blotter. That morning she had joined the other Amish families who had gone into town for the funeral of the deputy who had been slain defending their families and homes. After lunch back at the Yoder house, Augustine had lingered, and now he tapped gently on the open bedroom door. She glanced up and smiled. He gestured with his hand for her to come with him.

He sat at the kitchen table with a cup of coffee and asked quietly if she wanted one. She shook her head and took a seat. Rebecca had cleared up the lunch dishes with Lynndae and then disappeared upstairs. Augustine ran his fingers through his beard.

"He is getting stronger."

"Oh, yes. We are going to start taking walks this evening. It is warming up now that we are into March."

"It may rain. Keep his hat on."

"Of course."

Augustine played with his coffee cup. Looking into it as if he might find the words he needed there, he cleared his throat and said, "So, we have met, the pastors, and we talked about your brother and his burial."

Lynndae sat up. "Please don't trouble yourselves. I accept the restrictions for Amish burial that my brother's life have placed upon you. Mother was buried in the Lancaster cemetery. I intend to place him beside her as soon as Z is strong enough to join me at a graveside ceremony."

Augustine held up a hand. "We wish him to be buried here at Bird in Hand at our cemetery in the fields. It is also our wish to have your mother's remains returned so that she may rest beside him. Your brother Ricky's as well, if you would permit it."

Lynndae was astounded. She sat and stared at Augustine, who looked up at her and nodded. "Yes, it is not just the wish of the pastors and the bishop, but of all the people. We believe Seraphim truly repented, just as you described it, and that he is with the Lord. The excommunication has already been lifted from your family. Let mother and son be at peace, together again with their friends and neighbors."

Lynndae looked down at the tabletop. "I do not know what to say. I had not expected such an offer of—of—"

"My son David works well with wood, it flows in his hands. He will complete the coffin for Seraphim tonight, your mother's tomorrow. We will lay them by your grandparents. I would pray at the graveside, if that is agreeable to you."

"Oh, yes, oh, yes, Mister Yoder." Her eyes glistened. "I had not expected this."

"It is not simply our will, Miss Raber. It is the Lord's will." He stood. "Trouble yourself with nothing. I will go into town now and make the necessary arrangements for your mother's remains. Seraphim we will lay out in our *doed-kammer*, our dead room. The men will dig the necessary graves."

"When shall we do the funeral, Mister Yoder?"

"Is Friday too soon?"

"No, no, that is just fine."

"You will tell me, who you would like for pallbearers? We will need four carrying each of the coffins."

"Yes. I will make a list for you."

"Gute."

On Thursday evening men and women, dressed completely in black, walked or drove their buggies to the Yoder home. They sat on chairs and benches that had been brought to the house for that purpose. People spoke in hushed voices. Lynndae went from family to family, thanking them, asking if they wished to see the body of her brother.

Zeph sat in a chair in the dead room by Seraphim's body. Seraphim was in a coffin with a lid that had been left open to show the upper part of his body. When people arrived in the room in the company of Lynndae, Zeph nodded gently and pulled a sheet back from Seraphim's face and chest. His blond hair had been neatly combed and his body was dressed in a white shirt, vest, and pants. No cosmetics had been applied by the mortician, that was the Amish way, but Lynndae had requested the long sideburns be shaved off. The long scar was visible on her brother's pale cheeks, but Zeph considered that it did not look so long or so vicious as he had imagined. It seemed to him to be as thin as a faint line from a graphite pencil.

None of the neighbors had seen Seraphim since he was thirteen. Many wept silently. One older man gripped Seraphim's hand and said something in Pennsylvania Dutch, his tears dropping onto the corpse's cheeks, so that Seraphim, too, appeared to be crying.

The next morning began with a silver rain that washed over the fields and the remnants of snow. A number of women arrived early to help Rebecca cook food. They tried to chase Lynndae away, but she insisted on working alongside them. It was better for her to do something with her hands than to just sit and wait, she told them.

The carved coffins containing Lynndae's mother and her brother were placed side by side in the dead room. Augustine stood in the room and began to preach while the others sat without. He did not speak about Seraphim or his mother. He spoke about Christ, about His resurrection from the dead, about the resurrection of those who believe. "'Verily, verily, I say unto you,'" he quoted from the Gospel of John, without looking at his Bible, "'He that heareth my word, and believeth on him that sent me, hath everlasting life, and shall not come into condemnation; but is passed from death unto life.'"

It was all in the Amish tongue, but Zeph found himself experiencing a touch from God much the same way he had experienced it during the worship service almost two weeks before. So many things had happened since then. Yet God remained the same God. Zeph closed his eyes while Augustine preached.

Jesu Christi am kreuz.

A long line of buggies followed the two horses pull-ing the hearse from the Yoder house to the cemetery out in an open field. At first the rain rushed against them. But once they had reached the graveyard and were hitching their horses and buggies in the large fenced area set aside for that purpose, the clouds be-came silent, simply sitting over them, brooding and watching.

The four pastors carried Seraphim's coffin from the hearse—Augustine, Moses Beachey, David Lapp, and Malachi Kauffman. Lynndae's mother was lifted out by Bishop Schrock, Augustine's sons Daniel and David, and Aunt Rosa's husband, Aaron Christner. The graves were open. The men lowered the coffins with ropes. Augustine prayed. Then he opened the thick book, the *Ausbund*, and read a hymn while the people listened, heads bowed, and the pastors and bishop took shovels and covered the coffins with earth.

The headstones were the same as all the others in the cemetery, curved stone two feet high, set to face the gate, beautifully hewn. The name Angel Raber was on one and his mother's name, Sarah Raber, on the other. Once the graves were filled, Augustine invited every-one to recite the Lord's Prayer silently in their hearts.

Zeph waited, leaning on his crutch. People began walking back to their carriages, and a scattered line of buggies formed on the road, most of them heading back to the Yoder home for the meal. It was clear Lynndae wanted to be alone for a few minutes, so Augustine and Rebecca and Zeph held back. Zeph moved awkwardly among the rows, seeing the same names over and over again—Smucker, Zook, Glick, Riehl, Esh.

He gazed out over the broad fields of brown grass. They worked the land, and then they rested in the land. From the earth they were created, and to the earth they returned. There was a goodness to the pattern. So many men's bones were never gathered into one place and never remembered, left scattered among stones at a mining site or washed by cold waters to oblivion in some lonely mountain place.

"Hello," said Lynndae, taking hold of his good arm.

"How are you?" he asked, looking at her face.

"It is a sad day and a glorious day at the same time. My emotions are up and down and all over the place."

"But you are glad your mother and brother are resting here together?"

"Oh, very glad. I never imagined it. I never prayed for it. It seemed to me to be an impossibility beyond even the grace of God."

Zeph looked around him. "All the farms seem to fit into the folds of the land as if a master joiner and carpenter had put everything together. Even the graveyard seems right, though I've never been one for such places."

"There is a peace here."

"In this one. I've seen plenty of bone orchards that made a man restless, as if none of the spirits were content."

"I suppose some of the boot hills are like that."

"All of the boot hills are like that. The graves of the murdered and the hanged."

"I thank God that Angel can lie here and not in some hole in a prison yard or out under a desert sun that has no pity."

"Yes. This is a good land. It hasn't got mountains

and panthers, but a man could settle in and do some solid living here all the same."

"Is that something you're thinking about, Z?"

"I like it here. But I miss the Sweet Blue and the Two Back Valley."

"Well, me, too. I see the good in both Lancaster and Iron Springs. But sometimes missing the Sweet Blue can be almost painful."

"I know it."

Zeph continued to lurch on his crutch among the headstones. "Yoder, Mullet, Beachey. Anyone that's anyone is buried here."

"You, too, someday, if you live right."

"Well, you'll pardon me if I don't seem eager to rush on in, Miss Raber."

"I'd like to have you above ground a few more years myself, mister."

Zeph stopped. "I didn't know King was an Amish name."

"One of the finest and oldest."

"So William King, the attorney in Iron Springs, is Amish?"

"Well, I don't think he follows the *Ordnung*. But he has Amish roots. There's Kings he's related to in Lancaster County."

"Would they have known your family? Would they have known your father and brothers and Seraph?"

"The Kings? Of course. Some of them were very close to us before the excommunication."

Zeph had a flash of memory. *Billy King had the two pack horses that had been unloaded of their baggage. He raised his hat. "God bless you, folks, God bless you,*

Cody, Cheyenne. I pray time flows like a fast river for us all while we're apart."

"Seen enough, Z?" asked Lynndae. "The Yoders have the carriage ready."

"Yes, I'm done."

Zeph began to move toward the Yoders with Lynndae beside him.

"How's your leg holding up?" she asked.

"Give me a month, Miss Raber. I'll be right as rain, and you'll have a brand new name."

She laughed. "I've had so many, Zeph. I don't mind another."

Chapter Thirty-Three

Swore I would never come back here. Now I find it almost impossible to leave.

Lynndae sat by the train window, looking down at the families she had just finished saying good-bye to. Zeph was doing a final round of handshakes, including Samuel, tall and thin, and giving Bess a kiss on the cheek. Sheriff Friesen stood among the Amish in his three-piece houndstooth suit. His wife, May, was by his side, and she was no elf either, easily past his shoulder in height. Long brown hair framed her weather-tanned face. Her strong hand took Zeph's. Lynndae could just make out their voices through the open window.

May said, "My husband will be bored now. Nothing but horses, milk cows, and me."

Zeph laughed. "Time for that second honeymoon. Make sure you join us in the Rockies this summer for our wedding. That'll liven things up."

Then he was being embraced by Augustine and his toothpick. Lynndae could hear Augustine perfectly.

"We are sorry to see you go, Zephaniah. You two belong with our people."

"Pray for us," Zeph responded. "You never know what will happen."

The whistle blew twice. Zeph climbed on board and sat opposite Lynndae. The train began to move. Aunt Rosa, Bess, and Samuel waved. Lynndae and Zeph waved back. They rolled west for Harrisburg.

The fields were dark with plowing. Horses and cattle walked back and forth on the green pastureland. Swallows swooped and darted in the blue sky. Amish children in a wagon bouncing along a country lane looked at the string of passenger cars solemnly. A man stood waiting for the train to pass with a long fishing pole in his hand and a wicker creel slung over his shoulder.

"Heaven," murmured Lynndae. She felt empty inside.

Zeph nodded. "It's fine country."

She turned on him. "Is that all you can say? It's a fine country?"

"And it's full of good people."

"If you think it's fine country and full of good people then why are we leaving?"

"Well, where we're heading is fine country and full of good people, too."

"Things could have changed in our absence."

"Not that much."

"Yes, that much."

"I need a nap. That farewell supper kept us up late, and before we knew it the sun was shining in the windows and the train was heading in from Philadelphia." He settled back in his seat, pulled his hat down over his eyes, and folded his arms over his chest.

Another sentence was on the tip of Lynndae's tongue, but she held it back.

Fine, she thought, *sleep then. It must be awfully nice to just trim your wick like that and shut everything down.*

The train carried them through western Pennsylvania, Ohio, and Indiana before they made a change in Chicago.

Then they rattled and swayed on tracks that ran through Illinois and Iowa to Nebraska. In Omaha they booked passage on the Union Pacific to Ogden and had a three-hour stopover. Zeph touched the brim of his piker hat and vanished up a nearby street. "Meet you back here in an hour."

Lynndae protested. "Don't you want me to go with you?"

"No."

What was the matter with Z? In an unsettled mood, Lynndae wandered among the shops close to the station, but very little caught her fancy. She was in between two worlds and felt adrift. If only the train for Utah could have departed sooner. Restless, she paced back and forth on the station platform until she saw a man approaching with Zeph's carpetbag in his hand.

"Hello," the man greeted her.

Lynndae stared. "Zephaniah Truett Parker. What have you done with yourself?"

"Shave and a haircut, two bits. My Levi Strauss pants, my boots, my hat. We've crossed the Missouri, my lady. We're back in the West."

"I hardly recognized you."

"Weather's warm, so I don't need a coat."

"You haven't looked like this since—"

Zeph interrupted. "Now, this is a chit for a dress shop just two blocks thataway—"

But she wasn't listening. "—Eagle Rock or Ogden, I can't remember which—"

Zeph carried on. "—you can't miss it on account of how fancy the sign is. A Missus Willoughby will be happy to fit you into—"

So did Lynndae. "—but I would have to say it's a very pleasant change to have you less plain."

Zeph finished up. "—a brand new dress right off the rack, no waiting around for two or three weeks."

Lynndae finally listened to him, startled. "A new dress? Two or three weeks? Oh, Z, the train will be leaving in less than two hours."

"No, I said it *won't* take two or three weeks. They have ready-to-wear dresses hanging up in the store. They just need to open some parts out and pin some others in, at least that's what they told me."

Lynndae repeated Zeph's words. "You went into a dress shop—"

"I did."

"—to buy a dress for me—"

"Well, I wasn't planning on trying any on for myself."

"—when you don't even know my size or what colors I like or—"

"That's why I'm giving you this chit. The dress is paid for.

You just have to pick it out."

Lynndae looked at him in astonishment. Zeph touched the brim of his brown Stetson and placed the slip of paper in her hand.

"Two blocks north, right up that street, and then a

left. You can't miss it. Missus Willoughby. Can't miss
her either. The kind of woman who fills a chair. Very
sweet."

"Why, Z—"

He grinned. "It's your engagement present. I haven't
seen you in anything but blacks and grays for more
than three months. Time to let you be the wildflower
you are again."

"What if they don't have anything suitable?"

"Get going, palomino. You're burning daylight."

Suddenly realizing what Zeph had done, and that
she might not have time to pick a dress out and have
it fitted in time, Lynndae began walking rapidly up
the street.

Zeph watched her slender dark figure until she
paused and turned left, and then he went to buy himself an Omaha paper and relax with it.

After he bought the paper and had read a few stories,
Zeph remembered that he had gone past the telegraph
station earlier. He was debating whether or not to send
word to Matt that they were on their way back. If the
accomplice was still around, he would be sure to read
it. Zeph wasn't interested in being ambushed on the
stage between Virginia City and Iron Springs. Mull-
ing it over, Zeph wandered into the office. After waiting behind two other men dressed in fancy suits and
then asking for a pad, out of the blue the idea popped
into his head to ask for telegrams for Parker. The clerk
looked and said there hadn't been any.

"But I do remember the name Parker," he said. "I
sent a real odd telegram out to a Parker in Pennsylvania a couple of months back."

Zeph was hunched over the pad with a yellow pencil. His ears pricked up at the clerk's words. "Pennsylvania?"

The older man chuckled. "Sure, hard to forget. It was a passage from the Bible, from Revelation. I never get anything like that."

Zeph stared at the clerk. "Do you happen to recall who sent the telegram?"

"That's just it, how could you forget someone that went by the handle Angel?" The clerk busied himself with some papers. "Not that it was his real name, anyhow."

Zeph put down the pencil. "What was his real name?"

"Oh, he never told me. Just laughed about it. But then he went and left his business card in that basket there. All sorts of travelers leave one behind. People go through them now and then. You never know. Someone might get in touch about a business deal. Let me see."

The man came out from behind the counter and went to the large wicker basket that sat on a table by the door. There were hundreds of cards, but he was not deterred. Zeph came and stood beside him. After several minutes of riffling through the pile, the clerk exclaimed, "Here we go!" and held a card up to the sunlight from the window.

"WILLIAM S. KING, ATTORNEY AT LAW," he read out loud, "IRON SPRINGS, THE MONTANA TERRITORY, WILLS, ESTATES, PROPERTY. That's the one. You see, he puts a crown on the top of the card, his business logo, I guess, and that makes the card easy to pick out. Good head on his shoulders. Nice man. Gave me a tip, too."

"And you're sure this is the man who sent the Bible passage to Pennsylvania? And signed the telegram 'Angel'?"

"T'weren't no other."

"And he sent it to Parker?"

"He did. That Parker kin to you?"

"Yes. He is."

Zeph walked in a daze back to the counter and the telegram pad. He kept thinking of how many times Lynndae and the kids had almost been killed because the Raber Gang always knew where they were going and what they were doing. He saw King grinning and laughing through his thick beard, and the heat rose in him and the blood pounded through his head. Raber's gunmen had been deadly, but they had been strangers to him. King was a friend, someone he'd dined with and sat next to in church. The sense of betrayal was strong. Zeph felt he could knock down an Omaha brick wall with his bare hands.

He wrote out two telegrams. The one to Matt had Zeph and Lynndae coming into Iron Springs at least a week later than he knew the train and stage would get them there. The other he sent to Colonel Austen at Cheyenne.

He was seated with his paper at the depot when he spied a tall, slender beauty in a dress of white, yellow, and blue silks almost floating down the street toward him. Men were stopping to turn and look at her, even men who were escorting other women. Zeph folded the newspaper and got to his feet. Not for the first time he marveled that this lady should be excited about marrying him.

Thanks for the train ride, Lord, he prayed. *It wasn't*

an easy trip, but I'm grateful for how things turned out, and I wouldn't change a thing.

The sunlight danced all over Lynndae's hair and dress as if it were delighted to have a woman of her caliber back in Nebraska again. Zeph could not take his eyes off her. As she drew up to him, her face reddened.

"Must you stare so?"

He whipped off his Stetson. "I'm afraid I must, ma'am."

"Oh, don't act so foolish. You'd think it was the first time we've met."

"I've never seen you wear a dress like this in Iron Springs."

"Well, I never had the time to make one. And, I was never engaged before."

"I was looking forward to seeing the Rocky Mountains shining in the distance, and now I don't care. I got more of God's beauty in my eyes right now than any man has a right to see"—he put his arms around her—"and more of God's beauty in my arms than I'll ever know what to do with. I'll need time, a lot of time. Why, I expect I'll need a lifetime, and even then I won't get around to doing all the things a man would enjoy doing with a woman of such fine features and well-bred disposition."

She rested her head on his shoulder. "I'm sure it's the dress."

"No, ma'am."

"Or the heat."

"I put you in sackcloth, your beauty'd still shine. For the past three months it sparkled, even in your Amish wardrobe. It's just that this dress and these silks bring out all the different colors in your soul, and they show who you truly are: a woman of vast splendor, of awe-inspiring magnificence, and of exquisite loveliness. I really don't know what to do with you."

"Why don't you just kiss me then and stop talking? It's embarrassing."

So he did, while trains shunted in and out of the station and whistles blew and people streamed past and locomotives hissed steam and covered them in white mist. Finally, she pulled back.

"Was that a Western kiss?" She smiled.

"You only get those on this side of the Missouri."

"Well, then, I think I'd like to stay on this side of the Missouri for a little while."

"I am glad to hear it."

The train pulled them through Nebraska all that day and into the night. At sunset on the following evening, it began to slow as it came into Cheyenne. Lynndae was patting her cheeks with a napkin dipped in cool water and passing it over her throat when she noticed a man in black standing alone on the platform. People rushed back and forth all about him, but he was like a rock in the middle of turbulent waters, fixed and immovable. It so happened their car came to a stop right in front of him. Lynndae leaned forward out of her seat.

"Why, Z," she exclaimed in astonishment, "that's Colonel Austen."

"So it is."

"Well, come, come, we must get off the train and greet him before we miss this opportunity. There's so many things he will want to know."

"You'll have plenty of time for that."

"What are you talking about? We don't have plenty of time at all. The train may only be here twenty or thirty minutes." She rose out of her seat and gathered her skirts about her, but Zeph placed a hand gently on her arm.

"Lynndae."

"What are you doing? Aren't you coming out with me?"

"There's no reason to do so."

"What do you mean?"

"He'll be coming on board presently, and he will be with us, by rail and stage, all the way to Virginia City and Iron Springs."

"What?"

Lynndae stared at Zeph and then out the window at Colonel Austen. He had noticed her once she stood up, and he met her gaze with a smile. Then he gently touched the brim of his black Stetson. Coming aboard, he greeted her with a kiss on the cheek and shook Zeph's hand.

"Thank you for the watch, Colonel," Zeph said.

"Thank you for the memory," Austen replied. "A strong one and an important one."

He settled in his seat and turned to Lynndae. "I have exciting news I think you would like to hear. My family is alive."

"What? Oh, Colonel Austen, is it true?" She threw her arms around him and gave him a hug. "Where are they?"

"The Territory of Arizona and the Territory of New Mexico. I received the report from the US Army, which received the information from a trader by the name of Wilkes. They are indeed attached to an Apache tribe. I intend to go down there and get them back."

"Colonel, I thank God. You must feel like setting out this very day to bring them back."

"I do. But there is unfinished business in Iron Springs. And I intend to help Zephaniah and Matt set that to rights before I make my way into the American southwest."

"Oh." Lynndae glanced at Zeph. "Will that take long?"

Austen shook his head. "I believe, Miss Raber, that it will be short and sweet."

Chapter Thirty-Four

William King used a key to open the door of his law office. A passerby on horseback called his name, and he waved and went inside. It was early, only seven, and his secretary would not arrive for another hour. He checked her desk to make sure everything was in order. Then he went back to his own room and opened that door with another key.

Everything seemed to be as it should. His filing cabinet was in place and all the drawers intact. He moved around, going through his usual Monday morning ritual. His desk was neat and tidy, just the way he had left it on Saturday. He opened a drawer and brought out a short-barreled Colt 45 revolver that was deep blue in color. Turning it over in his hand, he admired the workmanship of the pistol then glanced at the cylinder to make sure it was loaded with six cartridges. He almost looked away before his eyes told him the gun was empty.

King frowned. The Colt was always loaded. All sorts of riffraff went in and out of his office on a daily basis. He had to be sure he could protect himself as well as defend his female secretary from assault. He reached back in the drawer for the box of 45 cartridges he stored with the pistol. It was gone.

King's heart began to thump rapidly in his chest. His office might look undisturbed, but someone had obviously been in here. The Colt was always loaded and the box of extra cartridges was always in the same drawer with it. He remembered looking at the gun and the box Saturday afternoon. Something was wrong.

"Looking for these, Billy?"

King whirled around and met the flat stare of Matt Parker. He was holding six bullets in one palm and a box of cartridges in another. King began to sputter.

"Matt—what—why did you take the bullets? Who let you in here? Give them back—"

"Well, Billy, I normally don't give a loaded gun to a wanted felon."

"What are you talking about? Have you gone loco? I'm an attorney."

"So I'll just keep ahold of these a little bit longer, until Judge Skinner decides what to do with them. And with you."

"You're out of your mind. I don't know what's going on, but I'm not about to subject myself to some sort of frontier justice you've cooked up with that old fool Skinner. What is this all about?"

Zeph stepped into the room. "It's all about two Amish kids named Troyer and Kauffman, Mister King, and a man named Seraphim Raber who was hunting them down because they'd seen his face."

"Zephaniah! I didn't know you were... Welcome back. I was expecting you next week."

"Expecting me? Why, I didn't tell anyone but Matt when I was coming in."

"And I didn't tell anyone else," said Matt.

King looked from one of them to the other. Suddenly he yelled and charged at them like a bull. King was a big man and he bowled them over. Then he raced down the short hall for the back door of his office, threw the latch, and jumped outside, prepared to jump on the horse he'd hitched there and ride it bareback out of town. Colonel Austen stood between him and his mount.

"Mister King?" he said. "I am Marshal Michael James Austen out of Cheyenne, Wyoming. I am afraid I must detain you, sir. The charge is, I believe, accessory to murder and accessory to attempted murder."

King stared at the man in black. He glanced to his right.

Matt's deputy, Luke, came out from behind a nearby building, and he was holding a coach gun, a shotgun with two short barrels that was often used by Wells Fargo guards. He pointed the weapon at King. "I'm guessing you know what this can do at close range, sir."

Matt and Zeph rushed out the back door and then stopped. Austen strolled up to King and put his face right up to the lawyer's. "Mister King, you endangered friends of mine. You endangered women. You endangered children. I have little use or patience for men such as yourself, masquerading as a champion of justice by day and doing the deeds of darkness by night."

He pulled out handcuffs and locked them on King's wrists. "I arrest you as an accessory to the crimes of the Angel Raber Gang. You will be accompanying me to the jailhouse in Cheyenne."

"You can't do that!" protested King. "You're way out of your jurisdiction. I'm staying right here."

"For this transfer, I have a court order meant to prevent two possibilities from occurring. One, that your two brothers attempt to release you from jail in Iron Springs unlawfully."

"Leave them out of this. They don't know anything about Raber. They were never part of any of it."

"And two, that a lynch mob might storm the jail and hang you by the neck for assisting one of the most notorious and blackhearted gangs that has ever crossed the Missouri River."

King went silent as he turned this bit of information over in his mind. Zeph walked up to him.

"Was it the money, Billy?" he asked. "Tell me there was a better reason than the money."

King could not meet Zeph's gaze. He dropped his eyes and studied the dirt under his feet. "How'd you know? Did Raber tell you before he died?"

"The clerk in Omaha recalled you sending the Revelation telegram to me in Pennsylvania."

King snorted. "You'll never be able to prove I did anything else. You don't have any of the telegrams I sent Raber."

"The clerk here talked."

"No."

"Yes. He did. He'll say whatever he needs to say to save his own neck."

King looked up and pleaded with Zeph. "You have to understand, the Rabers and Kings go back a long way."

"I know that. The Kings in Lancaster County told

me all about it. What I don't understand is how some old friendship turned you into a criminal."

"The Kings owed the Rabers. It's as simple as that. When my great-grandfather left the church seventy or eighty years ago, it was some of the Rabers who made sure my family had land and livestock and a roof over their heads. They saved us. When a telegram came for me demanding I return the favor, I couldn't refuse. I am a man of honor."

"Of honor!" Zeph was seething. "Helping Raber's cutthroats is your idea of honor? Helping them track us down so they could murder those children? Shoot Miss Spence? Shoot me?"

"It—it's complicated."

"No, it's simple. It wasn't just returning the favor. It was filling your pockets with gold, too, wasn't it? Your practice was a lot more lucrative in the gold rush days. This was a good opportunity to make up for the shortfall."

"I didn't take much."

"The clerk says you paid him ten thousand in gold. I'm thinking if you paid him ten thousand, well, you must have kept a whole lot more to yourself to live on."

King looked down again. "Just remember, my brothers didn't do anything."

"I guess we'll ask them for ourselves. Meanwhile, you've got a stage to catch."

They took him down the lane behind the buildings where the stage was waiting. It was empty. The driver saw King and spat down into the dust.

"We told the passengers there'd be another stage along in a few hours," he said.

"Thank you kindly," responded Austen, pushing King into the stage ahead of him.

Zeph stood at the window. "Charlotte Spence has another name, Mister King, and it's Raber."

King looked at him in astonishment.

"She talked with Raber before he died. A brother and sister heart-to-heart. I thought you might like to know he apologized for all the wrong he'd done. I guess the better word is repented. You recall that word from church, don't you, Mister King?"

"I don't believe it," King growled. "A killer like Raber wouldn't turn unless there was money in it."

"Well, there was God in it, I know that for sure, and love for his sister, too. He had to fight off what was left of his gang in order to save her life. They took exception to her preaching. It shamed him, but didn't sit well with the others."

"Raber would never turn, I tell you."

"But I was there that day, Mister King, and I tell you he did. I guess you've got the same choice to make as he did, heaven or hell. I hope you make it before the trapdoor springs."

"They'll never hang me."

"Well, now, don't you bet your life on it."

Zeph stepped back and looked up at the driver. The man nodded and flicked his reins.

"Hey yup, hey yup," he cried.

Austen leaned forward in his seat and touched the brim of his black hat. "My regards to Miss Raber. I will see her again at your wedding. It will be an honor to stand for you, Captain Parker."

"And an honor for me as well, Colonel Austen."

* * *

The stage rolled down the street, kicking up dust. Then it was gone. Matt was at Zeph's side.

"You still a deputy marshal?" he asked.

"I don't know."

"Well, let me know when you do know."

They walked back down Main Street with Luke. Their horses were tied off in front of the law office. All three of them swung up into their saddles.

"Luke and I need to pay a visit to the Kings," Matt said.

"You think there'll be trouble?" asked Zeph.

"I think they'll be as surprised and upset as we were. Don't know how they'll feel about it down the road."

"Will they hang Billy in Cheyenne, brother?"

"With his connections to the Raber Gang? I believe Wyoming might."

"None of this feels good to me. We were all best friends."

"I know it. Jude said something about it the other night, quoting the Bible, of course. Zechariah, I think it was: 'These are the wounds I received at the house of my friends.'"

Luke and Matt rode off, and Zeph turned his horse toward the trail north that led to the Sweet Blue. The town was waking up and wagons went rattling past. People crossed the street in front of him and behind him. He didn't pay any of the hustle and bustle any mind. He was thinking about how much a life can change not only from one year to the next, or one month, but one moment to another. And how you hardly ever saw it coming.

Chapter Thirty-Five

It was the middle of June and warm as a wood fire, Lynndae thought. She coaxed Daybreak along the ridge and looked at the mountains that seemed purple in the distance. A few still had snow, but most had sent it down by way of creeks and streams and rivers to water the valleys and pastures below. "Heartland," she murmured.

"Why, hello," came a cheerful voice.

Lynndae smiled as Zeph cantered toward her on Cricket from across a small stretch of meadow. He touched his hat brim.

"Hey there, palomino."

"I'm never sure if you're talking to my horse or you're talking to me," she teased.

"Maybe both."

"Which is it?"

"I think you know."

"Hm." She glanced around her at the vista that surrounded them on all sides. "I had my head down most of the way up watching her steps. My goodness, this land gets more beautiful as each day goes by."

"This land. And some of its inhabitants." Lynndae smiled over at him. "Always gallant."

"And always truthful."

Lynndae looked at her man, at the tan the western sun had already fashioned over the skin of his face and hands, at his brown eyes and hair, at his smile and rugged good looks, at the kindness as well as the strength that was there, and felt an enormous surge of gratitude toward God for the entire journey from the Montana Territory to Pennsylvania and back again. It had been fraught with danger, but the outcome had been blessing upon blessing. She needed to know if he felt the same way.

"Z?"

"Hm?" He was looking at the sun as it moved closer to the tops of the peaks.

"Was it worth it?"

"Was what worth it?"

"The trip, the journey, the whole thing we've been part of since February."

"What sort of crazy question is that?"

"My crazy question. If you had to, would you do it all over again?"

Zeph moved his eyes from the sun to her. "Let me see. You're in new denim pants, Levi Strauss, like mine, and a long-sleeved cotton shirt in pale white. You've got a black-and-white pattern bandana around your neck and your silver earrings are catching the sunlight. Your golden hair is pulled back and braided and dropping like a glittering rope down your back. Your Stetson is as new as your pants and black as midnight, and it ties together all your handsome whites and darks and golds at one beautiful summit."

Lynndae felt the heat in her face. "Z, please stop. A woman can only take so much of your chivalry in one go."

"Then there are your eyes. A man could live forever just gazing into that blue."

"Are you finished playing Romeo?" she asked. "When are you going to answer my question?"

Zeph smiled. "Was it worth it? Bess and Samuel are alive, so is the village of Bird in Hand, so are you. Your brother's in heaven, which he had small chance of getting into before, and the Raber Gang isn't around to terrorize innocent folk anymore. Colonel Austen and I met up again. I made a hundred new friends in Lancaster County, Pennsylvania. We discovered Black Jack gum."

She waited for him to continue. "So, is that it?"

"Our ranch'll be the biggest spread in southeastern Montana once we buy that little strip that separates Two Back from Sweet Blue. Your brother Ricky'd like that."

Lynndae felt an impatience stirring inside her. But she was also pretty sure he was toying with her. He laughed.

"What's so funny?" she demanded.

"You are. Because you think I'm done."

"Aren't you?"

"Not by a long shot."

He brought Cricket closer so that they were only inches from each other. "We finally got our sunset ride," he said.

"We did."

"Took a long time to get here."

"It seems that way, doesn't it?"

"Trains and stages and walking on foot. Might have saved ourselves the trouble by just staying put."

He reached out a hand and ran it gently down one side of her face. "Except if I hadn't made the journey, I wouldn't have gotten to know you half so well. Wouldn't have seen all your courage and tenderness and charm. Truth is, before we left Iron Springs, I thought I knew you pretty well. But I didn't know you at all. There's a difference between looking at a stretch of heartland from a distance, thinking it's fine, and riding through that same country for a week and seeing every well and spring and blackberry bush, and knowing for a fact it's fine."

He leaned over and surprised her with a soft kiss on her lips. Then he kept his face near. "Well, I guess you could say God took me on a ride through a heartland till I got to see every stone, every flower, every ribbon of fresh water, every green place, and once I made that ride, I understood what He meant when He said He made that land and called it good, very good."

Lynndae felt a flush rising to her cheeks. How was he always able to do that to her? He kissed her again, and she wished he would never pull away, never stop. Then he was cradling her head against his chest, and she could hear the beating of his heart.

"Was it worth it? I fell in love with the most beautiful woman God has ever placed upon this earth, a lady who outshines Esther or Cleopatra or Helen of Troy. But what's even more astonishing is that this woman fell in love with me and said she'd be my wife. Do you know how long we'd been gone when she said yes? Maybe two weeks. Do you think she would have promised to marry me after just two more weeks of living in Iron Springs and neither of us setting a foot outside the Sweet Blue or Two Back Valley? If I'd come to your door with roses and daisies and chocolates and kisses and said, 'Miss Spence, will you marry me, it's been two weeks,' would you have thrown your arms around me and cried, 'Oh yes, oh yes, marry me, Z, it's been two whole weeks of courtship, and we've scarcely seen each other in all that time?'"

Lynndae laughed into his shirt. "I would have got the boys to throw you out on your ear."

Zeph carefully lifted the new Stetson and kissed the top of her head. "So there you have it. The journey was hard and not without its moments of great darkness, but in the end it was a miracle. With the kind of ending to the story I'm holding in my arms right now, I'd do it again. And again. There is no doubt of that in my mind, and there shouldn't be any in yours."

"There isn't."

"Then we are in agreement."

All the land was sheeted in copper and gold now, and Zeph tilted her face back into the sunlight.

"Look at you," he whispered, "my lovely palomino, ready to throw back her head and toss her golden mane and fly across God's earth like a shooting star. I love you."

Lynndae was about to respond with the same three words when she felt him slip something cool and round and thin on her finger. She pulled back in surprise and sat upright in her saddle, looking at her left hand. A ring and its jewels sparkled in the setting sun.

"Z!" she exclaimed.

"The sapphire is for your eyes, of course, those eternal windows to your soul. But the amethyst is there for the same reason. I was able to procure two of a deeper shade of violet, the shade that comes over your eyes in certain moods and changes in the weather. Did you know the British crown jewels have amethyst? I had them put these four stones in a circle around the diamond. You understand that the diamond is you, all of you, in one perfect gem? It catches the light, makes rainbows, shines like the moon and stars and all the heavens. That about says it all, don't you think?"

Lynndae didn't want to cry, but the tears came anyway. "Oh, Z, what girl was ever given such a beautiful ring in such a beautiful place by such a beautiful man?"

"I just wanted to make it official. And I was waiting for the right moment." Zeph put his hand under her chin again and gently lifted her face toward his. "Lynndae Sharlayne Raber, will you make me the happiest man on earth? Will you be my bride?"

Lynndae cried out and threw her arms around his neck. She kissed him so hard and so long he didn't know if she would ever let him go. When she finally did, he caught his breath and asked, "Is that what you call a yes in Amish?"

She laughed a silver laugh and took him in her arms again. Just as she did so a shooting star streaked across the Montana night. A good shiver went up her spine.

"Don't ever leave me," she whispered.

He kissed her forehead so lightly she thought it was moonlight.

"Don't worry," he said, "in this story we ride as one from here on in."

* * * * *

About the Author

Author, Baptist pastor, and historian, Murray Pura began writing at an early age. He has since published numerous works of both fiction and nonfiction. Murray lives in Canada where he enjoys the frontier landscape and its people. To learn more about Murray, visit his website at www.murraypura.com.

Discussion Questions

1. Charlotte Spence is a woman on her own who has to run a large ranch. Can you identify with her situation in any way? Are there things you have had to do on your own, without help from a boyfriend or spouse, that have called on inner resources of faith and strength you might not have been sure you had?

2. There are many men in Charlotte's life, including a pastor brother of Zephaniah Parker's. What traits or aspects of Zephaniah's personality do you think draw Charlotte to him rather than to the other men around her? Would you feel the same degree of attraction or not to those traits?

3. Charlotte has many secrets, and she does not confide in Zephaniah regarding many of them. Why do you think she chooses not to do so? Do you think keeping her secrets from Zephaniah was a good decision? Is it right to keep secrets from those you love?

4. Charlotte has no children of her own, yet she treats the two orphaned children like gold. Can you explain why she might have such strong affection for the boy and girl and why she is willing to risk her life to save them? Do you know people like Charlotte?

5. What is it about Charlotte's personality do you think Zephaniah likes the most? Do you understand why he reacts so strongly when he finds out she has been keeping secrets from him? Do you feel he is overreacting? How would you feel if someone close to you did the same thing to you?

6. Zephaniah is reluctant to carry a firearm because of his negative experiences during the Civil War. Do you empathize with him, or do you feel he is being unrealistic about what is required for self-defense or the defense of others? Why does he finally feel he must use a gun? What is your stance on self-defense and the use of guns and where God stands in it all?

7. How close do you think Charlotte is to the Amish and their faith? Out West in Montana, it seemed like she had severed her ties with them forever. Back in Pennsylvania, do you think her feelings about cutting herself off from all things Amish undergo a drastic change? Have you ever undergone such a thawing of hard feelings towards others over a period of time?

8. How important is the Bible Zephaniah carries with him and Charlotte? How often do they consult it?

Does their Christian faith make a great deal of difference to what they decide to do on a day-to-day basis or not? Do you try to use the Bible in the same way, or do you find it difficult to have quiet time with the scriptures every day?

9. What circumstances do you feel combined to make Charlotte's brother into a hard-hearted killer? Why did he finally repent of his life of crime and violence? Do you think his repentance was sincere? Have you known people like him—perhaps not murderers—who drastically changed their ways because of returning to God, whether on their deathbed or not?

10. Why are the Amish able to embrace Charlotte's brother in death when they could not embrace him while he was alive? Do you think they should have shunned the Raber family to begin with? Could they have done more to reach out to Charlotte's brother during his lifetime? What are your own opinions about church discipline directed towards individuals and families?

11. Charlotte (Lynndae Raber) and Zephaniah face a hard decision over whether to stay in Pennsylvania and adopt an Amish lifestyle or return to Montana. If you were in their shoes, what might you have done? Stayed or returned? How have you handled decisions to move or stay put when the choice to go or stay was in your own hands and prayers?

12. How do you think Charlotte (Lynndae) and Zephaniah will make out as a married couple? They

both have strong personalities, and Charlotte has been used to making her own decisions and running things her way—how will she adjust to making those decisions alongside a husband, and how will Zephaniah adjust to her strong will? How easy is it going to be to combine their ranches? If you were their pastor and counseling them before their wedding, what four things might you emphasize when it came to offering advice on how to work things through together?

SPECIAL EXCERPT FROM

❧

LOVE INSPIRED SUSPENSE

INSPIRATIONAL ROMANCE

*A K-9 trooper must work with her ex to bring
down a poaching ring in Alaska.*

Read on for a sneak preview of
Wilderness Defender *by Maggie K. Black,*
the next book in the Alaska K-9 Unit series,
available May 2021 from Love Inspired Suspense.

Lex Fielding drove, cutting down the narrow dirt path
between the towering trees. Branches slapped the side
of his park-ranger truck, and rocks spun beneath his
wheels. All the while, words cascaded through his mind,
clattering and colliding in a mass of disjointed ideas that
didn't even begin to come close to what he wanted to
say to Poppy. Years ago, he'd had no clue how to explain
to the most incredible woman he'd ever known that he
didn't think he was ready to get married and have a
family. He might not have even had the guts to tell her all
his doubts, if she hadn't called him out on it after he'd left
a really unfortunate and accidental pocket-dial message
on Poppy's voice mail admitting he wasn't ready to get
married.

Something about being around Poppy had always made
him feel like a better man than he had any right being.
Even standing beside her made him feel an inch taller.

He just hadn't thought he'd been cut out to be anyone's husband. Something he'd then proved a couple of years later by marrying the wrong woman and surviving a couple of unhappy years together before she'd tragically died in a car crash.

He heard the chaos ahead before he could even see it through the thick forest. A dog was barking furiously, voices were shouting, and above it all was a loud and relentless banging sound, like something was trying to break down one of the cabins from the inside.

He whispered a prayer and asked God for wisdom. Hadn't been big on prayer outside of church on Sundays back when he'd been planning on marrying Poppy. But ever since Danny had been born, he'd been relying on it more and more to get through the day.

Then the trees parted, just in time for him to see the two figures directly in front of him dragging something across the road. His heart stopped.

Not something. *Someone.*

They had Poppy.

Don't miss
Wilderness Defender *by Maggie K. Black,*
available May 2021 wherever Love Inspired Suspense
books and ebooks are sold.

LoveInspired.com